Dan Rix

Entanglement

Burning Ember Press

This is a work of fiction. References to real people, events, establishments, organizations, or locales are intended only to provide authenticity, and are used fictitiously. All other characters, and all incidents and dialogue, are drawn from the author's imagination and are not to be construed as real.

A Burning Ember Book
Published in the United States by Burning Ember Press, an imprint of Lavabrook Publishing Group.

Editing by American Editing Services
www.americaneditingservices.com

Cover by Eden Crane Design
www.edencranedesign.com

For Laura,

my inspiration.

ONE

28 Days, 19 hours, 15 minutes

"SCAR TISSUE," said the doctor, "here." She tapped the white lump on the MRI scan.

"Is that in my brain?" said Aaron.

"Just touching it, actually. Between the grey matter and the skull. Aaron, how long have you been having these headaches?"

"Since I was a kid. It's gotten worse recently."

"Well, the good news is it's not cancerous." The doctor stretched on a pair of latex gloves and probed the back of Aaron's head with two fingers. "The pain is always here?"

"Yeah, like something tugging back there." Aaron Harper shifted, still jumpy from the MRI, and his sticky palms suctioned the paper off the exam table with an irritating crinkle. "What's the bad news?"

"Pardon?"

"You said the good news is you don't think it's cancerous. What's the bad news?"

He felt the doctor's breath on his scalp.

"The bad news is that according to your MRI, that scar tissue is right here—" she tapped the very back of his skull, "in the region of your clairvoyant channel, possibly obstructing it. Since you're almost eighteen, my guess is you're experiencing a boost in clairvoyant activity with your half. Hence the inflammation in the surrounding tissue."

Aaron fought the urge to swallow. "But we're okay, right? Me and my half? I mean, I would have felt if something was blocking us."

"Well . . ." the doctor scrunched up her eyebrows, "not necessarily. I doubt you'll notice the symptoms until you meet her. After that, it really depends on both of you."

"The symptoms of what?"

With a whip-like snap that made Aaron flinch, the doctor peeled off her gloves. "Aaron, I'm sorry, but with that scar tissue blocking your channel, your half could literally be standing right in front of you—*kissing* you even. Part of you is going to feel like she's not really there."

In the Sansum Clinic parking lot outside the Radiology wing, Aaron jabbed at his Mazda's ignition but couldn't slot the key. His hand still trembled from the doctor's words.

His half.

The girl born at the exact same time as him, somewhere else in the world. Like all seventeen-year-olds, he was scheduled to meet her on his eighteenth birthday.

Now it felt like a death sentence.

The key lodged. He cranked the ignition and thrust his

foot down, and the tires burned out with a screech. Smoke rose in the rearview.

In twenty-nine days, he was supposed to meet his soul mate. Eighteen years of waiting, wondering, fantasizing . . . looking forward to someone perfect.

Now this crap.

That evening as the buzzer concluded the first league volleyball game between Pueblo High School and Corona Blanca, Aaron, Pueblo's starting setter, ripped off his jersey and flung it into the stands.

His coach grabbed his shoulder. "Cool it, Harper."

"Where the hell was Franco tonight?" said Aaron, stooping to catch his breath.

"He's eighteen now."

"Coach, it takes forty-five minutes to win a volleyball game. He can't leave his half for *forty-five* minutes?"

"And I wouldn't ask him to," said his coach. "Just like I won't ask you after your birthday."

With a nervous twinge, Aaron recalled his visit to the doctor. All the things he *didn't* get to look forward to. He stood, shrugged off the coach's hand, and made for the exit.

His coach called after him. "Put a goddamn shirt on, number eleven."

Aaron punched the wall on his way out. Outside the gym, the night cooled his sweaty skin, and Corona's fans parted around him. He never reached the bus, though.

Someone's hard shoulder crunched into his spine. In that split-second of contact, he felt a shock-like twinge at the back of his skull, then something crawling inside his scalp. He staggered forward and grabbed the back of his head. But the skin wasn't broken.

Aaron spun toward the culprit and saw a figure in a gray hoodie vanish into the crowd of Corona fans, oblivious.

Aaron started after him. "Hey!" he called, but the figure slipped out of view. Aaron charged through green-jerseyed fans. He shoved aside a Corona player and saw a flash of gray hoodie. He lunged.

But his hand closed on empty air.

The figure darted past the last cluster of students and receded into the night. Aaron tore after him, and for a brief, blind moment, the wind whistled in his ears—before he collided with a chain link fence. He caught his breath and peered into the shadows beyond the fence.

There, under a dark hoodie, two pale blue eyes—Aaron blinked. No, just shadows.

He slammed the fence in frustration. As the pain in the back of his head subsided, his skin formed goose bumps.

It was the same spot. Exactly where the MRI showed a lump of scar tissue in his brain. The headaches were one thing, just pressure on his brain, but this—this had felt like a piece had actually torn off. And all because a stranger in a gray hoodie bumped into him.

The doctor he had seen earlier wasn't the first to predict that he and his half would have problems. He had seen a dozen doctors the last year alone, brain surgeons and clairvoyant specialists, and they all said the same thing; the scar tissue would hamper his emotional connection to his half, they just didn't know how much.

No surgeon dared operate on him. The lump of scar tissue was pushing up against his clairvoyant channel. One mistake with a scalpel could sever it, destroying the already delicate connection between Aaron and his half. They would both die.

Aaron was still standing at the fence, a new wave of dread soaking through him, when he realized there was someone behind him.

"Number eleven, right?"

Aaron recognized the shaggy-haired guy as Corona Blanca's starting setter.

"Yeah, what's up?" said Aaron.

The other setter extended his hand. "I wanted to meet you," he said. "I was watching you set during the game, and with a pair of hands like yours, Pueblo should have won."

"Thanks," said Aaron, as they shook hands, "the better team won."

Corona's setter shrugged. "Hey, a couple of our players are heading down to the beach. We got a bonfire going and a couple of coolers. You feel like a postgame party?"

"Maybe next time."

"No pressure," said the setter, and he headed back to the cluster of green jerseys.

Aaron rubbed his scalp again. It still felt raw. As he lowered his hand, he wondered if the doctor had been optimistic. Maybe symptoms would show up even before his birthday. Like tonight, the searing pain caused by the hooded figure. Maybe this was his last night as a normal seventeen-year-old.

If it was, he damn well wasn't going to waste it lying in

bed.

"I changed my mind," Aaron called. "Where's the bonfire?"

The setter glanced back, grinning. "Arroyo beach. Once you hit the sand, turn right. You can't miss us."

He really couldn't miss them. Aaron felt the bonfire's heat a good sixty feet from the flames, which leapt above the silhouettes of what looked like Corona Blanca's entire school. And some.

They had taken over the whole beach, crowding around open coolers and sitting on pieces of driftwood, drinks in hand, their faces glowing reddish-bronze. Aaron wished he hadn't come. This wasn't his school.

At least he could have changed out of his damn red and white Pueblo volleyball jersey—

"Number eleven, over here!"

Aaron spotted Corona's setter along with the rest of the Corona Blanca volleyball team chowing down on pizza off to his right. As soon as Aaron reached them, he felt an icy sting as the setter slapped a can of soda into his palm.

Aaron took a swig and scanned their surroundings. A brief flicker of red by the base of the cliffs caught his attention. At first he thought it was an ember from the fire, but as his eyes adjusted to the darkness, he made out two seated figures on the beach just beyond the lighted radius of the bonfire. He recognized one of them.

The figure in the gray hoodie.

The other one was a girl, a blonde with long, wavy hair,

and Aaron couldn't quite tell from the distance, but she looked pretty—and very bored. As Aaron watched, the hooded figure slipped a bright red object into his pocket.

Aaron grabbed the sleeve of Corona's setter, his heart racing. "Who is that?" he said, nodding to the pair of them. "Over there in the dark." He didn't want to lose sight of the figure again.

The setter and a few of his teammates followed Aaron's gaze. They all laughed.

"You noticed her too, huh? Welcome to the club," said the setter. "That's Amber Lilian. New student at Corona Blanca."

"Sure, she's eye candy," said number ten, "she's also sassy as hell."

"I mean the *guy*," said Aaron. "He bumped into me earlier."

The team went silent. Then the setter spoke in a much quieter voice. "That's Clive Selavio. Also new."

"Her half?" said Aaron.

"Her boyfriend, but they have the same birthday, so it's pretty much a sure thing. I think their families moved here together."

Aaron nodded. Same birthdays. Given that halves were usually born near each other—often within the same city—halves did sometimes find each other before their birthdays. But people got it wrong too. He looked back at the boy and girl seated on the driftwood only to find that once again, the hooded figure had vanished. The girl sat alone.

Aaron scanned the beach, now frantic. Something weird had happened when Clive bumped him, and he needed to figure out what. Aaron couldn't find him in the crowd, though, and his eyes darted back to the girl. Maybe she could explain.

"I'm going to go talk to her," said Aaron, making up his mind before she, too, could disappear. He barged through what was now a Corona Blanca team huddle and slogged toward the girl.

A player muttered behind him, "Where do these Pueblo guys get their nerve?"

"It's because he doesn't have to live with the embarrassment of seeing her at school. I'd talk to her if she was a Pueblo chick."

"Nah, it's because he was running behind-the-back quick sets all night—"

Aaron ignored the rest. As he trudged through the sand, he was more concerned with what in God's name he was going to say to this girl once he got to her.

Amber Lilian was way more than just pretty, he realized, when she finally glanced up at the sound of his approach, the gleaming whites of her eyes warning him not to take another step. Caught in the girl's predatory stare, Aaron felt his pulse quicken as he covered the last few feet.

"I need to talk to you about your boyfriend," he said, sitting next to her.

She eyed the narrow gap he'd left between them and, without a word, edged away from him.

He tried again. "You know, that guy in the hoodie—"

"Why are you even here?" she said, interrupting him.

"You guys lost."

"I'm aware of that." Aaron undid his laces and kicked off his shoes. "So, about that guy—" He glanced up, but the sight of her up close caught him off guard, and he trailed off. She brushed her hair behind her ear, still watching him. So it was a staring contest. Fine. Except staring into Amber's strikingly green eyes gave Aaron the same bad feeling he got at zoos when he accidentally locked eyes with the caged panthers—the ones that could rip his throat out.

Aaron felt his gaze slipping and broke their stare, noticing with relief that she broke at the same time.

"He's not my boyfriend," she said.

Heart still racing, Aaron nodded to the group of green jerseys he had come from. "Your school's volleyball team says he is."

"I think I would know," she said, flashing him another warning look.

"Then who is he?"

"Do you actually care or is this just an excuse to talk to me?" she said.

On any other day, Aaron would have juggled coals as an excuse to talk to this girl, but tonight, he worried more about the throbbing pain at the back of his skull and what Clive Selavio had done to cause it. He tried another angle. "What was that red thing he showed you earlier?"

"Nothing," she said, a threatening tone in her voice as she edged away from him again.

"So you guys are the real deal," he said, "same birthdays and all?"

"So what?" she said. "Why is everyone so obsessed with

birthdays? I'm going to belong to my half for the rest of my life. Can't I just be a normal seventeen-year-old right now?"

Aaron blinked. She had just put into words exactly what he felt about his own birthday. Before he could respond, though, he sensed the tension in her body as she fought a shiver.

"Are you okay?" he said. "You look cold."

"Don't even think about putting your arm around me."

"That wasn't the question."

Amber glared at him, then laughed to herself. "As if you would understand. You probably downloaded that dumb birthday countdown app on your cell phone and check it every five minutes just like everyone else."

"Actually, I do understand," said Aaron. "I'm dreading my birthday too. I have scar tissue in my brain blocking my clairvoyant channel, so when everyone else gets to meet their soul mate, I get to see what's missing. And I *didn't* download that app."

His answer must have surprised her. She stared at him, mouth open, and forgot to brush away the curtain of hair that fell in front of her eyes.

Just then, a commotion near the bonfire drew their attention. A group of juniors was talking excitedly, and as others joined in and cheered them on, they took off their shirts.

Two guys ran over to Aaron and Amber's log. "Hey, like twenty of us are going skinny dipping, you guys want to come? Dominic's already in the water."

It was obvious they were here to recruit Amber. Big surprise.

"No thanks," said Aaron. "We're good."

"Is it just pervy guys?" said Amber. "Or are there actually girls too?"

"There's girls too. It was their idea, in fact."

Then, to Aaron's bewilderment, Amber said, "Okay. I'll come in a second."

"Cool, see you down there!" The two guys raced back to the water, and when they thought they were out of sight, they grinned and high-fived.

"Can I hide my cell phone in your shoes?" Amber said, facing Aaron.

He gaped at her. "You're kidding, it's freezing out there—"

But she was already pulling her sweater over her head. He felt a rush of air as her hair came loose from the hood and swished back. She smelled like the beach, like salt and sunscreen.

"So do you have a name, number eleven?" she said, removing a large pair of peacock feather earrings that had been hidden under her hair.

"Aaron Harper," he answered, still in disbelief.

"So when's this birthday you're dreading, *Aaron?*"

"March thirtieth."

Amber froze, and for the first time that night, it seemed, she let down her guard. "Mine too," she whispered.

Aaron felt his heart leap, and for a moment they couldn't look away from each other—

"Amber, put you goddamn clothes back on," said a cold, drawling voice behind them.

Aaron turned around as Clive Selavio, the figure in the gray hoodie, emerged from the shadows at the base of the cliffs.

Two pale, milky blue eyes glowed beneath the shadow of his hood. Though muscular, he was shorter than Aaron by a few inches, with perfect, if not cruel features. Like Amber's. Too perfect.

So this was the guy who knocked into him. Aaron's first impression was that Clive couldn't have been seventeen. Twenty, maybe.

"You—" Clive said to Aaron, "thanks for babysitting her. Now you can leave."

Aaron didn't budge. His mind was still reeling with the news that he and Amber had the same birthday. Plus he had unfinished business with Clive. "You shoved me after the game, remember? What the hell was that?"

Clive ignored him to deal with Amber, who was now shivering in just a T-shirt. "Put your sweatshirt back on."

"Actually, I'm going skinny dipping," she said.

"You are not fucking *skinny dipping*," said Clive.

"If she wants to take a dip, let her take a dip," said Aaron.

Clive's gaze snapped back to him, and Aaron felt the corner of his mouth twitch as their eyes burned into each other. "I thought I told you to leave," he said.

"I asked you a question," said Aaron.

Clive's eyebrows shot up. Then he ran his hand over his scalp and behind his head, nudging off his hood, and Aaron saw that both sides of his thin, shaved head were etched with deep scars. As though his face had been peeled off and reattached. "The thing is, number eleven . . ." he said, rounding the log to Aaron's side, "you know this beach belongs to

Corona Blanca, and you know that Amber is off limits, so why are you still here?"

Aaron noticed a red glow in the pocket of Clive's shorts. Clive saw where he was looking and quickly covered it.

"What'cha got there?" said Aaron, certain he could now feel a gentle tugging behind his head. Maybe provoking this guy was a bad idea.

"It's nothing," said Clive.

"No, it looks like you have something in your pocket."

"It's just a glow stick. It's nothing."

"If it's just a glow stick, then show it to me," said Aaron.

Clive's eyes became slits, and without another word to Aaron, he spun, grabbed Amber's sweatshirt, and forced it back over her head. "Get up. We're leaving."

"Clive, *stop it!*" she yelled, shoving him off. "People are watching."

He pinned her against the driftwood. "Think I give a damn?"

"Clive, you're hurting me—" She scratched his arms, but Clive was stronger, and he dragged the fabric down over her face, suffocating her screams.

It was crossing the line.

Aaron lunged forward, closed his fist around Clive's collar, and yanked him back. "Not while I'm here, jerk—"

He ended up in the sand, Clive on top of him.

"Cut the crap!" Aaron yelled, flinging Clive's hands off his neck. Then he heard a sound like the rumble of crashing surf—the sound of running feet.

Clive jumped away from him, and Aaron stood as Corona Blanca's entire student body jammed into a ring with them at its center. The excited mutters quieted when a dripping wet senior stepped into the circle.

From his braided rat tail and the green letterman jacket the senior wore over nothing but a wet pair of boxers, Aaron recognized him as Corona Blanca's rugby star, Dominic Brees. He grinned, flashing a broad mouth packed with shining white teeth. Then, to Aaron's horror, he chanted, "*Fight—fight—fight—*" and within seconds, the whole school joined in.

Clive grabbed Dominic's jacket. "You better be able to get me out of this," he said. "I'm *dead* if my father finds out I got in another fight." Evidently, Clive didn't want the attention any more than Aaron did.

Dominic laughed and raised his hands, silencing the crowd. "We've had a change of plans," he yelled. "Corona Blanca's Clive Selavio will now race number eleven from Pueblo High School all the way out to the buoy!"

Aaron scowled. Clearly this was Dominic's ploy to get more people in the water. Unfortunately, it worked. The spectators roared and changed their chant to, "*Buoy—buoy—buoy—*" Dominic slapped Clive on the back and receded into the circle, deserting him before he could protest.

Aaron scanned the shouting faces, trying to calm his breathing. How the hell had he gotten himself in this situation?

Of course it was that girl, Amber, who he noticed was conveniently nowhere in sight. For a night out, it was fairly typical, he supposed, as the crowd started booing him; he never quite managed to keep his damn mouth shut. At least not when it counted.

Aaron glanced back at Clive, and their eyes met across the ring. He had a hunch Clive would back down, and he prayed he was right because he wasn't about to humiliate himself and disgrace his school. He whipped off his shirt and flung it to the sand.

The crowd cheered. Point for Pueblo.

Slowly, the corner of Clive's pale, chapped lips tightened into a smirk. He tugged his hoodie over his head and laid it carefully on the driftwood, then he started on the buttons of his collared shirt, and the crowd went berserk.

Aaron stared at him. So they were actually going to do this.

Clive cheated, bolting for the water a full second before Dominic shouted, "*GO!*"

Aaron kicked off the sand and tore after him. He felt a deep rumble followed by a spray of mist, and from out of the darkness, a film of foamy surf slashed across his ankles.

There was no sign of a buoy, not even a line marking the horizon, just blackness. Thankfully Clive had kept his undershirt on because all Aaron could do was follow his bobbing white silhouette as they hurled themselves into the pounding surf.

Aaron dived under a wave and icy brine flooded his nostrils. He broke out into the open water, neck and neck with Clive. After a few minutes, he lost track of time. Gradually every square inch of his skin went numb with cold.

Then Clive's splashes stopped.

But there was nothing up ahead. Aaron panicked. Had he

followed a rogue wave? Was he in fact miles past the buoy, lost?

He tried to find the shore, but the water stung his eyes and blurred everything. He couldn't even see the bonfire.

Something moved in the darkness ahead of him, and all at once, the pungent smell of salt and rotting fish rushed over him, filled his lungs, choked him. Right before a wave sucked him under, he saw huge masses shifting and blotting out the stars. He surfaced, terrified, to the sound of barking—violent, piercing barks that echoed off the water. Aaron clutched his ears.

There were splashes all around him, and he was aware that something else was swimming in the water with him—something big. He felt a thrust of cold water against his knees as a huge creature swam past him.

From somewhere behind him, he heard Clive shout, "Sea lions!"

More barking, more splashes, and more things swimming past him. Aaron twisted to get away from them, but the turbulence from their flippers pulled him back.

A moment later a white shape loomed in front of him, and he reached his arms out just in time to stop his face from colliding with hard metal. The buoy.

With Clive's help, he tipped it over so they could rest the upper halves of their bodies. Underwater, Clive's pocket emitted an eerie red glow, tinting the water around them purple.

"I won't drown you for talking to Amber," said Clive, after they caught their breath, "but do me a favor, okay? Don't go near her again."

"How about you quit treating her like dirt," said Aaron.

Clive snickered. "Number eleven, you know better than to tell a man how to treat his own half."

"Too bad she's not your half," said Aaron. "She's only seventeen."

"Yeah, but we were both born on March thirtieth."

Aaron spat into the water, cleansing the salty taste from his mouth. "Then it sounds like we got a problem, Clive, because I *also* was born on March thirtieth."

Clive faced him abruptly, sinking his face into shadow so only the glint of his pale, unblinking eyes shone in the darkness. As a passing swell tugged at Aaron's feet and weakened his grip on the buoy, he wondered if he could defend himself if Clive tried to kill him right now.

"I'm only going to tell you this one more time," said Clive finally. "*Don't* go near her again."

"Or else what?" said Aaron.

"Tell me you have a smarter question."

"Yeah, one. What's in your pocket?"

To Aaron's surprise, Clive actually reached into the water and pulled it out. Aaron thought the bright object was, in fact, a glow stick, until he leaned closer.

It was a glass vial, rounded at both ends so it was completely sealed. Inside, a glowing red liquid crawled along the glass.

"Do you know what this is?" said Clive, smirking, his face now fully illuminated.

"Plasma?"

"This is what drips out when you cut a hole in your clairvoyant channel."

Aaron felt a wave of cold, separate from the ocean. "Is it *yours?*"

Clive shook his head. "Whosever it is, they're sorely missing it right now. Want to hold it?"

Aaron took the vial from Clive, but when the glass touched his skin, the sudden stabbing at the back of his scalp nearly made him drop it, like something trying to exit his head through too small a hole. The red fluid scurried inside of the vial, forming tendrils, as if searching for cracks. And Aaron had the impression that the vial was somehow filling up, glowing brighter and brighter, too bright to look at—

"Hey, how'd you do that?" said Clive.

"Hold on," said Aaron, now mesmerized by the luminous substance. The glass, he noticed, was stamped with some sort of ID code.

"Give it back—" Clive lunged for the vial.

Aaron held it out of reach, straining to make out the letters, but Clive caught his wrist. The impact splayed Aaron's fingers wide open, and in slow motion, the vial flew from Aaron's palm, bounced off the buoy, and plopped into the water.

"Shit!" Clive plunged his arm in, but the vial slipped through his fingers, briefly lighting their toes on its way to the bottom.

Clive dived. And Aaron had no choice but to dive in after him. About eight feet down, blind and out of breath, Aaron clamped his arm around Clive's ankle and took a bare heel to the forehead. He held on, though, righted himself, and thrust down hard. With sheer will, he hauled Clive out of the ocean and forced him against the buoy.

"Let it go!" Aaron yelled. "It was my fault."

"You *idiot*," Clive gasped, "you stupid idiot! Now we'll never find it."

"Then it's lost," he said. "It could be thirty feet to the bottom. What was that thing, anyway?"

They both looked down as they caught their breath, and their last glimpse of the vial was a fuzzy dot, no brighter than the reflection of a star, before it was gone.

"My father's going to kill me for this," said Clive.

Aaron let go of him and lowered himself into the water. "Come on, let's go back. It's freezing out here."

When Aaron made it back to the beach, he was relieved to find that most of Corona Blanca had gone home, and the few smoking weed by the bonfire's dying embers had forgotten about his and Clive's race to the buoy.

Aaron reached his shoes, still disconcerted by what he'd seen in the vial and determined that he would have nothing to do with Clive Selavio, his vial, or Amber Lilian ever again, Clive's half or not. No point in trying to see her if the guy was that protective. Besides, Aaron and Amber's birthday was only a month away. Then they would know.

There was something in his shoe, wedged down by the toe. Aaron pulled out a bright, powder blue smartphone.

Amber's cell phone. *Damn.*

When Amber pulled in front of Dominic Brees's gate to drop off Clive, she felt his body go tense—as it usually did when she was doing everything wrong.

"So you're making me walk up the driveway?" said Clive, and Amber barely heard the vulnerability beneath his irritation. He was getting better at hiding it now when she pushed him away, which made her nervous.

"Can you just go?" she said. "I'm really tired."

"You sure got cozy with number eleven, didn't you?" he said.

She sighed. "Why do you always do this?"

"I'm keeping you safe," he spat.

"Wow," she said, "I must really be something if *every* guy I meet is trying to steal me away from you."

"I saw the way he looked at you," he said.

"Actually, Clive, he was asking about *you*," she said, and all at once, her frustration came rushing back. Of course she would *finally* meet an interesting boy with the same birthday as her, only to have Clive obliterate her chances, as always, of the boy ever talking to her again. She sighed, wishing she knew more than just his name.

"Amber, he lost the vial."

"Then maybe you shouldn't have stolen it from your dad." Amber relished the wounded flare in Clive's eyes. To torment him even more, she smiled sweetly, twirling her hair around her finger, and decided he would be the one who looked away first.

But Clive leaned over her instead, and his breath prickled her eyelashes. "You're going to be powerful because of who I am."

Amber rolled her eyes and gazed out her window. "Do you think I care?" she said.

"Look at me," he whispered.

She didn't say anything, just stared straight ahead.

"*Look at me!*"

Finally, skin crawling, she faced him.

"Your pure blood," he whispered, "mixed with mine—*imagine* our inheritance, Amber."

And then, while she was still glaring at him, he came the last few inches and kissed her. She let him, because it was easier to surrender the little things. Because she knew the part of her that resisted him was wearing out, and eventually there would be nothing left.

She used to think Clive was sexy in a scarred up, feral kind of way, but now it hardly mattered what he looked like. What frightened her was the part inside, the part she could taste.

When Clive had finished, Amber edged away from him and let her hair fall between them, though she could feel his gaze lingering. She knew it was miserable for him, knowing she never kissed back, knowing he would never feel her lose control and *really* kiss him.

"Amber, you get to have everything," he said. "Start appreciating it." He climbed out and slammed the door.

Amber sat in her car for a whole minute, her stomach squirming, before she pulled out and drove home.

She hardly paid attention to the road. The yellow paint strip slithered into the darkness, and as her VW Bug squealed around a corner, she half wished the tires would slip. She shot down a dark straightaway and the gas pedal bottomed out under her toes. As the car's speed pressed her into the seat, gnarled branches of oak trees swung past her.

The moon flickered, faster and faster.

She closed her eyes.

You get to have everything. Start appreciating it.

Amber kept her eyes closed, and she knew it would be too late to slow down once her headlights illuminated the next corner, too late to make the turn.

She knew what Clive would say, her father, her mother, Clive's father, everyone who said they cared about her. *Amber. You're much too important. Don't you dare be reckless.*

But the rush made her dizzy, tingly all over, lightheaded. It was so easy not to look, like falling asleep—like being held.

Then her mind returned to Aaron Harper, the strange boy who'd shown up out of nowhere and made things interesting for a night.

She opened her eyes—and slammed on the brakes. The car shuddered and threw her forward. Her heart squashed against the inside of her chest as the vehicle sank toward the edge of the road.

Then silence.

Her headlights blazed two feet from the trunk of an oak tree. *Two feet*, that's how close she had come. Slowly, Amber let out a breath, which she realized she'd been holding the entire time. Feeling numb, she reversed and got back on the road. She was full of helium, practically floating away already.

Who *was* he? Okay, so he was gorgeous. Amber shivered when she remembered his dangerous, jet black eyes. In her entire life, she had never been so devastated by a stare.

Nor had she met anyone else who dreaded turning eighteen like she did. And their shared birthdays . . . Her heart had been racing since he told her.

But years ago, Amber had resolved never to get her hopes up; it was easier that way, and a random guy she'd just met at a bonfire was *not* about to change that.

She already knew her fate.

TWO

26 Days, 3 hours, 59 minutes

A BURST OF rap music jolted Aaron awake. He glanced around, disoriented, until he located the music's source—Amber's cell phone.

He silenced the call, which he noticed was from Clive Selavio, and swiveled his feet to the ground. Since Amber's phone was locked and he didn't have the passcode, he couldn't access any of her contacts. He would have to return the phone to her in person. *Great.* More opportunities to royally piss off her psychotic boyfriend—or half, or whatever Clive was.

Aaron sighed, running his fingers through his hair. He tossed her phone in the trash. Cute as this girl was, she wasn't worth the trouble.

As he stuffed his backpack for school, though, he realized that was a total lie. For some reason he couldn't get Amber out of his head; she was just—*different.*

In the dim hallway outside his bedroom, Aaron felt the

crunch of paper under his foot. He picked up an envelope, clearly marked with the silver seal of the Chamber of Halves, and slid out an official-looking letter.

Dear Aaron Harper,

In preparation for your upcoming eighteenth birthday, the Chamber of Halves would like to arrange a meeting with you on Saturday, March 30 at 11:00 A.M. We strive for a successful union between you and your half. Unfortunately, your case involves some complications, which your correspondent from the Chamber will discuss with you in confidence.

Regards,

Walter Wu
CHAMBER OF HALVES
TULAROSA BRANCH
Est. 1939

Aaron blinked and read it again. *Complications?* He had never heard of complications. On your eighteenth birthday, you went to the Chamber of Halves, you met your half. It wasn't complicated.

Unless, of course, they knew about the scar tissue. Aaron stuffed the letter in his backpack and tried to ignore the flash of queasiness. On his way to the front door, he passed the breakfast table, where his mom was scanning the news headlines on her laptop.

"A student from Corona Blanca High School was reported

missing on Friday," she said, without looking up.

"Who?" said Aaron.

"Justin Gorski, he's a rugby player."

"Never heard of him," said Aaron.

"Says here he was last seen right after school with a classmate, Amber Lilian," she said.

Aaron halted, his hand on the doorknob. "*Amber Lilian?*" he repeated like an idiot.

"Why, do you know her?"

"No," he said quickly, but when his mom wasn't looking, he slipped back to his room and fished Amber's phone out of his trash can. Aaron could already tell this girl was nothing but trouble.

Unfortunately, he had a chronic inability to stay away from trouble.

"So how was the water, Buddy?" said Aaron's best friend, Buff Normandy, as the six-foot-four, two hundred and forty pound, curly-haired and baby-faced rugby player squeezed into the adjacent desk before first period. "Heard you took a dip on Friday."

"You should have been there," said Aaron. "Dominic Brees was working the crowd."

"No bullshit, *Breezie* was there?" said Buff. "Tell me you punched him in the face for me?"

"I kind of had my hands full," said Aaron.

"You heard about that missing kid, right?" said Buff. "He's the one who dropped that pass during the finals last year, Justin Gorski. Cost Corona the game. I bet Breezie snuffed him out because the season's about to start."

"Couldn't have been a rugby player," said Aaron, "Gorski was last seen with a girl."

"No bullshit, Breezie put her up to it," said Buff. "Hey, are you still trying out for rugby this year?"

"Yeah, now that the volleyball team's whole starting lineup is eighteen," said Aaron, "I guess I don't have a choice."

"Not sure why you're even bothering . . ." Buff grinned and glanced at his phone "You're up in twenty-six days."

Just then a girl came through the doorway, her dark hair sailing in slow motion behind her. Emma Mist. She glanced at Aaron briefly, then let her hair fall over her shoulder to block him from view.

"Yep, she hates you," said Buff.

"It's that obvious?" said Aaron. He had recently broken up with Emma because his birthday was coming up. It was the right thing to do—but standing her up the night of winter formal after she'd already done her hair and makeup was the wrong way to do it.

"Please turn in your essays on quantum mechanics and the discovery of halves," said Mr. Sanders, walking in just as the bell rang.

As the sounds of shuffling papers and sliding desks filled the room, Buff produced a crumpled sheet of notebook paper covered with barely legible scribbles. He glanced at Aaron, whose hands were still jammed in his pockets, and gave a disappointed headshake before he ambled to the front.

Aaron tried to catch Emma's eye, but she was decidedly oblivious, twirling her hair around her finger and gazing firmly out the window. If she would just let him apologize . . .

Ten minutes into lecture someone knocked on the classroom door, and Mr. Sanders paused to let in another girl who hated Aaron. Tina Marcello. Today she wore big sunglasses and chewed bubblegum.

"Ms. Marcello, I'm glad you're here," said their teacher with a smile. "I didn't think it was fair for us to talk about you behind your back."

She stopped chewing and brushed her straight, highlighted hair out of her eyes. "Huh?"

"Take a seat, Tina." Mr. Sanders went back to his lecture. ". . . so although quantum entanglement was well documented by 1935, we credit Schrödinger with the discovery of halves. Mr. Harper, why does he get all the credit?"

Tina sat right in front of Aaron. As usual, she glowered at him as she walked toward her seat, chewing her gum like it didn't taste good.

Aaron mouthed, "*Bite me.*"

"Aaron, how did he prove it to the world?" said Mr. Sanders.

Buff kicked the side of Aaron's calf, making him wince.

"Prove what?" he said.

"That every human is born with a half."

"Uh—he used an aitherscope?" said Aaron.

"Wrong. Aitherscope technology wouldn't exist for another decade." Mr. Sanders swept to the chalkboard. "Schrödinger said if humans formed in quantum entangled pairs, then in every case we would find that the halves were born simultaneously . . . therefore all we have to do is look at birth times." The chalk made a nasty scrape on the board.

"Nice one, *Aaron*," Tina said under her breath. She was

putting on makeup.

Aaron kicked her desk, causing her to smear her lipstick.

"*Jerk*," she said, wiping the smudge with her tank top.

Their teacher scanned the classroom for the source of the commotion, and his eyes settled on Aaron. At the same moment, Amber's cell phone went off in his pocket, turning all the heads in the classroom with a shrill, hip-hop beat and a chain of rapid-fire cusswords.

Lovely.

Over the next six hours, Clive called Amber's cell phone so many times that Aaron found himself humming the ring tone between periods. When it rang for the twentieth time on his way to volleyball practice, he picked up.

"Clive, this is Aaron—"

But the caller hung up before he finished. Aaron lowered the phone from his ear, and his heartbeat felt heavier than usual. He had just made a huge mistake. Now Clive Selavio, Amber's abusive boyfriend, thought she and Aaron were hanging out.

He had to get the phone back to her. Soon, before the guy did something to her. Maybe if he ditched practice and drove straight to Corona Blanca High School, he could catch her before she went home.

Don't go near her again, Clive had said.

Too bad.

There were still cars in Corona Blanca's parking lot when Aaron rolled in around four. But how to find her . . .

From what he remembered, Amber looked athletic,

probably played a sport and stayed after school for practice. If she had a car, it would be here.

Outside, he slid on his sunglasses and leaned against his Mazda, feeling oddly nervous about talking to her again. At the campus entrance, a bronze statue of the Austrian physicist, Erwin Schrödinger, glinted in the sun. Its shadow crept closer.

The man who changed everything.

Just then Aaron saw her coming out. A smile pulled at the corners of his lips when he saw Amber approach a bright, Crayola-style powder blue Volkswagen Beetle. Same color as her cell phone.

She wore a white tennis skirt and a green tank top with '*Corona Blanca Varsity Tennis*' written in white cursive along the front. Her skin was damp with sweat, and a few wisps of hair had escaped her ponytail and stuck to her forehead. She walked slowly, her eyes downcast.

He waited until she reached her car before he called out her name.

Amber glanced up, saw him, and froze. "*Aaron?*" She combed her damp hair off her forehead.

"What's up?" he asked. "Lousy practice?"

"Why are you here?" she said, and when Aaron pushed off his car and came closer, she narrowed her eyes, tracking him.

In the daylight she was even more stunning. Once again Aaron found himself lost in her green eyes, not sure what he had been about to say.

Luckily, a distraction behind her snapped him out of his

daze. The rest of the girls' tennis team came into the parking lot, chatting and giggling. They paused, and after a few wary glances in Amber's direction, continued on their way.

Aaron dug through his pocket. "You left this." He tossed the phone to her, which she caught. "Does Clive always call you that much?"

Without even a thank you, Amber keyed in her passcode and thumbed through the list of missed calls. "It's because he's worried," she said.

"Worried about what?"

"You. He's worried you might have a crush on me," she said, slipping the phone into her backpack with a hint of a smile, "and that you're going to wait by my car after school with some lame excuse about having to return my cell phone just so you can talk to me again."

"Oh?" Aaron raised his eyebrows. "So he's not worried about the fact that you left the phone in my shoes on purpose then?"

She didn't take her eyes off him. "Did that make your day, Aaron?"

"Actually, I was kind of dreading this," he said, "since our first conversation resulted in me freezing my ass off with some sea lions while your boyfriend threatened to kill me if I ever went near you again."

"Then you probably shouldn't be near me. Why did you race him, anyway? It's not like anyone was impressed."

"It's a guy thing."

"Uh-huh," she said doubtfully. "You know, he's done things to guys like you before."

"Like me?"

"Egotistical and stupid."

"Why, is that your type, or something?" said Aaron, returning her glare. When it got ridiculous, though, he gave up trying to outstare her and squinted into the horizon. "So you really think Clive is your half?"

"You sound jealous," she said.

"Just confused," said Aaron, pushing his sunglasses halfway up the bridge of his nose. "Halves don't treat each other like that . . . and I could tell he was nervous when I told him we had the same birthday."

"Oh, right," she said. "I forgot."

Aaron peered sideways at her, but this time she broke eye contact first.

"No, you didn't," he said.

"I think I would know," she said, rolling her eyes. Though now she was blushing.

"Well, have you thought about—"

"Just drop it," she said.

"You don't buy it, do you?"

"Buy what?"

"Halves. The whole bit."

She set her gaze on him and the sudden force of her green eyes jolted him. "We've known about halves for barely eighty years. We don't even know what causes it . . . I mean, nowhere does it say we're meant to be soul mates. We just *assumed.*"

"Yeah, because that part was obvious."

"There's another explanation."

Aaron nodded to the bronze statue. "One your man over there didn't think of?"

"You know . . ." she said, without looking back, "Schrödinger kept a mistress."

"Ouch," he said. "Alright, let's hear your theory."

"Halves are more like siblings. Like cosmic twins . . . which would make this all incest."

"You are aware most people say its love at first sight when they meet their half."

"Easy." She held his gaze. "Power of suggestion."

"You're saying it could be anybody?"

"I think that depends."

"On what?"

"The person," she said, watching him with a tinge of daring, "and what they believe."

"Most people believe halves are perfect biological matches," he said.

"That's what scares me," she said. "What happens to the human race if we no longer evolve through natural selection, but instead allow ourselves to be artificially bred by a force we haven't even begun to understand?"

"You think it's breeding us?"

She shrugged. "I wouldn't be the first."

A few students walked past them, and Aaron chewed his lip, waiting for them to pass out of earshot. Like the tennis players, their eyes darted between the two of them but lingered on Amber, and then Aaron remembered—

"What happened to Justin Gorski?" he said, changing the subject.

Amber glared at him as if he had just asked the stupidest question on Earth, and Aaron regretted asking her; the poor girl had probably gotten nonstop stares at school, and it was still only her first week.

Yet part of him doubted her innocence. "Weren't you the last one with him?" he said.

"He offered me a ride home, which I didn't take," she said, "and I *wasn't* the last one with him."

"Then who was?" he said, ignoring her look. "Was it your boyfriend, Selavio, jealous maybe? Am I next on his hit list?"

"It was Dominic Brees," she said, "and that's because they're both on the rugby team and they carpool home after practice."

Aaron turned away from her and closed his fist. "Just like Buff said," he muttered.

"Why do you even care? You don't go here."

"One more thing," said Aaron, as he recalled Friday night, still believing Clive was somehow involved. "What was in that vial your boyfriend brought to the beach?"

"What are you, Aaron, some kind of private detective?"

"He said it was liquid clairvoyance."

Amber pulled her keys out of her backpack and reached for her car door. "I'm kind of done talking to you," she said, "and for your information, it was just a glow stick."

She slammed the door in his face.

Well, that went well, Aaron thought, as her tires squealed on the asphalt and left him in a puff of burnt rubber.

"It's too suggestive," said Amber's mother.

Amber stood on a pedestal wearing the dress, still fuming inside from her conversation with Aaron. Just who did he think he was? At the moment, a dozen people were looking her up and down.

She felt André's hands on her waist. "We want to display her athletic figure," he said. "The fabric accentuates movement, lightness. Step down, Amber, try walking around a bit."

She stepped off the stool and walked a few feet then turned around. The group murmured its approval.

"And what are those ruffles, André?"

André smiled. "It's a fabric, Mrs. Lilian. It has to move."

"Can you tighten that up along the side?"

"Quit nitpicking," said her father. "He's done a fine job."

"You have no idea how camera flashes can amplify these imperfections," said her mother.

"*Imperfections?*" scoffed Dravin, one of her parents' friends, as his vulture-like eyes inspected Amber favorably from behind his glasses. "All I see is perfection."

"Quiet," said her mother. "André, do you have any brighter lights? I can't see anything properly in your cave of a studio."

André brought out two halogen lights on stands and they, like the eyes of her dozen admirers, were trained on Amber's body.

"Congratulations," said her mother. "You've wrapped her in vinyl."

"There needs to be luster," said André.

"Can it be charmeuse?" she said.

"Mrs. Lilian, the dress is done," he said. "We're just making the final adjustments."

"Then do it again," she said.

"But there isn't enough time," he muttered.

"Can we put padding in the cups?" said her mother.

André scowled.

"Ignore her," said her father. "The dress is flawless."

"It is *not* flawless," said her mother.

While they bickered, Amber wandered into the corner and stared at herself in a mirror. Her hair was pinned up so every part of the dress could be seen, admired, and scrutinized for flaws. Just like her.

The silk was whisper-light on her skin, barely touching her, but not so loose they couldn't see what she was shaped like underneath. It was André's most appealing design so far—and probably the one she'd wear on her eighteenth birthday, although the thought made her stomach squirm.

She couldn't stand the idea that once she met her half—once she *belonged* to him—she would never again be considered her own person. Irresistible as she was in André's dress, she felt the urge to rip it off and don baggy sweatpants. The worst part, though, was she doubted there was even a single seventeen-year-old in the world who could empathize with her.

Well, maybe *one* seventeen-year-old.

Amber realized she was about to start thinking about Aaron all over again and sighed in frustration. She had thought about him way too much ever since he came to her school last week. But that *wasn't* because she liked him. He was a jerk.

She just couldn't figure him out, and though she didn't trust him at all, she wished she had told him what she knew about the missing boy from her high school—at least to get it off her chest. Now he probably thought she was hiding something. Which she was.

And *why* did she care what Aaron thought? For all she cared, he could curse her name in his sleep.

Dravin appeared behind her, his half at his side. "He'll be lovesick when he sees you, sweetheart."

"Fine. As long as he doesn't puke on me," said Amber.

He ignored her tone. "With you at his side, he'll be chosen as the heir."

"Dravin, please do your scheming with my father," she said.

Amber caught his half's eye in the mirror and regretted it immediately. There was a reason Dravin usually left his half home when he visited. The woman's unfocused eyes lolled between them, only loosely timed with their speech.

Amber averted her gaze, but not before her lips curled with disgust. Dravin must have read her expression.

"That's not polite, sweetheart."

"She's gross."

If the comment stung, Dravin didn't let it show. "I was born in the early days, sweetheart. Before they understood premature contact. We first touched when we were only three days old; her body wasn't ready . . . her channel tore open and she lost most of her clairvoyance."

The detachment in his voice chilled Amber. "Aren't you even upset about it?"

"You were almost like her, you know. Only your parents were more . . . *skittish.*" He said it like an insult.

"Yeah, well not everyone's perfect," said Amber. Despite her biting tone, her face flushed.

He was right.

Dravin and his half were victims of juvengamy. They had been forced together as infants.

So had Amber's parents.

And as a pureblood, descended from an unbroken lineage of juvengamy halves, so had Amber.

At least that's what they told her. She and her half were separated before she could remember. Before any permanent damage could happen to her channel . . . she hoped.

Amber heard shouting behind her and turned around. Her parents were yelling at each other now.

André sat in the corner while his half, the studio's other designer, massaged his shoulders, throwing mutinous glances toward Amber's mother. André and his half were both men. Homosexual halves did occur, though not as often as heterosexual halves.

Suddenly, Amber's mother slapped her father and marched toward the exit, toppling one of the halogen light stands. The tripod crashed to the floor and the bulb popped. On her way out, she shouted over her shoulder, "I don't care if you don't sleep, André. I want another dress next week."

When she got back to her purse, Amber had a missed call from Tina Marcello, Dominic Brees's girlfriend, and a message asking if she wanted to hang out, maybe watch Pueblo High School's rugby tryouts.

Definitely. She could use some time with someone normal.

"*Well?*" said Buff furiously as he and Aaron hobbled to the stands after rugby tryouts, both of them drenched in mud.

Behind them, the goal posts sank into the mist.

"You saw. I scored three times," said Aaron. "You tell me why your coach is an idiot."

"Buddy, what was that bullshit? You're a ball hog; you didn't pass once. Have you ever even played rugby?"

"Just drop it," said Aaron.

"No bullshit," Buff grabbed his shoulders and faced him, "the closer it gets to your birthday, the more you creep me out. Look, Buddy, I know you're freaked about that stuff in your head, but it's not the end of the world, okay?"

Aaron shrugged off his best friend's hands and continued walking.

"Okay, be a prick. Fine." Buff walked in stiff silence next to him.

For a week, Aaron hadn't stopped thinking about Amber. Clearly, she didn't belong with Clive, yet she acted like they were unofficial halves or something . . . and he was beginning to hate it.

But his birthday was way too close to risk getting hung up on her—only nineteen days now. Besides, whether Clive Selavio, Aaron, or someone else entirely was Amber's half would be revealed on March 30, and no one could do a damn thing about it.

So why was it so hard to let her go?

"Hey—" Buff nodded toward the stands, "look who came to watch."

Aaron glanced up. It was Tina Marcello, but when he saw whom she was with, his skin tingled.

"And who might *that* be?" said Buff, suddenly very interested.

The two girls were sitting right where they had left their backpacks.

Amber wore a baby-blue sweater, the sleeves rolled up to her elbows, damp with mist. Her hair glistened. Aaron stopped right in front of her.

"*You* again?" she said, making no attempt to sound excited. Aaron wondered whether she'd consulted Tina about him or whether they'd concluded separately that he was a jerk. Maybe they could form a club with Emma Mist.

Aaron wiped his brow with the back of his hand, and his sweat ran red down his fingers. A cleat must have nicked his forehead. He lifted the bottom of his shirt and wiped away the blood.

Amber blinked. "Do you really have to do that right in front of me?" she said.

"What are you doing here?" he said.

"Oh, so it's okay for you to lurk by my car and ambush me after practice, and it's not okay for me to watch the tryouts?"

"Fine. Next time I'll leave your phone in the trash," he said, "and just so you know—" he nodded over his shoulder at the rugby field, "I got distracted back there."

"It's not like I came to watch *you*."

"Oh yeah?" he said. "Who'd you come to watch?"

Buff pushed him out of the way and held his hand out to Amber. He put on his most dignified expression, which wasn't much. "Buff Normandy."

Amber took his hand and smiled. "Amber."

"So you like rugby, Amber?"

She shrugged, and her eyes darted to Aaron. "It's okay," she said.

"I didn't really need to try out—" said Buff. "I'm actually already on the team." He chuckled, and his cheeks reddened. "Actually, I was last year's MVP."

"Knock it off," said Aaron. "She's a friend."

Buff stepped in front of Aaron, blocking him. "You got any plans for later?"

Aaron smirked and rolled his eyes, and Amber glanced at him again. She smiled too.

"Could you please leave us alone now?" said Tina, wrinkling her nose. "You guys stink."

A lined notebook lay open on her lap, which Buff snatched and proceeded to dangle above her head.

"Buff—" Tina lunged for the notebook and missed. "Give it *back*!"

While they squabbled, Aaron scanned the bleachers for his backpack. He had left it right here. He inhaled, and his chest stung. More sweat drizzled into his mouth.

Then he saw it stashed under the bench, shoved out of the way right behind Amber. He leaned over her, and her eyes narrowed suspiciously.

"Excuse me—you're in the way." He reached past her.

But she refused to budge, and his shoulder brushed her cool skin. He felt her tense up. Aaron flexed and dragged his backpack onto the bench next to her. She stared at the spot of mud he left on her arm, then at him.

"What makes you think I'm your friend?" she said.

"I didn't say you were," said Aaron.

"You did two minutes ago." She glanced at his forehead.

"I think you need a Band-Aid."

Blood dripped from Aaron's chin. He wiped his forehead with his shirt again—it came back bright red.

"I'm fine." He unzipped his backpack. Then he grabbed the collar of his shirt and pulled it over his head. Caked mud and sweat stuck to his skin. He crumpled the shirt into a ball and wiped his face another time. That was when he noticed the bruises along his rib cage.

While his shirt was off, he saw Amber steal a glance at his torso, then quickly avert her gaze and fix her eyes firmly on the horizon—until a grunt from Buff made them both look in his direction.

"Buddy, she's scouting for Breezie!" he shouted, staring wide-eyed at the players' names written neatly in pink ink in Tina's notebook. "And why isn't my name here?"

"Buff, forget about it," said Aaron. "She doesn't know jack—"

"Huh Tina? Why isn't it on here?" Buff repeated.

There was a dark glint in Tina's eyes. "Because your GPA is below the league minimum. You won't be allowed to play."

"That's not true."

"Is too."

Buff tore out the page, ripped it into little pieces and dropped them on Tina's lap. "No more of this bullshit," he said, grabbing his backpack.

"You freak!" said Tina, staring at the scraps.

"When we play rugby, Breezie's going to need more than just a cheat sheet," said Buff, kicking the riser on the bench.

"Well that was lame." Tina brushed the scraps of paper into a puddle and grabbed her purse. "Amber, let's get out of here."

"Hang on," said Buff, "let me get Amber's number." He rummaged in his pockets for his cell phone, came out empty-handed, then unzipped his backpack and started digging out crumpled wads of schoolwork.

Amber gave him a coy smile. "Buff, you hardly know me," she said.

Buff's face reddened. He stood and scratched his head. "Maybe I should give you my number instead," he said.

"She doesn't want your number," Aaron scoffed.

Amber shot him a glance. "Maybe I do."

Meanwhile, Tina made a point of sighing loudly.

"I got an idea!" said Buff. "Buddy, give me your phone. I'll get her number that way."

"Too bad," said Aaron, "didn't bring it."

Amber glanced at the side of Aaron's backpack, at the mesh pocket—where the bulge of his cell phone was clearly visible.

"Didn't bring it, huh?" She slid Aaron's phone out and flipped it open, keyed in her number, and called her own phone with it. Then Amber and Tina squeezed between him and Buff on their way out.

As Amber brushed past Aaron, she slipped the phone into the pocket of his shorts. "That's for *Buff*," she whispered, her breath right in his ear. Her green eyes lingered on him for another second before she turned away.

"Buddy, *who* was that?" said Buff, gaping at him.

"Don't worry about it," said Aaron. "She's out of her

mind."

"Who cares?" said Buff. "Give me the phone number, it's obvious she likes me."

"She goes to Corona Blanca," said Aaron.

Buff lunged for the phone in Aaron's pocket, and Aaron had to beat him off with his backpack.

"Fine, I'll just wait until she calls me," said Buff, leaving Aaron to go talk to his coach, "which she *will!*"

"Say hello for me when she does." Aaron slung his clean shirt over his shoulder and headed to his car alone. So much for forgetting about her. After that last sizzling look she gave him, that was going to be impossible.

Aaron sighed, imagining how much simpler his last month as a seventeen-year-old would have been if he'd never met her—and wondering if he'd ever have the courage to delete her number. Or call her.

His Mazda waited, black and sleek. Aaron was almost at the door when he noticed the damage, and his heart jolted.

He scanned the lot, hardly breathing. Nobody lingered. Nobody had left a note.

Aaron stared at his car. A dent stretched across the door, broken glass and crumpled metal, bashed inward. Bare steel glinted underneath, deformed and scraped white. Black flecks of paint streamed in rivulets along the asphalt under his feet.

"No—" he whispered, and he laid his palm on his car's frame.

It wasn't a fender bender. The dent was too deep, as if someone had deliberately driven into it, their toe to the floor—or beaten it with a crow bar.

Aaron pulled the handle, and the door collapsed an inch and screeched open. He stared at the ruined door, and pressure tingled in his sinuses, like two thumbs pressing under his eyes.

The driver's seat was soaked from the mist, and the door didn't close. It just banged against the side and swung back open. Aaron squeezed his shirt into a ball and flung it across the parking lot.

Then his cell phone rang.

"Hello," said Aaron.

"Aaron Harper, how are you?" said an icy drawl.

A chill slithered up Aaron's spine—Clive Selavio.

He scanned the deserted school, the houses across the street. "Who gave you my number?" he said, his heart pounding. All he heard was Clive's heavy breathing infused with static.

"I told you to stay away from her," said Clive.

"How'd you get my number?"

"But you didn't *listen*," said Clive.

The air stirred in Aaron's ear, like someone breathing behind him. He spun.

Nobody.

"It was you—" Aaron's eyes darted across the street. Down in the shadows between two bushes, hunched over. Nobody.

"It was *you*—that was my car, asshole!"

Clive chuckled. "Next Friday," he said. "Expect me. I have a little surprise for you, Aaron Harper." Then he hung up.

THREE

18 Days, 2 hours, 45 minutes

Aaron didn't know whether to feel terrified, pissed off as hell, or betrayed. He was sure Amber gave Clive his number, unless Clive hacked it off her phone somehow. Or threatened her. Still no excuse.

By morning, pissed off as hell won out, and Aaron hunkered down at his desk before first period, kneading his fists. He'd spent everything he had on his Mazda, he loved that car. Sure, he wasn't always on time with the oil changes and he had to hotwire the thing each time he started it, but to him, his car meant freedom—and Clive Selavio had defiled that.

If Clive thought Aaron was just going to disappear like Justin Gorski, just another name off his hit list, he was dead wrong. Next Friday, Clive was going to lick asphalt.

Emma Mist came in late and slogged to her seat, and Aaron noticed something off about her. Her face was pale, and her hair, usually full and glossy, looked wilted. He caught her eye as she slumped into her seat, and Aaron knew this was his chance to apologize. Before she could look away, he mouthed, "*Can we please talk?*"

She stared at him, her brown eyes clouded by weariness, then gave a stiff nod. Aaron felt a weight off his chest already.

But while his eyes were still on her, her back arched suddenly. She gasped, and her bony shoulders tensed before she fell forward, shivering. Students' heads swiveled toward her, and Mr. Sanders, who had started his lecture, trailed off.

"*Emma!*" Their teacher ran to her desk and knelt beside her. "Emma, talk to me—what's wrong?"

She clutched her stomach, and a tear slid down her cheek from her wide, terrified eyes.

"Is it a stomach ache?" said Mr. Sanders.

When Emma spoke, her voice was a whimper. Almost too low to hear across a classroom, but Aaron heard.

"I . . . I can't feel him," she said, and another tear splattered on her desk. "I can't feel my half."

"Let's get you to the nurse," said Mr. Sanders, helping her to her feet. "It's going to be fine."

Emma touched the back of her own head, winced, and collapsed against his chest. She was breathing too fast, hyperventilating.

Mr. Sanders looped his arm behind her knees, scooped her up, and carried her to the door. Only Buff ran forward to help. The rest of the class sat white-faced and frozen.

Mr. Sanders addressed them before he left. "Explain how the discovery of halves pushed the world toward greater international cooperation in the late thirties, I want at least a page from each of you when I get back—and NO talking!"

Then the door slammed.

All eyes turned on Aaron. Nervous, shifty-eyed stares, wary of his reaction to what had just happened to his ex-girlfriend. They knew the symptoms.

Her half was dead.

Emma's condition had gotten a lot worse when Aaron and Buff visited her on Sunday, five days later.

Sunlight spotted the peach wallpaper in Emma's bedroom, and Aaron felt a strange twinge in his stomach when he saw her. She was buried under comforters and fluffy pillows. Her pale skin gleamed with sweat, and her eyes made endless circles as she watched the blades of a ceiling fan.

Her mother managed a weak smile from her rocking chair and leaned over her daughter. "Baby," she said, her voice cracking, "look who came to see you!"

Buff squeezed Emma's hand. "It's us, Emma. It's me and Buddy from school."

She opened her mouth but only managed to drool.

Emma's father cupped her head in his palm and edged the pillow out from underneath her. Right where the back of her head had been, Aaron saw a red stain in the indentation on the pillow—blood. Her father laid her down again and glanced at his half.

"It's getting worse," he said.

There was no cure for what Emma had, for half death. The scientific explanation was quantum entanglement, the spooky phenomenon whereby two entangled subatomic particles could be separated by light-years yet react instantaneously to changes in each other's states.

In humans, it was termed *clairvoyance.*

Up close, Emma's eyes were vacant, unfocused, cloudy. There was only a glimmer of the girl Aaron once knew, and he felt a lump form in his throat.

Emma was innocent. She was normal. There were only six weeks left before her birthday—six weeks until she met her half. And that was stolen from her.

Aaron was the one whose clairvoyant channel was clogged. It should have been him in that bed, drooling and bleeding from the back of his skull. It should have been him with half death, not her.

Aaron knelt by Emma's bed and peered into her half open eyelids. "I'm sorry, Emma."

Too late.

He felt a hand squeeze his shoulder—Emma's father. "What happened to her at school wasn't the first sign that something was wrong," he said.

"What do you mean?" said Aaron.

"She had a similar attack a couple weeks ago," said her father. "We thought it was a false alarm and that she was still okay, but now the doctors are telling us her half was already dead." The man shook his head. "Something strange happened to her half that first time. Whatever it was, it managed to keep her going for a few weeks."

"When do they think her half actually died?" said Aaron.

"They haven't quite pinpointed it yet, but they're pretty sure it was March first."

Aaron nodded, not sure what else to say.

"Wait a sec," said Buff, "March first? That's the day that

kid from Corona went missing."

"Right, Justin Gorski." Emma's father managed a weak smile. "We thought about that too, but the Chamber of Halves won't release the identity of Emma's half until she's gone—or until they find Justin's body . . ." His voice faltered and he trailed off, tears in his eyes.

Aaron caught Buff's eye, and they left Emma's parents alone with their daughter. On their way out, Aaron's cell phone beeped, interrupting their mournful silence. He opened his phone and stared at a text message from Amber Lilian.

Can I come over? There's something I need to tell you.

By eight she still hadn't shown. Aaron bounced his volleyball off his wall, straining to hear a knock on the front door, a scratch . . . *anything* over the evening news blaring in the living room. Jesus, were his parents deaf or something?

Besides, it wasn't good news playing. He could tell from the bits he overheard. A hundred-and-something year old woman who had refused to meet her half for eighty years, now famous as the sole survivor from the pre-halves era, had died earlier today. Apparently, she had been in her early thirties when halves were discovered, but chose to stay with her husband.

The doorbell rang.

Aaron's heartbeat quickened. He beat his dad to the door, fumbled with the lock, and yanked it open.

Her usual knockout self, Amber stood in the doorway, cheeks flushed, a green flower pinned to her hair. Aaron recalled vaguely that it was St. Patrick's day—and that he had thirteen days left until his birthday. He grabbed her hand and pulled her inside, his heart still jittery. At the sight of her, his dad did a double take.

But before Amber could say, "Hi mister—" Aaron hurried her down the hall, pushed her into his room, and shut the door.

"That was rude," she said.

"My parents are easily disturbed," he said.

Amber tucked her hair behind her ear. "And you think I would disturb them?"

Aaron studied her green eyes, and it occurred to him that she might be the reason his heartbeat wasn't slowing. "Never mind," he said, and he grabbed his volleyball off the floor and collapsed onto his bed. "So what did you want to tell me?" He set the ball to the ceiling and caught it.

"It's about Clive," she said.

Of course. She was here to confess that Clive was her half. Suddenly, he didn't want to hear it. "Look," he muttered. "Whatever weird thing you have with Clive, you can keep it to yourself. I really don't care."

But he was a bad liar.

Amber's eyebrows nudged upward. "You *do* care?"

"I said *I didn't*."

"You kept my phone number," she observed.

"I was keeping it for Buff."

"Uh-huh." There was a teasing glint in her eyes, as if she now had a secret she could use against him. "Well, I wasn't going to tell you about that anyway."

"Then what?" said Aaron, frustrated she had gotten to him so easily. He set the next ball so it landed in her lap, and she jolted back in surprise. He smirked and sat up next to her. "Does he know you're here?"

"I *hope* you don't think I'm that stupid," she said.

"No, but I think you're trying to make him jealous."

"Yeah, Aaron," she said, rolling her eyes, "I drove all the way out here just to make him jealous."

"Good plan," he said. "Are you going to tell him you're with me? Or do you want me to do it this time?"

"I *didn't* tell him last time."

"Then why is he paying me a visit this Friday and why is there a fat dent in my car?"

"Probably because you're dumb and you keep taking his bait." And without missing a beat, Amber surveyed him from head to toe, announced, "You're not wearing green," and pinched him on the waist.

He pinched her back. "Neither are you."

She pointed to the flower in her hair. "What do you think *this* is?"

"Nope," he said with a smirk, "It's got to be clothing." And he pinched her again.

She flung the ball at him, and he caught it. They gazed at each other struggling not to laugh, but for a moment too long. Aaron felt a tingle at his sternum, pressing down on his heart—before she blinked and looked away.

Then she spoke all at once. "I lied to you about Justin Gorski. The last person with him wasn't Dominic . . . or Clive. It was Clive's father."

"Clive's *father?*" said Aaron.

"He's a doctor," she said, "and they're staying with Dominic's family until they find something more permanent. All I know is Justin was supposed to have an appointment with him. When Justin and Dominic offered me a ride after school, they were on their way over to see him. That was the last time I saw him."

Aaron rolled the volleyball to the floor. "Why are you telling me this?" he said.

"Because I heard what happened to that girl at your school, and because . . ." she trailed off.

"Because what?" said Aaron.

Amber brought her legs onto his bed, brushing his arm with her knee. She sat cross-legged and faced him. Straight on, he noticed her eyes were layered, like gold dust sparkling at the bottom of a stream. "You aren't looking forward to your birthday either," she said.

"You remembered?" he said.

She held his gaze. "You're different."

"Yeah. You could say that."

"Did you know her?" she said. "That girl?"

Aaron nodded, and he realized how tense his own body was, how his muscles felt taut—because of how close Amber was. "I saw it happen."

In a quiet voice, almost a whisper, she said, "What was it like?"

"It was like a hand tugging at something inside her," he said, remembering the unnatural recoil of Emma's body. "She was tense for a few seconds, and then she just went slack. Like it finally ripped out."

"You know, it's getting worse," said Amber. "Every generation."

"You mean half death?"

"People were fine living without their halves for millions of years," she said. "Like that old woman on the news. Her half probably died ages ago and she didn't even feel it." Amber pulled her legs up to her chest. "It wasn't even until the second generation that people started dying of half death . . . our grandparents' generation. And back then it took years. Now it's only a few days."

"I know. Soon you won't be able to take a piss without holding Clive's hand."

Amber arched her lip in disgust. "*Eww*, Aaron . . . Why am I even talking to you?"

"Not appropriate?"

"What I *meant* is I think it's doing something to our genetics."

"Like what?"

"Like we're inbreeding."

"I get the feeling you know a lot more about this stuff than . . . most people."

Amber didn't respond. She rested her chin on her knee and continued to watch him.

"Why did Justin have an appointment with Clive's dad?" he added, forced to fill in the silence himself.

"Clive and Justin got in a fight," she said, "and Justin had these chronic headaches afterward. He was threatening to sue, so Clive's father offered to treat him so he'd keep his mouth shut."

"Justin made a pass at you, didn't he?"

Her eyes flashed a warning. "Don't act like you know my life."

"Fine. So the vial Clive brought to the beach . . . That stuff came out of Justin?"

"I don't know, but Clive didn't have it the day before."

"There was something written on the side of the vial, some kind of code," said Aaron. "You remember what it was?"

Amber shot him a glare. "Yeah, Aaron, I have photographic memory."

"It was four letters," said Aaron. "I'm not asking you to memorize the bible."

Amber was about to snap out another retort when her eyes brightened. "Hold on," she said, reaching into her pocket. "I think Clive took a picture on my phone." She flipped through her photos then showed one to Aaron.

They stared at the photo on her cell phone screen together. The vial, just as Aaron remembered, now with an ID code clearly silhouetted against the fluid.

`JGEM130301`

"The numbers are a date," said Aaron, "March first."

"No duh," said Amber, "I can read too. That's the day Justin disappeared. The letters are initials."

Aaron nodded, feeling a wave of chills. "Justin Gorski and Emma Mist."

They both fell silent. Slowly, Aaron released his breath and cupped his face in his hands. Amber quietly returned the cell phone to her pocket, and by an unspoken agreement, they didn't bring it up again. There was nothing else they could do.

Amber broke the silence first. "Why are you scared of meeting your half?"

"Because I don't want to spend my life with a stranger," he said.

"You know the first second you see her, you're going to change your mind," she said. "You don't need clairvoyance to love someone."

"I know, but it's supposed to be more than that with your half."

"It's not," she said. "The high wears off after a few months. Then you're just two ordinary people faking it like the rest of the adults."

"At least it's better than it was before."

"You mean pre-discovery? Clearly you haven't seen the bad ones."

"What bad ones?"

"Like my parents. They're rotten and they hate each other's guts. Just because they're joined at the hip doesn't make them saints . . . They actually bring out the worst in each other." Amber swiveled away from him again. "And that's what I get to look forward to." A few strands of her hair came loose and dangled in front of her eyes.

Aaron resisted the urge to brush them back. "Is that because you're Clive's half?" he said, dreading the answer.

She bit her lip and edged away from him, and a single teardrop teetered on her eyelid. Aaron recognized right then what he should have seen from the beginning. The redness of her cheeks. Amber had been crying before she came to his house.

"I'm sorry—" he began.

"I have to go," she said, and without a glance backward, she fled for the door.

"You don't have to," he blurted out, halting her in the doorway and immediately regretting it. "I mean—you're allowed to stay."

"Oh, really?" she said, "Actually, Aaron, what I'm allowed to do isn't up to you." Then she gave him one last look that set his skin on fire and vanished into the hallway. A few seconds later, he heard the front door close.

Aaron grabbed his volleyball again and lay on his bed, loathing the pounding in his chest. He tried to set the ball to the ceiling, but it struck the shelf above him and dislodged a T-ball trophy, which fell on his face.

Aaron sat up and rubbed the cut on his forehead. Clearly, he had to stay away from her. He couldn't afford to fall for her, not with his birthday in two weeks.

To clear his mind of Amber's green eyes, he thought about the vial instead, and the question neither one of them had dared voice: what in God's name was Justin and Emma's clairvoyance doing inside a vial?

Health class wrapped up on Friday afternoon with a video on half disorders. Still preoccupied with the vial, Aaron didn't bother watching. He already knew *his* disorder wouldn't be covered.

But the next section drew his attention back to the screen for a different reason: "Premature Contact."

"You meet your half at age eighteen for a reason," said the

narrator in his British accent, while a cheesy movie played in the background of new halves holding hands. "Just as touching a wire to a battery creates a surge of electricity, first contact with your half literally creates a surge of clairvoyance within your channel. Until you've gone through puberty, though, your clairvoyant channel is too soft to withstand this surge—and it's liable to burst. Because of this unfortunate reality, juvengamy remains illegal . . ."

Content the video wasn't going to reveal any horrifying truth about Amber and Clive's relationship, Aaron relaxed a little and leaned back in his chair. Though he still listened.

Apparently, juvengamy was still practiced in cult circles for the very thing that made it illegal. It made a man's half docile by emptying her out.

The exposure was timed carefully. A girl's body was more sensitive to clairvoyance, so her channel broke first. Most of her clairvoyance leaked out or collected in the boy.

All under the guise that juvengamy forged a stronger bond between halves.

Weird.

Aaron was waiting at his car after class for Buff when he heard squealing tires. He jerked his head up as a steel gray Beamer swerved through the parking lot, skidded around the speed bumps, and pulled up next to him. Dominic Brees sat at the wheel, Clive Selavio in the passenger seat.

Dominic leaned out the window. "Number eleven, don't be a loner. Get in."

Aaron stepped up to the window and casually surveyed

the leather interior, which gave off the stale smell of marijuana. Finally, he stared at Clive.

"That's eight-hundred and twenty-five dollars you owe me for my car," he said.

"Why don't you get in," said Clive, patting the back seat. "We'll talk while we drive."

"No, you get out. We'll talk right here."

Clive reached for his seatbelt, clicked it, and the strap recoiled. His fingers closed on the handle.

"Not now—" Dominic grabbed his knee and nodded out the back. "Look who's coming."

Aaron glanced up and saw Buff trudging into the parking lot.

Though his fingers whitened on the door handle, Clive stayed in the car. "Lucky bastard," he muttered, licking his chapped lips.

"So where's my present?" said Aaron, leaning in through the window. "I was hoping you were going to bring me a puppy or something."

A smirk crept onto Clive's face. "Actually, Harper, I was thinking you and I could have some *adult* fun tonight—since we're both turning eighteen next Saturday. Ever heard of the Pelican?"

"I'll pass," said Aaron. Clive was talking about a nightclub on the pier that had a reputation for underage sex. The Pelican was where seventeen-year olds with fake IDs got drugged up and lost their virginity to strangers, not realizing the consequences. Sex was meant for your half, no one else. If you broke that rule, something would forever be missing between you and your half.

"You know I'm going to take good care of you," said Clive.

"Yeah? You can start by fixing the dent in my car."

"Oh, did that make you sad?" said Clive. "Well guess what? Next time you see Amber, I'm going to put a dent in your skull."

Aaron felt an itch in his fingertips. "She came to me," he said.

Clive leaned across the seat toward him. "If that's the story you prefer, Harper, then I'll put a dent in *her* skull."

It was too much. Aaron yanked open the door. But Dominic had already shifted into first, and the Beamer lurched away from him, the door slammed.

"Oh, I forgot to mention—" Clive yelled from the window, "Amber's going too." He broke into laughter.

Aaron kicked the rear bumper as hard as he could before the car accelerated away from him, his blood burning in his veins.

Clive was taking Amber to the nightclub.

A second later Buff was at his side. "That was Breezie, wasn't it?" he said, smacking his palm with his fist. "I can smell his stink."

"Tonight," was all Aaron managed to say, his stomach turning queasy at the thought of Clive forcing himself on her, "we're going to the pier. We have to stop a girl from ruining her life."

Amber picked up after the first ring.

"Hey," she said, as if Aaron calling her was totally normal.

"Amber, could you promise me something?"

She was silent while Aaron continued to fiddle with his car door in his driveway, trying to get it to latch.

"Probably not," she said finally.

"Promise me you won't go out with Clive tonight."

"Let me guess, you'd rather I go out with *you?*" she said.

"Sure, whatever. I'll take to a movie or something."

"I didn't say I *would* go out with you."

"Look—" Aaron held the phone against his ear with his shoulder, "you might end up in a situation tonight where you could get hurt."

"Then protect me," she said.

"Amber, just promise me."

"No." And she hung up.

Calling her was a mistake, Aaron decided that night, as he scanned the swaying mass of halves grinding against each other inside the Pelican nightclub, their sweat glittering under green lasers and disco balls, because even if Amber hadn't been planning on it, now she would probably come here just to spite him.

But what worried him even more was the way he'd risen to Clive's taunts after school—how *protective* he'd felt toward her—when the odds seemed increasingly slim that they were halves. In fact, he wasn't sure he even wanted Amber as his half; she'd be a nightmare.

Yet here he was at the Pelican because she meant more to him than he cared to admit, and if Clive date raped her in a filthy nightclub eight days before her birthday, if he scarred her like that, the loss she and her half would suffer for the rest of their lives was unthinkable. Aaron couldn't let that happen.

He spotted Dominic dancing with Tina Marcello against the far glass walls. Clive would be near them. "Over there," said Aaron.

Next to him, Buff pulled on his red and white rugby hoodie.

"Seriously?" said Aaron.

"I didn't come here to dance, Buddy. Breezie needs to know what hit him."

"Whatever. Just hold him off while I take care of Selavio." Aaron straightened his leather jacket and plunged into the crowd. He focused on the rainbows cascading down Dominic's back to stay oriented as he squeezed around pairs of bodies. In the sweaty fog, someone knocked him in the jaw—and he froze.

He had walked right into Clive, and the guy still hadn't noticed him. It was too perfect.

Aaron reached for his shoulder, his heart thumping, and yelled, "Surprise!"

But right then a gap opened and he saw exactly what he dreaded most. She was rubbing up against Clive's torso in a club dress with tiger stripes, lips shining with lip gloss, her arms draped seductively around his neck like they were already halves—Amber Lilian.

Clive whipped around to face him.

Aaron had three inches on Clive. It should have been an easy fight. A few punches. He could have broken Clive's nose, knocked him out cold.

Instead he just stood there, stunned by the sight of Amber, as Clive attacked.

Aaron had been struck off guard before, knocked to the ground even. He had taken blows from other seventeen-year-olds, kicks, punches in his jaw. They didn't faze him.

This was different.

The strobe light split Clive's movement into frames. His fist burned in the white flash, a blur, before it smashed into Aaron's jaw.

Pain rattled his teeth. Aaron toppled backward, dizzy, and hit the floor. Clive knelt over him and coiled his arm back again, ready to strike with his full weight. Aaron rolled, crawled through someone's legs and jumped up. His ears still rang from the blow.

People scattered, shouted. Aaron tackled Clive in the stomach, pinned his neck. Clive squirmed out of his grip, a sour musk rising from his armpits.

Somebody's hands closed on Aaron's shoulders, dragged him backward.

"She's not your half!" Aaron yelled, but it was pointless. More bodies crowded around him, grabbed and shoved him, their ugly faces hardly human. He flung off their hands, only to suffocate in their hungry perfume. Everything was in black and white. An entire club filled with shadows, halves of people herding him backward.

Aaron never took his eyes off Amber. She was the only thing real. Her orange and yellow tiger stripes. She returned his stare, speechless, just as shocked as he was.

Clive stood behind her, smirking, and with his long, pale

fingers, he caressed Amber's neck, her collarbone, then reached lower—

Aaron averted his eyes, disgusted, as every last inch of his skin caught fire and burned with jealousy.

Aaron stumbled onto the balcony and gulped fresh air, still seething—and pissed at himself for overreacting. No shit Amber got touchy feely with Clive on the dance floor, she was his damn *girlfriend*; Aaron just hadn't really believed it until tonight. A moment later, she came out behind him.

"So that's why you called me?" she said. "You're an asshole."

Aaron rolled his jaw, and the pain from Clive's blow gnawed inside his skull. His teeth still didn't align. "Go back inside and finish what you started," he said. "Clive brought you here for a reason."

"No duh," she said, brushing her damp hair from her eyes. "They don't check IDs."

"You think *that's* why he brought you here? Come on, Amber, you're smarter than that."

"Apparently not the whiz you are," she said.

"Fine, I'll spell it out for," he said. "It's called date rape. You're nothing but a trophy to him, he's not going to wait until you're eighteen."

Amber stepped in front of him, and her eyes were stunningly bright. "He's not like that, Aaron. You're just *jealous*."

"*Oh, please*," he said, "I'm stopping you from throwing your life away . . . because you don't seem to give a damn. Jealousy's got nothing to do with this."

"And what exactly is *this?*" she said, motioning between them.

Aaron leaned against the railing, as the techno beat numbed his thoughts. "What makes you think he's your half?" he said.

"Does it matter? It's not like I get a choice."

"Yes you do," he said. "You still have a choice for one more week, and this is when people screw it up. It might not be him next Saturday, so don't do something you'll regret."

"Who are you, my *parents?*" she said. "I have enough people fussing over my safety without you preaching to me."

"Fine, but believe me you're with the wrong guy," he said.

"Why don't you just say it already and stop wasting my time, Aaron—*you* think I'm *your* half."

"Well, since you brought it up," he said, "maybe you shouldn't be dating Clive eight days before our birthday."

Amber stepped closer to him, and the ocean breeze lifted her hair across her forehead. "I'll date whomever I please."

Aaron could smell her lip-gloss—cherry flavored—and feel the heat emanating from her skin. "At least until Clive kills them, right?" he said.

"He only does that when I get bored and tell him to," she said, her eyes challenging him.

"Really?" said Aaron. "Then why has he known about every time you've seen me? Bored already?"

"Slightly."

"Then let's make things interesting. Dance with me."

"No," she said, staring him straight in the eye, "didn't you just lecture me about not doing things I would regret?"

Before he could answer, yells from inside the club

interrupted their conversation. Aaron and Amber spun as Buff staggered out onto the balcony, two bouncers right behind him, their torsos bulging inside black T-shirts.

Buff planted his palms on their chests, one on each, and halted them. "No more bullshit—I swear!"

They rolled up their sleeves and hustled him backward, shoved him against the railing. Buff's eyes froze on the dark, sloshing ocean behind him. They were going to pitch him over.

"I said no more bullshit!"

Aaron and Amber jumped to the rescue.

"There you are bud—"Aaron threw his arm around Buff's shoulder and dragged him away from the bouncers. "Been looking all over for you! See that sailboat over there . . . *marvelous*, isn't she?"

Amber intercepted the bouncers. "Oh my God, thank you guys *so* much for your help!" She smiled and batted her eyelashes at them. "He's my half."

Aaron stole a look at her and had to turn away to suppress a snicker.

The bouncers grunted and retreated into the thumping, flashing darkness.

"Buddy, I got him!" said Buff, smacking his palm. "Broke Breezie's nose, just like that." He grinned, and blood dribbled down his chin from a split lip. His eyes were bruised too.

Amber came up next to them and rubbed her arms. "It's cold," she said to Aaron, shivering. "I changed my mind. Let's go dance now."

"Forget it," said Aaron. "It was a bad idea."

"Fine," she said, and her gaze darted to Buff. "I'll dance with your best friend then—"

But before Buff had a chance to accept, Aaron snatched her hand away from him. "Alright, *one* song," he said. "You still think you're going to regret this?"

"Actually," she said, catching his eyes with a sizzling glance as she pulled him into the club's sweaty heat, "I'm counting on it."

A scan around the club revealed that Clive and Dominic were absent, and it made Aaron nervous; they were up to something.

The song was in transition as he and Amber headed for the corner, just the synthesizer. The lasers made slow sweeps across the ceiling.

When they reached a good spot, the strobe lights flashed and the bass kicked in, obscuring Aaron's thoughts. Amber faced him, blushing, and glanced down. He watched the lights flashing across her face, and his heart fluttered, weightless. He pressed his eyelids shut. His birthday was too soon; dancing with Amber was a mistake. He needed to get out of here.

But then she draped her arms around his neck, and already, he felt himself giving in. He held her waist, unable to pull away. Blood surfaced under his skin. The thrill was almost palpable.

The music pressed them together, the club dissolved. They were alone. Together.

He felt her hair on his cheek, silky. She smelled like sweat and flowers. Holding her was easier than it should have been. Excruciating, yes, but easier. Intoxicating, in fact.

Very intoxicating.

Aaron felt her mouth near his ear. "None of this is going to matter when we're eighteen. Why are you so tense?"

But she was tense too. Her body felt taut, as if she was holding her breath.

She moved closer, and he felt her cheek against his neck. He could feel her heart racing—or was it his? His nerves felt tingly wherever their skin touched.

"What are you thinking about?" she whispered.

"Take a guess."

"I can't read you," she said. "Tell me."

"Oh, you know . . ." he said, "just my Anthro essay."

"Butthead."

It felt like only a moment passed, and then the song was over. It hardly seemed fair. But they still didn't let go of each other.

"I think the song's over," he said.

"Then why are we still dancing?" she said.

Just then, Buff burst out of the crowd and grabbed Aaron's arm.

"Buddy, your *car*—" he gasped, out of breath, "Breezie and Selavio are pushing it into the water!"

FOUR

7 Days, 11 hours, 29 minutes

OUTSIDE, THE COLD, salty breeze stung his eyes, blurred his vision. Dominic and Clive leaned over on either side of his Mazda, their arms flexed on the inside of the frame. They had turned the car around, and now they were picking up speed, jogging toward the end of the pier where white foam frothed up onto the planks.

Aaron unclasped his fingers from Amber's hand and started after them—and slipped, slamming his face into wet, slimy wood. He jumped back to his feet.

"Turn it right," Dominic yelled, nearly running now. "Turn the wheel right!"

The car veered left. "I said *right!*"

They jumped away from the car, just as Aaron shot past them. He sprinted for the driver's side, where the door swung open. Salt clogged his nostrils, his thighs burned.

It was rolling twenty miles per hour into the wind, and there was forty feet of pier left. He couldn't gain on it.

But he loved this car.

Aaron took one more step and lunged, grabbed the frame. The door slammed on his fingers, but he held on. The car bounced, and he got his other hand on the door and swung himself into the driver's seat.

Now he was inside a car barreling toward the edge of a pier with twenty feet left before blackness.

Now what?

He yanked the emergency brake and jammed his foot down on the brake pedal. It was stiff; they were hydraulic brakes which hardly worked when the engine was off. He pushed harder, strained against the ceiling for leverage. The car slowed, barely.

"Buddy, get out of the car!" he heard Buff yell from somewhere far behind him.

To Aaron, it seemed to take a whole minute with his leg flexed, foot crushing the pedal, before his bumper crashed through the railing. Splinters scraped the windshield, the car pitched forward. The sea rose before him, white caps churning in the darkness, and he felt the undercarriage grind off the edge of the pier. Then everything stopped.

Balanced on the edge of the pier, the car had stopped. Aaron let out his breath.

Buff ran up and yanked the door open. "No bullshit," he yelled, dragging Aaron out of his seat.

After the two of them heaved the car back onto the pier, Aaron noticed the driver's side door hung looser than before. He pried the panel off the underside of the steering column and started twisting wires together. Since he lost the keys last summer, he had to hotwire the thing every time he wanted to start it.

The engine sputtered, and all the warning lights flashed. Aaron sighed and let the engine die.

He didn't have to check under the hood; the oil pooling under the car gave it away: a cracked oil pan. Behind him, Amber was demanding that Clive and Dominic give them a lift home.

"Are you crazy?" said Dominic, pointing to the bloody wads of toilet paper stuffed up his nose. "*Look!*"

"Wow," she said, "you're comparing a nosebleed to almost killing him."

"Why don't *you* drive him if you're so concerned?"

Her eyes flashed in Aaron's direction, suddenly fearful. "Because I don't *want* to," she said.

"Make him walk," said Clive.

"How about I just tell your father?" she said

Clive went pale.

And that settled it.

Aaron knew it was a bad idea, but they were fresh out of options. The buses didn't run past ten, and after paying twenty each to get inside the Pelican, he and Buff couldn't pool enough for a cab. Nor did Aaron have any intention of waking his parents, as that would lead to too many questions.

Aaron didn't bother saying goodbye to Amber. There was something in that last look she had given him that seemed to erase everything that had happened on the dance floor.

"Anything happens, we got each other's backs," Aaron murmured, as he and Buff slid into the backseat of Dominic's beamer, behind the guys who had just tried to sink Aaron's Mazda in the Pacific Ocean.

"Always, Buddy."

"Let's take these fuckfaces home," said Dominic, once they were all in the car.

"I bet you know where I live," said Buff, "since you egged my house fifty times."

Dominic spun around. "Make one more sound, Normandy, and you will not make it home alive."

"What are you going to do, Breezie, call another bullshit play like you did back in the Junior League rugby championships?"

"I was right with you," said Dominic. "We could have scored and you know it."

"Yeah, if you listened to me."

"There were scouts that day," said Dominic. "I'd be playing for the Eagles right now."

"A prissyboy like you?" said Buff. "Go play football if you want to be a hero."

"Both of you shut it!" said Aaron, feeling things were escalating.

Buff was talking about an old offshoot of rugby that died off in the thirties, during the exchange of international culture that followed the discovery of halves. The tougher, more dynamic rugby had won out.

They dropped Buff off first. Dominic rolled down the window, sniffed, and spat bloody snot at him—and then Aaron was alone.

"Now you have to fix my oil pan too," he said to Clive, sounding braver than he felt.

"You knew how it was," said Clive. "You knew what I had with Amber."

"Actually, I'm still confused."

"Didn't she tell you the truth?"

"That's not why she ran after me."

Clive's lips whitened. "She's my half," he said. "And if you touch her again—"

"You're seventeen," said Aaron. "You don't know who your half is."

"I thought we'd be past this by now, Harper."

Aaron leaned forward. "How about when you kiss her?" he said. "Does she kiss back like a real half?"

It struck a nerve, and once again, Aaron wished he'd kept his stupid mouth shut. Clive swiveled his body and clamped his hands around Aaron's throat, digging his fingers into his jugular.

Dominic slammed on the brakes. "*Clive!*"

Aaron clawed his face, but the guy held on.

"Clive, let him go!" Dominic yelled.

Aaron's felt dizzy, and he was only half-aware of Dominic trying to drag Clive off of him. He was more focused on Clive's hand as it reached around his head, his thin fingers probing the back of his scalp—until he touched the farthest point back.

As if he'd pressed a button, the strength deflated from every muscle in Aaron's body, and the last thing he remembered before losing consciousness was the pain, like molten lead dripping into his brain through the back of his head—that and wishing he'd had more time to live.

Because he really wanted to see Amber again.

After Amber dropped off Tina Marcello, she drove home, relieved she wouldn't have to deal with Clive after what happened with Aaron—and convinced Aaron had been put into her life just to tempt her.

The drive home was miserable. The smell of Aaron's sweat was all over her body, in her hair, and she couldn't breathe without tasting him. She needed boiling water, shampoo, a loofah, maybe even scented bath salts to get rid of it—but then she had a crazy and exhilarating thought.

If she didn't shower, if she went to bed just like this, she could fall asleep to his smell. She could sleep the entire night with a constant reminder of him, and nobody would ever know her secret. The notion gave her such an intense, nervous rush that she immediately felt herself blushing—and was furious with herself.

As if she would *ever* fall asleep like that.

As it was, she would have enough trouble forgetting the feel of his torso through a thin cotton T-shirt.

Amber sighed and closed her eyes. She couldn't allow herself to see him again, not after tonight. And that was how it should be. She loved Clive.

Her cell phone rang . . . Dominic's ringtone. Feeling faint, Amber answered her phone,

"What now?" she said.

"Your lucky number eleven is unconscious," he said.

It took Amber a moment. "*What?*"

"Selavio pulled the same exact shit he did with Gorski," he said. "Remember at school?"

"Where is he?" said Amber, swerving briefly into oncoming traffic.

"Selavio? I left him by the side of the road, he's still walking back—"

"No, where's *Aaron?*"

"Never gave me his address. I brought him back to my house."

"I'm coming over," said Amber, and she squealed to a stop before he could tell her no. There were honks behind her. As she turned around, her insides felt prickly and cold. This was her fault.

At every high school she attended, Clive did things to boys if they so much as glanced at her in the hallway. Yeah, it was frustrating enough that every boy she dated was too scared to acknowledge her existence in public, but she should have known Aaron would be much worse. He *tried* to piss off Clive.

After she parked up his driveway, Dominic stopped her at the door. Amber was breathless for a second, thinking it was Aaron.

"You probably shouldn't be here," he said, "at least not until Clive gets back. I don't want him thinking anything."

"Where is he?"

"I left him down by the freeway."

"I mean Aaron."

Dominic's eyes narrowed at her. "Amber, why do you do this to Clive?"

"Why do you even care?"

"Because his father is an incredibly talented doctor, whom I'm honored to have as a guest in my house—and he's asked me to look after his son," he said.

"Well," she said, "you're not doing a very good job of it, are you?"

"Just give Clive what he wants."

"And what does he want, Dominic?"

"He wants you."

"Doesn't he already have me?" she said.

"You could be better about it," he said.

She pushed past him. "Just let me see him."

He chased her and grabbed her arm. "You can't right now," he said.

"Is he alright?" she said, sounding more concerned than she would have liked.

"He's being examined," said Dominic stiffly.

Her eyes widened. "By—by *Clive's father?*"

"I didn't know what else to do," said Dominic. "He wouldn't wake up."

Aaron opened his eyes on a bed in a room he didn't recognize. The air tasted sour, prickly. Like static electricity and stale glue.

He felt the back of his head, but there was no more pain. Had Clive pulled some kind of Ju-Jitsu move on him?

Aaron glanced around the bedroom. The only furniture was a dresser, topped with a wrought iron sculpture depicting two cupids. The floor was layered with slivers of cut up photographs and empty cans of Red Bull. Someone had made a collage with the photos that spanned the entire opposite wall, and though he couldn't say why, something about it didn't look right.

Feeling dizzy, Aaron sat up and swiveled his feet to the floor, stepping onto a Swiss Army duffel bag that was stashed between the bed and the windowsill. A baggage claim ticket on one of the straps revealed the owner. Clive Selavio.

So this was his bedroom.

Aaron's gaze snapped back to the photos on the wall, and he realized what was off. They were all photos of the same person. Playing tennis in high school. Swimming in middle school. Even younger. Baby pictures. Everywhere he looked, a thousand snapshots of her blonde hair.

All of Amber.

The sour odor of static and dried glue seemed to thicken. He went to the sculpture on the dresser. They weren't cupids like he'd thought, they were simply babies. Two infants, their bodies wrapped around each other in a sexually suggestive way. On the base of the sculpture, carved into the iron, were the words:

Halves joined at birth
The Juvengamy Brotherhood

Hot with disgust, Aaron stared at the infants' faces, sculpted into vague expressions of ecstasy, as every puzzling facet of Amber and Clive's abusive relationship clicked into place.

They were juvengamy halves; their parents had put them together shortly after birth. There were still a few who clung to the old belief that nature intended it that way, even though juvengamy had been illegal for decades. It damaged halves, thus Amber and Clive's love-hate relationship.

Aaron's skin prickled with sweat, and he licked his lips, which had dried to scabs. If Amber was Clive's half, it didn't make sense to feel jealous anymore. He would meet his own half in a week. So why, he asked himself as he stormed into the hallway, did he still have the squeamish feeling that Clive had stolen her from him?

Dominic Brees was on his way in, though, and they collided in the doorway.

"*You?*" said Aaron, but before he could act, Dominic grabbed his collar and slammed him against the wall outside the door.

"This is my house, fuckface, and nap time's over. You owe me now for saving your life . . . Clive almost killed you."

"No shit," said Aaron, peeling Dominic's fingers off his collar one by one. He could see why Buff hated this guy. "What the hell was that anyway?"

"It's what he does to idiots who hit on Amber," said Dominic, lowering his hand. "You're lucky his father was here to examine your head. Dr. Selavio wants to check you again later."

Dr. Selavio. Clive's father. the same man, Aaron recalled, who was likely responsible for Emma Mist's half death. "We'll see about that," he said, surveying the huge candlelit hallway. "By the way, where is our wonder boy?"

"If I were you, I would stop provoking him."

"Once he fixes my car," said Aaron. "This is his room, right? I think I'll wait for him here."

"No, you won't. His father's going to deal with him," said Dominic. "Your job right now, number eleven, is to go downstairs and end whatever fling you got with Amber."

Aaron's heart stammered. "She's here?"

"And she shouldn't be," said Dominic. "If Clive comes back and finds both of you, you're dead."

"So they're halves, then?"

"What's it to you anyway?" said Dominic. "She's not available. End of story."

"I'm just curious, I'm not interested in dating her."

"Oh yeah? And what was all that on the dance floor?" said Dominic.

Aaron turned away, wishing Dominic hadn't reminded him. "It was her idea," he said.

"I'm sure you begged her to stop."

He ignored the comment. "So are they really juvengamy halves?"

Dominic laughed. "What moron told you that?"

"On Clive's dresser," said Aaron, feeling a twinge of hope as he nodded to the sculpture through the doorway.

"Yeah, he's kind of twisted like that," said Dominic, "but no, the Chamber hasn't confirmed them yet. I don't know their full story, but I do know they're going in on their birthday just like everyone else. Now, go downstairs and deal with her . . . tell her you have rabies or something."

Aaron forgot Dominic's request, though, when he found her biting her nails in an empty downstairs bedroom, her face hidden by her golden hair. Though she wasn't a juvengamy baby—and Aaron was still shaky at the good news—he still had his doubts.

When Amber saw him, she jumped up from the bed and tried without success to hide her relief. "What did Clive do to you?" she said.

"I'm fine." Aaron stopped right in front of her, and he felt the same rush he'd felt while they were dancing. Like the nervous, lightheaded excitement that comes on a roller coaster before the big drop.

Aaron had to resist the temptation to move even closer. "Tell me the truth," he said, "are you his half?"

"I'm seventeen," she said.

It wasn't even an answer. "Why is he making a collage of your face on his wall?"

"He's a family friend," she said.

"Who happens to be obsessed with you?"

Amber smoothed her fingers slowly through her hair then let it swish back, fanning Aaron with the smell of her vanilla shampoo. "Isn't that what boys do?" she said.

"The sick ones."

"Maybe I take cute pictures," she said.

"Yeah, except most of them weren't that cute."

She stared at him. "Aaron, what *am* I to you?"

"I have no idea," said Aaron. "We're not friends, we're not dating, and you don't think we're halves. Why don't you make something up?"

"You're infuriating," she said.

Aaron raised his eyebrows. "Oh, but *Clive's* no big deal?"

"It was a compliment," she said.

"I'd hate to get an insult."

"You're about to."

Her hair fell in front of her face again, and in a dizzy flash,

Aaron realized he wanted her as close to him as possible—or as far as possible. Because one dance had burned the silky feel of her body right into his skin, and that was a clear sign he couldn't trust himself around her. It was stupid to care this much; halves were predetermined.

"We shouldn't be doing this to each other," he said finally, his conviction already wavering, "especially not a week out. We'll know who it is on Saturday, so let's just hunker down and wait." He hated the way those words sounded.

"Did Dominic tell you to say that?" she said.

"He's right," said Aaron, "we're just stringing each other along—and you should go before Clive gets back."

"I liked you better when you didn't listen to anybody," she said.

"Yeah, well, I got smarter," said Aaron, his throat tight as he held the door open for her. "Maybe I'll see you in a week."

Amber shrugged and sauntered through the door, flinging her hair to the side so it whipped him in the face.

"Classy," he said.

She paused in the doorway and locked eyes with him. "You *won't*," she said.

"Won't what?"

"Ever see me again."

Aaron held her gaze. "Then you're just going to have to miss me."

"Don't hold your breath," she said, but instead of leaving, she just stood there—and Aaron felt the weight of their looming birthdays more than ever. Next time she would be with her half, he with his, and they wouldn't even notice each other. Their pre-birthday fling would be as unmemorable as if it had happened in their mother's womb. They couldn't say goodbye like this.

Aaron shut the door, and as if the sound had freed them both, he swept forward and she collapsed into his arms, tugging his shirt to her chest.

Aaron wrapped his fingers around her hand, and she let go of his shirt to squeeze back. His lungs felt tight. It was the coolness of her skin, the bristles of electricity climbing his fingers, the shallow beat of his heart.

Staring into her green eyes, he knew they were about to kiss, and the rush made him dizzy. He could feel her heartbeat through her hand, like a butterfly's wings. They moved closer.

But just before their lips touched, the door burst open next to them, and Clive Selavio strode into the room.

Aaron stepped in front of Amber to protect her. Clive, who hadn't seen them yet, heard the movement and halted in the middle of the room, his shoulder's flexed under his gray hoodie. He raised his head and sniffed the air, and as he faced them, Aaron caught a whiff of antiseptic—and saw why.

Blood dripped from gashes under Clive's eyes. Dark bruises gleamed with Neosporin, polished and shiny. He had been beaten.

As Aaron watched, he touched his eye and caught a drop of blood, which crawled down his finger like a black beetle before his tongue flicked out and licked it clean. "Amber, I didn't say you could be here," he said.

Aaron felt her tense beside him. "Isn't that up to Dominic?" she said.

"It's up to me," said Clive. "It's what I *let* you do, and until you behave—"

Aaron cut him off. "Buy a pet if you want to make rules, Clive."

Amber flashed him a warning look. "*Don't*," she said.

"You're wasting your breath," said Clive. "Harper doesn't know the negative command."

Amber glared at him. "Do you want me to get your *father*?" she said.

At the mention of his dad, Clive flinched. "Amber, could you do me a favor and go home?" he said.

Aaron starting rolling up his sleeves. "Wait outside," he said to Amber. "This'll just take a second,"

Amber watched him nervously. "Aaron, you'll *lose*," she said, and then she left.

Clive's pale eyes tracked her out the door then flicked back to Aaron. "My father will see you now," he said.

"What the hell happened to you?" said Aaron, rolling his sleeves back down.

Clive stepped toward him, and his eyes flashed treacherously. "I said my father will see you now. You wouldn't want to be late for your appointment, would you?"

Back upstairs, Aaron watched the quiet hallway from Clive's bedroom. His heart thundered impatiently, and Amber's playful smile winked at him from every wall, driving him crazy.

Unable to bear it, he forced his eyes to the opposite wall, to a poster above Clive's headboard. The famous photo of Schönbrunn Palace, Vienna. Taken 1939, when ninety thousand people packed the courtyard to learn the identity of their halves.

The first generation.

Aaron envied their pre-discovery lives. Everyone just living, loving whomever they pleased . . . sometimes loving *no one* . . . no ticking clock—

There was a quiet knock at the door, and Aaron's heart slapped against the inside of his chest. But the man who entered was nothing like what Aaron expected.

Dr. Selavio ducked through the doorway, clipboard in hand, and stood to his full height; he nearly reached the ceiling. His white lab swished in behind him, parting to reveal a beige collared shirt and matching tie. His skin glowed bronze, and although his eyes sagged from lack of sleep, they were bright, heroic.

Aaron breathed a sigh of relief.

Dr. Selavio saw him turn away from the poster and grinned, revealing a wide, immaculate row of white teeth. "A world transformation in just a few years," he said, nodding to the poster. "I pity all their lives before the discovery. All those wars and all that hatred. All that loneliness." He reached out his hand. "Casler Selavio."

Aaron took his hand and felt calm wash over him. It was only after the handshake that he noticed the black flakes of blood on the man's knuckles.

Casler saw where he was looking and rested his hand out

of view behind the clipboard.

"I apologize for my son's behavior this evening," he said. "He has trouble coping with his condition, and he often lashes out. It's always something. Lately, he's been sneaking off with my things." He scanned the room before his eyes settled on Aaron again. "In fact, I don't mean to pry, but has he ever showed you anything curious?"

"Curious?" said Aaron. "Like what?"

"Perhaps a vial?" he said.

Aaron swallowed. "What was in the vial?"

Casler just smiled. "You will tell me if that vial turns up, won't you?"

Aaron nodded.

"Excellent," said Dr. Selavio, beaming at him. "Now about what happened to you tonight . . ." He scanned his clipboard. "Clive discovered his ability to inflict pain on others a few years ago, quite by chance, actually. We've seen counselors about it, and by now, he knows the risks of permanent injury, both to himself and his victims. His slipup tonight was unacceptable."

"How does he do it?" said Aaron.

The corner of Casler's mouth twitched. "Sadly, my son's connection to his half is weak," he said. "The attractive forces that hold his clairvoyant channel together tend to drift. When he touched you in just the right spot, those loose forces tugged at your channel and caused you tremendous pain—and in your case, knocked you out. Your reaction did concern me a little, so I hope you don't mind that I took the liberty to examine you earlier." Casler nodded and glanced up, his eyebrows low and brooding. "What troubles me,

Aaron, is that curious lump of scar tissue you have blocking your channel."

Aaron was used to hearing bad news from doctors, and he zoned out most of what Casler said, but this surprised him. "How'd you figure it out so fast?" he said. "You can't possibly have an MRI machine *here?*"

With a smile, Dr. Selavio reached out and bent Aaron's head sideways. "Ever felt pain in this spot before?" he said, his thick finger probing the back of Aaron's skull.

"Sometimes," said Aaron, suppressing the urge to shiver.

"I understand you and Clive share the same birthday," he said. "You must be excited."

"Yeah," said Aaron, unnerved as Casler continued to feel around the back of his head, "just about as excited as anyone with a blocked channel can be."

"Hmm—" Casler pulled his hand back. "With your permission, Aaron, I'd like to run a simple test to see what we're dealing with here. I've got some equipment down in the cellar."

"What kind of test?" said Aaron, wondering if Justin Gorski had ended up in Dominic's cellar after his "appointment."

"There's something about that scar tissue that really troubles me," he said. "I'm actually not authorized to test minors, but since this is a private home—and since you only have a week until your eighteenth birthday anyway—I'm willing to make an exception. I'd like to reveal the identity of your half."

Aaron's eagerness to know his half switched to utter dread when he stepped into the musty wine cellar ahead of Dr. Selavio and saw the tripod-mounted, powder-white glass globe affixed with an orbiting brass scope.

Aaron had only seen them in pictures. Now he was looking at a real one—an aitherscope—a device that used a property of fused quartz to allow a viewer to peer inside his own clairvoyant channel, thereby revealing his half. They were rare, and you had to be licensed by the Chamber of Halves to even own one. Now, faced with the truth so soon, Aaron wished he still had a week-long buffer. Yet he couldn't resist his morbid curiosity.

Up close, the contraption smelled like rubbing alcohol, and Aaron saw why the globe looked opaque from across the room. There were millions of web-like cracks spreading out from its core. Aaron felt the urge to look away from the glass, as if he was staring someone in the eye.

A data cable ran from the back of the aitherscope to an open laptop on a stool. Dr. Selavio unlocked the eyepiece with a key and slid it along two concentric, grooved tracks, one labeled with the month and day, the other with the year. He clicked it into place at the intersection of March 30 and the year Aaron was born.

"Go ahead and peer through the eyepiece," said Dr. Selavio. He pulled a pen from his breast pocket and leveled his clipboard. "It's streaming video, so I'll have the same image on my laptop."

"And what am I supposed to see?" said Aaron.

"Should be an image of your half's eyes—her iris pattern, essentially. Sort of like a fingerprint. Once we get a clear picture, we'll get it analyzed."

Amber's green eyes flashed in Aaron's mind before he could stop himself, and he wasn't prepared for the nervous rush that shook his body. He stepped up to the brass eyepiece, and his heartbeat ratcheted up. He was scared to look, scared of what he might see—or might not see. He inhaled slowly, but his pulse kept climbing. Maybe just a quick glance. He leaned forward, closed one eye, and touched his eyebrow to the cold brass.

Aaron blinked, and a white circle filled his vision, cracks whizzed out of view. Then it went dark. He shifted to get a better angle.

"It's a piece of junk, it's all black—"

Just then an image flashed into focus. He saw threads of white static, so bright they stung his retinas. Aaron shoved the eyepiece aside, head spinning, and staggered backwards. A throbbing pain gnawed at the back of his skull. He clutched his scalp.

"Is this some kind of joke?" he said. "It's broken!"

"Why, what did you see?" said Casler, glancing between Aaron and the laptop screen, now blank.

"Nothing," said Aaron, "just static."

Dr. Selavio's eyebrows shot up, almost to his hairline. He scribbled something on the clipboard.

Aaron leaned forward to see what it was, but Casler tilted the clipboard away from him, still writing. "I'm sure Clive's explained my work," he said.

"Actually, I'm confused," said Aaron, and he pulled out the crumpled appointment reminder. "What is *Abnormal Obstetrics* anyway?"

Casler continued his frenzied notes. "Think of me as a plumber," he said, "I fix leaks in the clairvoyant channel. Mainly, I deal with childbirth, since virtually all abnormalities in the clairvoyant channel originate during its formation at birth."

"Is that what I have?" said Aaron, trying to peek over the clipboard again, "an abnormality in my channel?"

Casler finished jotting notes in Aaron's file and glanced up. "If it's alright with you, Aaron, I'd like to see you again. Preferably before your birthday."

"What'd you write in my file?"

"You have my card, Aaron," he said, tucking the clipboard under his arm. "You should grab Dominic now so he can drive you home." He flashed his brilliant set of teeth one more time and reached out his hand.

"Is something wrong with me?" said Aaron, but he didn't need to ask. Dr. Selavio's too-firm handshake confirmed his fears.

"I'm sure it's nothing," said Casler.

Aaron eyed the medical forms on the clipboard, suddenly convinced that Dr. Selavio knew something about him the other doctors didn't. He needed to read those notes.

Casler wore a ring on his middle finger, which he clinked against the clipboard. It was the only sound in the damp, concrete space. Frozen under Dr. Selavio's impatient stare and unable to formulate a plan fast enough, Aaron trudged toward the exit.

"One more thing," said Casler, when Aaron reached the stairs, "I'm glad you're curious about my work. I think you should come on Wednesday."

"What's on Wednesday?" said Aaron.

"It's kind of like a support group for men. We all need some time by ourselves, you know, without our halves." He winked. "Dominic attended last week, and I think he enjoyed himself. Think about it, Aaron. Oh, and shut the cellar door on your way out, would you?"

Aaron snapped out of his daze when he emerged from the cellar and found himself in the grandiose marble-tiled entrance hall of Dominic's mansion. He simply had to get his hands on that clipboard.

Feeling ridiculous, he hid in the bedroom where he'd found Amber until Dr. Selavio came out a few minutes later—empty-handed, he noticed.

When the sound of footsteps vanished, Aaron rushed back to the cellar. Once again in the dingy chamber, he scanned the floor around the aitherscope for the clipboard, but the only other thing in the cellar was wine. Casler must have carried it out with him. But the laptop too? Surely, he would have seen it under Casler's arm.

Aaron twisted to leave, thinking he'd been an idiot, when he caught movement out the corner of his eye. A rack of wine bottles against the far wall.

Heart thudding, Aaron scanned the racks, but everything lay still. Then he saw it again. The wine in each bottle was gently sloshing back and forth.

Dr. Selavio must have bumped the rack. Or moved it. Aaron crossed the room, and his scalp tingled against his skull like it wanted to peel away. Electricity hummed in the air near the back wall, cold as frost.

He knelt and felt along the edge of the wood frame, in between the wine bottles. Yes, the rack was on hinges.

With a tug, the entire section came loose and swung open, exposing the bare wall—and a gaping hole the size of a doorway, jackhammered right through the concrete. No wonder Dr. Selavio had stayed in the cellar.

From out of the dark pit, dank air rushed up Aaron's nostrils. Just inside the hole, jagged steps dropped into the earth, and he couldn't see the bottom. The cellar was already underground, the stairs went deeper.

Before he chickened out, Aaron stepped into the blackness and descended, pulling the rack closed behind him. He had done enough stupid things tonight already. What difference would one more make?

The stairs got steeper, thinner. Slimy roots hung from the ceiling—at least Aaron hoped they were roots. It was too dark to tell. Thirty feet down, he hit the bottom. The air purred with the warm smell of machinery. Drips echoed around him.

The stairs had opened into a chamber, and a light switch glowed red on the wall next to him.

He flipped the switch.

The scene that flickered into view made him gasp. It was manmade—but hardly. An enormous granite cavern expanded around him, with rough columns carved into the rock. Bulbs dangled from the ceiling, blinking like sick fireflies.

And Aaron was certain he had found the source of the static electricity he felt upstairs.

Anchored to the bedrock and rising to the ceiling was a device that, if fitted with lenses, could pass as a giant telescope in an observatory. From the machine's base, power cords snaked into the darkness. Something massive oscillated inside its metal core, and the nauseating rhythm thumped against Aaron's ribs.

Slouched in a chair at the foot of the machine, casually winding a spool of rope, was Clive Selavio. Blood had dried on his face in crusty black trails.

He made another coil as he watched Aaron enter the chamber. "You know we're supposed to be together," he said, "me and Amber."

"What the hell is this place?" said Aaron, and his voice echoed.

"Be honest," said Clive, letting the rope unwind through his fingers, "did you kiss her?"

They glared at each other, and Aaron's blood prickled. Neither one of them blinked.

Aaron nodded to the machine. "What's this?" he said, still not looking away.

"It's my father's."

"What's it do?"

"It makes an incision in the clairvoyant channel," said Clive. He leaned back and ran his hand along the steel shell.

"I thought he *fixed* leaks?" said Aaron.

"He does, but it's very much like surgery," said Clive. "You ever gotten surgery?"

"Not my thing," said Aaron.

"They have to cut you open first."

Aaron finally broke their stare. He circled the machine,

too curious to hold off any longer. Around back, panels were missing. They hadn't been installed yet, and Aaron saw what was inside Casler's device.

A spider web of crystal fibers, sewn together and pulsing like strands of mucous. They were organic, alien—*living*. But nothing was spinning—the thumping came from the fibers themselves. Aaron smelled burnt ammonia and wrinkled his nose.

The machine telescoped down to a dull metal spike, which was aimed at an operating table crisscrossed with thick nylon straps. The straps were meant as a harness.

"Don't tell me someone lies here," said Aaron.

Clive laughed. "I guess you could say that."

And Aaron noticed the odor of ammonia rose from a stain at the center of table—urine.

The machine had been used recently.

Aaron's heart gave a jolt. Justin Gorski. So this was how Dr. Selavio sucked out his clairvoyance.

The clipboard lay on a broken concrete slab behind the machine. Aaron unclipped the medical forms and began folding them. It was time to get out of here.

"Put that back," said Clive, "it's my father's."

When Aaron didn't comply, Clive lunged and closed his fist on the wad of paper. He yanked so hard Aaron thought his wrist would snap, but Aaron held on, and the folded stack tore in half.

Aaron had the side with the most writing, though, and before Clive realized, he stuffed the wad in his pocket.

Clive's forearms tensed, but he didn't attack him. Aaron wondered if it had anything to do with the wounds on his forehead.

Clive's lips curled into a smirk. "You'll be going on Wednesday, won't you?"

"Yeah, I'll bring a bag of potato chips for the potluck afterwards," said Aaron.

"We provide the refreshments," said Clive.

"Who's *we?*"

"The Juvengamy Brotherhood."

Aaron raised his eyebrows. "Is this the weekly social?"

"It's a bit more formal than that," said Clive.

"Is Amber going?"

Clive's smirk only grew. "You know, juvengamy halves get marked for each other," he said. "Matching tattoos."

"I've heard about that," said Aaron.

"Ever seen one?"

Aaron felt his heart quiver. He didn't say anything.

Clive turned his side to Aaron and removed his gray hoodie. He reached for the bottom of his shirt and lifted the hem to his shoulder—giving Aaron a full view of his side and back.

Aaron stared at the marks on Clive's torso, and a chill sank into him. The lines were white scars, etched into his pale skin—as they had been since the day he was born. The tattoo resembled a fingerprint, only more symmetrical, more spiral-like. It wrapped around the side of his rib cage and over his shoulder blade, but cut off at his spine.

"It's only half done," said Aaron.

Clive let his shirt fall back into place, and his lips twisted into a cruel smile. "That's because Amber has the other half."

FIVE

7 Days, 9 hours, 1 minute

AT TWO IN the morning, Dominic skidded to a stop in front of Aaron's house.

"That's twenty dollars for the gas, fuckface."

"What is this, *Europe?*" said Aaron, the image of Clive's tattoo still vivid in his retinas. He threw his last two ones at Dominic and stepped out of the car, hardly caring that now the rugby player—and probably in a few minutes, Clive too—would know where he lived.

Amber has the other half. Those words haunted him still, as Dominic's Beamer roared away from the curb, shattering the quiet of the sleeping neighborhood. But Aaron had to see the tattoo on Amber to know for sure. Her shoulders had been bare while they were dancing, but he hadn't looked. The club was too dark.

Aaron knew he had to quit agonizing over her, his birthday was too close, but he couldn't think about anything else. No way could he forget her enchanting green eyes, her maddening overconfidence, her nerve.

Seven days—seven days until he turned eighteen and never saw her again.

Back inside his room, Aaron dragged the torn stack of medical forms from his pocket and spread them out under his desk lamp, hands shaking. Under the "complications" section on a form titled "Physical Examination," Dr. Selavio's sloppy cursive was barely legible.

Scar tissue obstructing clairvoyant channel. Likely result of massive trauma to channel during birth.

Trauma during *birth?* But Aaron hadn't sustained any trauma during birth. Not unless you counted the false alarm story his parents always bragged about to family—how an intern had misread one of the synchronized clocking machines and declared Aaron a stillborn, even though he was crying right in front of them.

With the uneasy feeling his parents hadn't quite told him the full story, Aaron read the scribbles concerning his condition on the next form, titled "Aitherscope Imaging"—and felt his insides seize up.

Aitherscope registers zero clairvoyant activity and patient experiences inexplicable pain. Suggests extreme vulnerability to clairvoyance. Patient MUST NOT meet his half; initial surge of clairvoyance upon first contact will likely rupture his channel . . .

The rest was torn off, but those three sentences were more than plenty.

Darkness swallowed the bubble of light around Aaron's

desk. He tried to neaten the stack of forms, but they slipped through his jittery fingers and floated to the floor. He rose, tipping the chair backwards. His eyes throbbed, blurry.

Dr. Selavio's notes about him made two things clear. First, if he met his half on Saturday, his channel would rip open and leak like Emma Mist's. They would both die. Second, Amber wasn't his half, otherwise they would already be dead.

Aaron shrank onto his bed and grabbed his volleyball, but instead of setting the ball to the ceiling, he just curled around it, hugging it between his knees.

For his whole life he had worried something would be missing when he met his half, when in fact he *couldn't* meet her—No, *shouldn't* meet her. No matter the risk, he still had to show up on his birthday.

Life without one's half was no life at all, everybody knew that. Once mature, the human body required constant physical contact with its half. Aaron faced a simple choice. He either died on his birthday with his half, or withered away months later without her.

There was a third choice. It involved Amber and running away from their halves, and it burned him with such a deep sense of shame, he thought he would puke.

Aaron didn't know how he made it through the weekend, or why he even bothered patching the crack in his oil pan on Saturday afternoon, but by Monday morning, he had successfully relegated Dr. Selavio's medical report to the back of his mind. By first period, he even rekindled his delusional hope that he and Amber could be halves. Now, if he could just convince himself she wasn't a juvengamy baby.

From what Aaron remembered of the video they watched in health class, juvengamy girls had been emptied of the most precious thing they had.

Clairvoyance was like your soul. It was the conscious, living part of you, and should you lose any of it—well, it wasn't hard to imagine what that was like.

The worst part was that Amber Lilian supposedly had a scar branding her as one of them.

Aaron leaned toward Buff's desk. "Besides the matching scars," he said, "what else you know about them?"

"They're spooks," said Buff. "Ghosts. People say they're hollow."

"You can tell?"

"The girls act like their half's pet. They're not all there."

"The parents must be out of their minds."

"It's in their blood, Buddy. Ever since that first generation."

"So it's like their inbred—"

"Mr. Harper—Mr. Normandy!" Mr. Sanders yelled from the front of the class. "Shut it."

Buff leaned closer so he could whisper. "Their founder's like a hundred-and-twenty years old. I heard they're choosing an heir to replace him when he dies."

"How do they know who goes with who when they're putting kids together?" said Aaron, "Wouldn't they need access to the Registry?"

"They keep their own records," said Buff. "Most halves stay within juvengamy families."

"And they're always weird and empty?" said Aaron. "I

mean, let's say I met a juvengamy girl, would I be able to tell she's one of them just by talking to her—"

"Congratulations, Mr. Harper," said their teacher, his eyes intent on Aaron, "you've just earned yourself a detention." He turned back to the board. ". . . as I was saying, in response to Saudi Arabia's ongoing refusal to legally recognize halves, the League of Nations imposed sanctions on any country that prevented, hindered, or in any way deterred halves from meeting safely . . ."

Aaron slouched until his butt almost slid off the chair and fixed his eyes on the ceiling.

"However," Mr. Sanders continued, "it wasn't until almost fifty years later—about the year you guys were born—that Saudi Arabia became the final member state of the Chamber of Halves . . ."

When the bell rang, Jessica Lim, a girl who sat at the front, bounded over to Tina Marcello's desk.

"Oh my God! Can you believe it's tomorrow?" she said, squealing and clapping her hands. "And guess what I overheard? My parents are sending us on a honeymoon *cruise!*"

Out in the hallway after class, Aaron thought about his conversation with Buff. So there was no way to determine if Amber was a juvengamy baby. Not unless—and the idea gave him a nervous twinge—he accepted Casler's invitation to the Wednesday meeting of the Juvengamy Brotherhood.

Not the smartest idea, since he guessed the urine stain on Casler's operating table came from Justin Gorski. On that night, Casler must have drained the boy's clairvoyance into the vial, the same vial Clive brought to the beach a few hours later. Aaron couldn't imagine what it must have felt like for

Justin—and for Emma.

If only Aaron hadn't dropped the vial out at the buoy, he could have brought it the police, maybe gotten the substance analyzed. He wiped the sweat off his forehead and swung his gym bag to his other shoulder. Today was going to be hot.

"Buddy, it's ninety degrees out," said Buff, collapsing into an empty picnic table at lunch. "We're ditching practice and going to the beach."

"Not me," said Aaron, sliding on his sunglasses.

"Yes—you, me, Tina, and Amber. Tina invited us all to Arroyo beach."

At the mention of Amber, Aaron's heart fluttered. "Since when does Tina invite us to the beach?"

"She's okay now," said Buff. "She broke up with Breezie because his birthday's in a few months . . ."

Aaron missed the rest of Buff's explanation. Even in the scorching heat, the prospect of seeing Amber again gave him goose bumps.

So she was fine with breaking their consensual goodbye. Okay, so they hadn't *really* said goodbye. In fact, as Aaron recalled, their goodbye was interrupted . . .

Through his sunglasses, the sky blinded him. The sun's heat seared his scalp and the back of his neck. His black T-shirt scalded him, and he clawed at the material, trying to pull it off his skin—at least he could take his shirt off at the beach.

Amber would take hers off.

And he could check her back for the mirror image of

Clive's tattoo.

At two in the afternoon, Aaron and Buff trudged through the sand to Amber and Tina, who were sunbathing on two fluffy beach towels—and the center of attention of three chatting teenage boys. Amber lay on her back with one knee raised, stunning in a bikini, Aaron noticed.

"You three," he said, once they'd made it to the boys, "beat it."

Buff smacked his palm. The kids, probably juniors, took one look at the rugby player and stumbled away.

"So you're rude to everybody," said Amber, perching herself up on her elbows as Aaron approached her.

Now was his chance.

Heart racing, Aaron tossed his shoes behind her, and while he pretended to stash his wallet and phone inside them, he glanced at her exposed back. At first he wasn't sure, the way sunlight glanced off her bare skin, silvery white. A spiral shaped scar, or was it sunscreen? It was almost too bright to tell, even with sunglasses.

Aaron squinted, shifted positions, then perceived her back clearly. He felt a wobbly twinge in his knees. Amber's skin was unblemished, and he let himself sigh his relief.

Next to them, Buff and Tina were arguing.

"Stop blotting out the sun," said Tina, arching her upper lip in disgust. "I'm trying to tan!"

"Why'd you bring this bullshit washcloth?" said Buff.

"Oh my God," said Tina. "Don't you own a towel?"

To Aaron, their voices sounded distant, hollow. Still

feeling faint, he crouched in the sand next to Amber and scrutinized her face. Today, her eyes sparkled brighter than he'd ever seen them. Her golden hair winked at him in the sunlight.

"So . . . I kind of missed you." she said, holding his gaze.

Those simple words made his heart race. Up until now, he doubted she felt anything for him. This was the closest she had ever come to admitting she did.

"Yeah, you might have crossed my mind once or twice," said Aaron.

"Per second," she said.

"Has Clive tried to see you?"

"I've been ignoring his calls." She scooted over to make room for him on her beach towel. When he didn't move, she said, "What? Am I too cool for you?"

He eased in next to her, careful not to brush her skin. She tugged his shirt over his head again and dropped it in the sand.

Buff, now sick of Tina, paced a few feet away.

"First league game this Friday," he muttered, mostly to himself. "We play Corona Blanca, and coach won't let me play because of my grades—this is *bullshit!*" He kicked a crater in the sand. "I bet Breezie set me up."

Tina sighed. "All you and him ever talk about is getting revenge on each other—it's so lame."

Buff threw a practice punch through the air, then another. His fists whistled. "Friday, Breezie's gonna get it."

Aaron scanned the distant line of buoys lost in thought, and his eyes settled on the one he and Clive swam to the night of the bonfire, hardly more than a dot on the horizon.

What did it all mean? If Amber didn't have the matching tattoo, then who did?

And why had Clive insisted all this time that Amber was his half?

Aaron blinked. It was right in front of him.

The buoy.

The buoy marked the exact location where the vial sank. He could swim back out; he could dive to the bottom. He *could* recover the vial.

A wave of sweat soaked his skin, and he peeked at Amber, afraid she might have read his thoughts. At the same time, she glanced at him too, and their gazes snapped apart.

It was a stupid idea, he decided, now hyper-aware of Amber as she played with her hair. An underwater current would have swept the vial away by now, or buried it in the sand.

Amber leaned against him and whispered in his ear, her breath hot. "Aren't we supposed to say goodbye to each other?"

He tensed up, doing all he could to resist bringing her into his arms. But he nodded. That's what they had come here for.

He hadn't seen a tattoo, but that didn't prove anything. Obviously, Clive knew something about her he didn't. But what? Aaron scooped up a palmful of sand and watched the grains slip through his trembling fingers.

"Fine. If you're just going to sit there, I'm going to leave," said Amber, shoving him off her towel so she could fold it up. "Can you at least give me a ride home?"

"Look, I'm not really in the mood to be chivalrous right now," he said.

"So you want me to *walk* back? My house is way up on Mission Ridge."

"Then take it at a jog. You're athletic."

"In sandals?"

"How'd you get here anyway?" said Aaron, standing up next to her.

"I got a ride like a normal person," said Amber. "How do you *think?*"

Aaron cocked his eyebrow. "Would it kill you to be polite for once?" he said.

"Polite to *you?* Maybe if you weren't about to blow me off . . ." She gave up and sighed, "*Whatever.*" Then raised her voice. "Buff! Aaron's being a butthead."

Unable to resist, Aaron gave into the urge and tousled her hair—and was stunned how soft it felt.

"I thought you weren't touching me?" she said, smoothing her hair back again.

"I shouldn't be," said Aaron. "But you're . . ." he trailed off, not sure what he'd been about to say.

Amber stepped close to him. Kissing distance. "But what?" she said, "But I'm getting hard to resist?"

Aaron studied her face, the mischievous glint that lit up her eyes—concealing everything behind them that was dark. "I think I can manage to keep my hands off you for five days," he said.

Her piercing green eyes held him captive. "What about a lifetime?"

After Amber slipped into a jean skirt, she and Aaron walked across the sunbaked asphalt toward his Mazda. She held his shirt hostage.

When they reached the car, Amber faced him. "Did you have fun today?" she said.

Aaron held open the passenger door for her.

She didn't budge. "Did you?"

"If I was bored I would have told you," he said.

"What kind of answer is that?"

"I did."

She cocked her head. "Did what?"

"I did have fun." But even before the words left his mouth, a lump formed in his throat.

Amber's golden hair shimmered in the sun and blew across her cheek. "Me too," she said, and she climbed into the car.

Once inside, Aaron pulled off the panel under his steering wheel and dug through the wires. His fingers trembled.

"Are you stealing this car?" she said.

Aaron pressed the wires together and jerked his thumb away as they burnt him. His car rumbled to life. "It's my car," he said.

"But you stole it?"

"I lost the keys."

"Uh-huh," she said, eying the wires doubtfully.

Aaron revved the engine, yanked the wheel, and they flew out of the parking lot. He was aware of Amber's gaze on the side of his face.

"Why didn't you steal a nicer car?" she said.

"I didn't steal it," he said.

She wrinkled her nose. "This one smells."

For the next few minutes he followed her directions up Mission Ridge, past glinting red convertibles and glass mansions. The ocean glittered through the palm trees.

But he hardly noticed. He focused on Amber, radiating heat right next to him, just as tense as he was. Her warm scent floated through the car, and the thought of saying goodbye to her was unbearable.

Aaron spun the wheel, shifted into second, and carved around a switchback.

Below them, the green valley shimmered under waves of heat, and the sun's reflection winked off hundreds of tiny cars. Up here, the mansions were even bigger.

"This is my house," said Amber, pointing to a Mediterranean-style palace.

Aaron parked in front of a blue Corvette on Loma Sierra Drive. He unwound the ignition wires and his car shuddered to a stop.

The moment the AC quit, a yellow heat flashed through the car and the sun blazed their skin. For half a minute, neither of them spoke.

Because now that it was silent, now that they were alone—

Aaron faced her and slid off his sunglasses. She fidgeted with one of the laces on her bathing suit top.

"So I guess this is it then," he said.

"No duh," she said. "You're horrible at goodbyes . . . and you're not getting a steamy goodbye kiss if that's what you're fantasizing about."

“I think that would be inappropriate,” he said.

“You’re worried about your half, aren’t you?” she said, her tone daring, and he hated the way she referred to his half like she didn’t expect it to be her, didn’t even *want* it to be her.

“It’s complicated,” he said, facing forward again, his mind in turmoil. It was true; their involvement with each other this close to their birthdays could damage both of them. Like underage sex, enough emotion for the wrong person right now could drain clairvoyance from their channels, never to be replaced. Not a lot, but enough to notice, and they would feel what was missing the second they laid eyes on their halves.

A thick, sticky heat smothered the inside of the car. Amber shifted in her seat. “Do you ever get scared?” she said.

“I’m scared right now,” he said.

“I’m not.” Her green eyes sparkled. “You make me forget.”

“Stop it,” he said.

“What if this is all we ever get?”

“This is not all you get,” he said. “You get to spend your entire life—”

“With the wrong person,” she said, finishing his sentence. “Do you want to meet my parents and see for yourself?”

“Amber, you don’t have to be like them,” he said. “You’re not Clive’s half; halves love each other. That’s the only thing that’s real.”

“And what’s this?” she said.

“It’s fake.”

At first she didn’t move, but then she clicked open the door and stepped onto the curb. “Then maybe I was just being naïve," she said, her voice flat. The door latched behind her.

It was done.

Aaron took a deep breath and tried to connect his ignition wires. They sparked, but he couldn't hold them together.

Something felt wrong. He and Amber turned eighteen in five days. Halves or not, they both knew the danger of falling for each other. The decision to wait should have been easy, an obvious precaution. Anyone would have done the same in their shoes.

Instead, she acted exactly how he felt—as if these five days were her last. Ever. She acted like she didn't want to say goodbye. He didn't want to say goodbye, either. Because in five days, his own connection to his half would be uncertain, unlikely even. It might not even exist.

But Amber was real now.

Aaron kicked open his door. He caught her halfway up the broad, terra cotta steps leading to her front door and grabbed her by the hand.

"We don't have to end this—" he said, pausing to catch his breath, "if you still want to do this."

"I changed my mind."

"No you didn't." He pulled Amber closer, and her hair loosened and gathered over her eyes. The ocean reflected in her irises like glitter.

Suddenly his sprint up the stairs caught up with him. He tried to catch his breath but couldn't, or was it *her*, the heat emanating from every inch of her bare skin? Because he felt dizzy just looking at her.

And then he did it.

On impulse, while his brain was infuriatingly absent, he did the very worst thing he could have done. He kissed her.

The kiss surprised her at first, but then she sank into him, and he felt her fingernails digging into his back, squeezing him even closer. In his arms, her body felt naked and hauntingly appealing. Around them, the horizon's silver haze swirled endlessly. They were weightless. And Aaron realized his nerves had been frozen up until now, numb, asleep for his whole life.

Waiting for her.

He pulled away slowly, and the citrusy, salty taste of her lips lingered pleasantly in his mouth. But before he could speak, movement in one of the windows drew his gaze. "Are your parents home?" he said.

"Are you hoping they saw?" she said, goose bumps spreading down her forearms.

"They're inside, aren't they?"

"I don't actually want you to meet them."

Aaron tried to read her expression, but she was closed off once again, guarded. "Amber," he said, "is it a bad idea for me to keep seeing you? Will I end up hurting you?"

She stared at him, biting her lip, but said nothing.

"But you want me to anyway?" he said.

Slowly, she nodded.

And she looked very different than the girl he had met at the bonfire—disturbed, more dangerous. Involved in things she shouldn't be. Instinct told him this was wrong.

He should have let her go.

But the feeling passed quickly, like a wave of vertigo. Maybe he was still unsteady from the kiss. Yeah, that was it.

He and Amber climbed the rest of way to the front door. A sea breeze followed them through a marble archway, and into her house through two glass-inlaid mahogany doors.

Inside, the peach colored carpet was spotless. Someone had even vacuumed it in perfect rows, like farmland. The scent of lavender and orange soap wafted over them.

Aaron knelt to unlace his shoes, but Amber yanked him back up. She pressed her finger to her lips, then hurried him past a living room, where her dad was watching television.

Aaron strained his neck to get a look at the man's face. But all he saw was gray hair, cut military style—before he tripped on a staircase and slammed his knee into the riser, rattling the whole flight.

Amber shot him a furious look and dragged him up the stairs and out of view just as her dad turned around. Upstairs, her bedroom had a balcony and a view of the islands.

"Sorry, it's a mess," she said, shutting the door quietly.

"Amber!" her dad yelled from downstairs.

"Fine Dad!" Amber rolled her eyes. "He wants me to leave the door open." She kept it closed, though.

Aaron narrowed his eyes. "Am I in danger?"

"Only if you do that again," she said.

"And then what?"

"He'll get his rifle."

Amber circled her room, tossing laundry into the closet. Meanwhile Aaron reclined on her bed next to a powder-white teddy bear the size of real bear. His body sank into the turquoise down comforter, and his elbow struck an object.

An open shoebox, doodled with hearts. He looked closer . . . letters.

Amber saw the shoebox and snatched it up. Blushing, she shoved it out of view.

"What are those?" said Aaron.

"Love letters."

"From wh—?" But before he could finish the question, an odd stiffness gripped his chest. "Oh." He sat forward, kneading his palms. "Never mind."

"Well since you're *jealous*," said Amber, plopping down next to him, "they're letters my great-grandparents wrote each other." She slid closer to him, and he felt his breath stop in his throat.

"You still have their letters?" he said, sounding more relieved than he should have.

"I'm weird. I know," she said.

"How old were they?"

"Our age. It was right before everything changed."

He understood what she meant. "So they weren't halves."

Amber nodded. "Don't you think it's scary that everyone from before the discovery is dead?" she said. "I guess that's why we're special . . . the *fourth* generation and all that. Because there's no one left who *remembers*."

"You mean what it was like?"

"What true love is."

Aaron felt a chill. "Is that why you keep their letters?"

She glanced up. "I want to know what it's like to have a choice." Over her head, dust swirled through shafts of sunlight, blazing like flecks of magnesium. "You're the only boy I've ever kissed like that. Are you proud of yourself?"

"No. Now I'm never going to get you out of my head."

Up close, her eyes appeared layered, freckled like jade crystals. "I wish I had more than five days to know you, Aaron."

"How do you know you don't?" he said.

She leaned forward to kiss him. "Stop asking questions you don't want to know the answer to," she said. "Let's just make it count."

At that moment, the door banged open, and Amber jumped away from him. Her father stood in the doorway.

"*Son*—" His gray eyes flashed between them. "I expect your folks are having dinner soon. It's best you headed home."

Aaron walked downstairs in front of Mr. Lilian, still drunk off the man's daughter, euphoric.

The TV in the living room showed a televised political speech of some sort. Aaron was almost at the door when he recognized the politician on the screen—and his scalp tingled.

It was Dr. Casler Selavio, towering over an audience of reporters and flashing his dazzling rows of teeth for the cameras.

Aaron halted to listen.

"Rest assured the Brotherhood does not endorse the juvengamy procedure," said Casler. "Our mission is to help past victims cope with their loss, not create new ones."

A journalist asked a question. "Doctor, you claim you've invented a cure for half death, but have you considered the ethical implications of such a cure?"

"I'll leave that to the Chamber of Halves," said Casler. "For those interested, a demonstration of the technology will be given on Wednesday." He signaled for another question.

"Dr. Selavio—" yelled a reporter. "Are the rumors true that you've been chosen as the heir to the Juvengamy Brotherhood?"

Aaron felt a hand grab the top of his head and aim it out the door.

"That way," growled Mr. Lilian, before Aaron could hear the response. More questions he might be able to answer if he accepted Dr. Selavio's invitation to the Brotherhood's meeting. Outside, a twilight breeze sliced through his hair.

"Just one last thing," said Mr. Lilian, before Aaron left, "and this is for your own good, son. My daughter isn't allowed to date. If you ever go near her again, it's going to be your ass."

SIX

3 Days, 19 hours, 56 minutes

AARON ARRIVED EARLY for his afterschool detention the next day and found Mr. Sanders's classroom empty, so he sat at a desk. He couldn't stop thinking about her, about their kiss, and whether their plan to meet up tonight after her parents fell asleep would work. The anticipation made his heart race, but in between the shallow beats, his body revolted.

He knew the stakes. They were both due at the Chamber of Halves in four days, and with the taste of Amber's lips now etched into his brain, there was no way he could truly be there for his half. Not all of him, at least. Their channel, malleable up until their eighteenth birthday, would congeal with whole chunks missing.

Still, given the scar tissue blocking his channel, he doubted it mattered. If four days with Amber was all he got, she was worth it. Or *was* she?

Reeling with uncertainty and beginning to feel nauseous, Aaron switched his thoughts to Dr. Selavio and his alleged cure for half death.

If he did possess a cure, he certainly hadn't cured Emma Mist and Justin Gorski; he'd done just the opposite. Aaron drummed his fingers on the desk, then stood up and paced back and forth along the front of the classroom.

Just the idea of a cure for half death grossed him out. That halves died together was only humane. Continuing on alone after your half died would be pure agony. Yet Aaron had to admit, the "demonstration of the technology" planned for Wednesday aroused in him a certain perverse curiosity.

Would Casler unveil his machine?

Aaron was still pacing when he noticed the door to Mr. Sanders's office was slightly ajar. The bolt hadn't latched properly.

He approached the office, hesitated, then tugged the knob. The door swung open—and what he saw inside made his heart lurch.

A human skull, propped up on his teacher's desk. Its cavernous eyeholes gazed vacantly at the ceiling, swallowing the white blaze of a halogen lamp. A microscope jutted out from one of the eye cavities. Based on the geometry, Aaron estimated that a spot inside the cranium, directly opposite the eyeholes, lay at the microscope's focal point.

Aaron stepped behind the desk and glanced around, his heart thudding. From out of the vacant eyeholes, the stink of ancient rot curled up his nose and prickled the hairs on his forearms. This picture was wrong. Whatever was down there at the back of the skull, it wasn't meant to be seen.

He felt a frantic urge to knock the whole setup over and run. Yet his curiosity pushed him closer.

He steadied his breathing, wiped sweat from his clammy forehead, and leaned forward. The instant he pressed his eye to the top of the microscope, the air stirred.

Light filled the eyepiece. An image came into focus, he blinked—

"Mr. Harper, what do you think you're doing?"

Aaron jumped back.

Mr. Sanders stood in the doorway holding a tray of bones. He raised his eyebrows.

"Mr. Sanders, why do you have all these . . . all these . . . ?"

"*Bones?* I'm putting together a lab activity we can do in class." He set the tray on his desk. "I read in Scientific American that in old human skulls you can actually see the marks left by clairvoyance." He nodded to the skull under the microscope. "This one dates back almost seventy-thousand years. Have a look."

Aaron swallowed and leaned forward. Once again, a faint image crystallized through the lens, and the hairs stood erect on the back of his scalp.

At this scale, the back of the skull appeared coarse, almost terrain-like through the microscope. Peaks of bone rose out of focus. But with eerie precision, the three-dimensional pattern of an iris—an eye—was burned deep into the cranium. Aaron wondered if *it* was scrutinizing him rather than the other way around. He pulled away from the microscope.

"That's what you get from thousands of years of clairvoyance eroding the minerals in the fossil," said Mr. Sanders.

"*Thousands* of years? But halves weren't discovered until—"

"Exactly. We're starting to find evidence now that halves existed all along . . . Either that or its somehow propagating backward through lineage, in which case this could be recent."

"But there's still clairvoyance even though this guy's dead?"

Mr. Sanders nodded. "It's proof that even death doesn't break the channel between halves. The channel stays intact no matter what, even after the halves are long gone. Ironically, that's what causes half death."

Aaron perked up at his teacher's words. "Half death? What do you mean?"

Mr. Sanders smiled. "Think about it. When your half dies, it's like removing a plug from the other end of your channel, thus your clairvoyance leaks out. If the channel closed instead, then nothing would leak out and you could keep on living—albeit, severed from your half."

Aaron twisted away from his teacher, his skin prickling. So that was what Dr. Selavio's meant by a "cure." His machine severed the connection between halves in an attempt to keep one alive without the other. He had severed Emma and Justin.

By the time Aaron's chills subsided after detention, though, an idea had crept into his mind that made his insides squirm.

He and his half might die as soon as they met each other, but if they let Dr. Selavio sever their channel, there was a chance they could still live—and that's what scared him the most. That, and how desperately he clung to the insanity of it, how the madness took hold and dug in its claws. And he knew—despite his body's revulsion—that he would go through with the cure if he had to. That if he had to, he would sever his channel to his half.

Aaron imagined how Emma must have felt when her link to Justin was torn out of her, how she must have grasped inside her mind, terrified and lonely, but felt only the hole where he used to be. And Aaron tried to imagine a lifetime like that, perpetually hollow. Wasn't it better than nothing, though?

Maybe. Probably not. Regardless, Aaron wanted to know what Dr. Selavio was actually capable of. Still queasy, he dragged his cell phone out of his pocket and dialed Clive's number.

And he accepted Casler's invitation.

Fifteen minutes before midnight, Amber finished straightening her hair and studied her reflection. She felt beautiful, a feeling that hadn't left since she last saw Aaron. Tonight, he wouldn't stand a chance.

Not that she stood a chance either. Their first kiss had ruined her. Now whenever she closed her eyes, she felt like she was falling into his arms all over again.

Amber heard the muted buzz of her cell phone. Heart pounding, she leapt onto her bed and dug it out from her comforter—but for the twentieth time, it was Clive.

She silenced the phone, both irritated and embarrassed by her sudden adrenaline rush.

She watched the screen flash Clive's name then go blank and wondered again if her parents' story was wrong. What if everyone was wrong?

What if Aaron was actually her half? But it was too much to hope for, and she knew it. Aaron would forget about her the moment he met his half on Saturday. Amber collapsed miserably into her pillow as she imagined a replay of their first kiss, but with another girl. His half would be tan and exotic—and she wouldn't deserve him.

Amber's phone buzzed again with a new voicemail. Amber stared at the screen, now uneasy, and something told her she needed to hear this message.

Six minutes before midnight, Amber pressed her cell phone to her ear and listened to the hiss of Clive's voice.

"Amber, if you don't call me back in the next two minutes, I'm waking up your father to tell him," he said, and even though he was carefully measuring his voice, she could tell he was livid. "And one more thing—"

For a moment he just breathed into the phone, as if trying to calm himself. "Your boy toy's joining us at the warehouse tomorrow. He's going to realize you've been lying to him." He let out a low chuckle. "You have one minute and thirty seconds."

Then he hung up.

Amber dropped the phone, horrified. What was Aaron thinking going to the warehouse with Clive?

She glanced at her clock. She was meeting him in five minutes. They had waited all day for her parents to finally fall asleep, and if Clive woke them up now—

The downstairs phone rang, making her jump.

It was also ringing in her mom's bedroom down the hall—and in her dad's bedroom upstairs. They would wake up any second.

Amber raced down the stairs and caught it on the second ring. "What do you want?" she whispered furiously.

"So you've been screening my calls," said Clive.

"Why did you invite him?" she said.

Clive was silent a moment. "Father did."

Amber breathed once, and her body's warmth was suddenly gone. *Casler* invited him? Surely after what happened to Justin, Aaron knew not to trust him.

"And he's going?" she asked, but Amber knew it was a dumb question—of course Aaron was going; he always got himself into this kind of trouble.

"I tried to talk him out of it," said Clive. "But you know how bad a listener he is."

Only to you. Amber checked the clock in the den. 11:57. She bit her lip. She was starting not to care if her parents woke up or not, just as long as she got to see Aaron right now.

"Clive—*good night*," she said.

"Hold on," he said, his tone suspicious. "What's the rush, Amber?"

"My *parents*."

"They're asleep," he said. "Otherwise they would have picked up the phone."

She ran her fingers through her hair in frustration, and Clive must have realized he was about to get hung up on, because he changed his tactics.

"I miss you," he said quickly. "I want you to come over."

"Don't you sleep?" she said.

"Not unless I'm with you," he said.

"Then pretend," she said and hung up anyway, feeling only a twinge of guilt. He'd be pissed tomorrow, but at least he wouldn't call back tonight. Tonight she was Aaron's.

But first, she had to make sure Aaron wouldn't go to the Brotherhood's meeting with Clive. She hated that she had to lie to him, but if he figured out how screwed up her parents were, or worse, if he found out what was really going on with Clive—she shuddered at the thought. She would tell him everything, just not tonight.

At midnight, the gardens on Loma Sierra drive glowed blue and magenta under landscape lighting. Tularosa twinkled in the valley below.

The night was electric.

Aaron was waiting, just as they'd planned. As soon as she saw him—wearing only a short-sleeved shirt, arms crossed, leaning against his stolen car like nobody's business—she fought the urge to throw her arms around him.

"I was just about to leave," he said with a smirk. "If you kept me waiting thirty more seconds—"

"Well aren't you impatient to see me," she said.

His stare made her feel faint, and Amber realized she wasn't hiding anything from him. She was still flustered from Clive's call and it was all over her face.

"It was my parents," she lied quickly.

"It was Clive, wasn't it?"

"I said it was my parents," she said. "Can we go?"

He unfolded his arms. "What did he say to you?"

Amber stepped closer to him. "Ask him yourself," she said. "You're going to see him tomorrow anyway."

Aaron raised his eyebrows, but said nothing. Then he

circled to the driver's side. Frustrated, she lowered herself into the passenger seat.

They flew down the ridge, around switchbacks, and then cruised along State Street, past halves stumbling home with each other, palm trees strung up with white lights, and empty, flashing clubs. A fog floated overhead, stained orange by the city's lights.

"Please don't go," she blurted out.

"I'm not going anywhere," he said.

"I mean tomorrow," she said. "That meeting. Don't go to anything he invites you to."

Aaron shifted gears forcefully, and they sped through a stop sign. "I have to go," he said. "Don't ask me to explain it."

Her heart plummeted. "He's lying to you," she said.

"Who? Clive?" he said.

"Casler."

"About what?" said Aaron.

"About whatever he told you when he examined you," she said. "He lied to Justin too."

All Quiet on the Western Front, a movie about the last big war before halves—the World War—showed in the Arlington Theater at midnight. It was mostly empty.

They chose the farthest seats back, and Amber raised the armrest separating them. She leaned into him, her hair draping over his shoulder.

She closed her eyes, breathing in his smell. It was like the poisonous, dizzying fumes that rose after the strike of a match, existing only for a moment before the flame went dark.

She closed her eyes and pressed herself closer to him. During the explosions, her eyelids flashed neon yellow, but she didn't want to open them. They were in their own world at the back of the theater, a world where they never had to say goodbye to each other, where they were halves, and where juvengamy was only a memory.

Aaron's body went rigid.

"What are you thinking about?" she said.

He trailed a finger down her arm, teasing the skin inside her elbow and giving her goose bumps. "Something my teacher said," he said.

"Wouldn't you rather think about us?" she said.

"I try not to," he said.

Meaning he can't stop. She smiled, and slowly draped her arms around his neck. "My parents won't be home tomorrow evening," she whispered into his ear with her most alluring voice. "We could hang out if you want?" And then she left him no choice by kissing his neck. He would, of course, no longer be accepting Casler's invitation.

"Nice try," he said, giving her a consolation kiss on her forehead. "But I'm still going to the meeting."

While Aaron waited for Clive and Dominic to pick him up the following evening, he opened his mom's laptop and googled Dr. Selavio.

The name popped up in medical journals and websites sponsored by the Juvengamy Brotherhood, but nothing of interest. Then, in an old article archive, Aaron stumbled across a strange headline:

Casler Selavio Fails to Demonstrate Cure for Half Death; Cites Privacy Issues

Curiously, the article was ancient, from the year Aaron was born. He glanced up at the kitchen clock: 9:05 p.m. They would be here any minute.

Aaron skimmed the article, and a few sentences jumped out at him. He reread them.

. . . though Dr. Selavio claims the March 30 test of the device (performed during birth) was a success, he still hasn't revealed the identity of the "severed" boy, citing a wish to protect his privacy until a much later date. Selavio states that the procedure may leave scarring at the back of the brain, but no external signs. Meanwhile, health practitioners are alarmed by the staggering rates of half death observed in recently widowed halves . . .

Aaron tried to swallow, but couldn't work the muscles in his neck. According to the article, Casler had tested his machine on a newborn on March 30, eighteen years ago—the same day Aaron was born.

Could it just be a coincidence?

He recalled that Casler had also written on his medical forms that his scar tissue was probably the result of a massive trauma to his channel during birth. Perhaps he meant a trauma like getting severed from his half.

Aaron's sweaty thumbs slid on the keys, and his heart made dull, echoing thumps in the hollow of his rib cage. Was *he* the "severed" boy Dr. Selavio had tested his device on?

There was a loud honk from Aaron's driveway.

Aaron snapped his head up, and his stomach plunged. He rose from the table, hands shaking, and tripped over his chair.

Dominic's Beamer purred in his driveway. Its high beams flooded Aaron's front yard with a blinding bluish haze, while a full moon glowed on the horizon.

Aaron slid into the backseat, willing the panic from his mind. He would find the error in his logic later.

"Put this on," said Clive, handing him a cloak without looking at him.

Aaron held the material to the window, and it shimmered in the moonlight—a luminescent royal red. Dominic and Clive were already wearing theirs.

In addition, Clive wore a gold sash over his shoulder—*membership*. He fingered the scabs around his lips and eyebrows, which still hadn't healed from Friday.

"Amber's not your half," said Aaron, trying to distract himself with the first thing that came to mind. "She doesn't have your tattoo."

Clive smirked. "Not yet," he said.

"What the hell does that mean?"

"You'll just have to wait and see, won't you?"

On the freeway onramp, Dominic downshifted and put on a burst of speed. Aaron's stomach scrunched against the seat, then sloshed back. He laid the cloak in front of him, queasy all over again.

"You know the exit," Clive said to Dominic.

Layers of Eucalyptus rushed by outside the window, black and silent. And through the gaps, the full moon burst through a silver veil of clouds.

For several minutes they drove in tense silence. Then Dominic took his eyes off the road and twisted around in his seat. A white bandage covered the bridge of his nose.

"I swear to God, if Normandy tries anything this Friday—" There was a click, and Aaron saw a thin switchblade glint in his hands. He raised it to Aaron, blade first. "He's dead. Got it?"

Aaron felt his muscles tense, but he didn't flinch. "You might want to stab me right now then," he said.

"Sounds like fun." Dominic smirked and flipped the knife closed. A minute later, holding the steering wheel between his knees, he lit a joint and the reek of marijuana wafted through the car. Clive took the next hit, held it in. Two wisps of smoke seeped from his nostrils as he offered the glowing tip to Aaron.

"I don't smoke," said Aaron.

They got off the freeway and drove for miles down a deserted road, past dry fields and empty warehouses. Every quarter mile, a street lamp flooded the car with orange light and deepened the hard creases in Clive's face.

"Pull in here," said Clive. "We're in that warehouse."

Aaron saw what he was pointing at and realized coming here was a big mistake. Nature had tried to reclaim the warehouse but abandoned the job half done. Ancient graffiti flaked off the pitted concrete into tall, dead stalks of grass. Yellow bulbs flickered over twisted steel doors. An old backhoe had been driven into the wall, and the hydraulic rams had long since rusted over with hard, black scabs.

The only sign of activity was the white light spilling onto the dirt through a crack in one of the boarded up windows. At this point, Aaron figured he would rather strap himself into Casler's device than step inside the place.

Dominic parked behind the warehouse, and two men walked out to meet them. The hoods of their red cloaks covered their eyes.

One man was a whole head taller than the other—Casler Selavio. Aaron's heartbeat quickened.

Casler signaled for Dominic to roll down his window, and then he leaned in and stared around at the three of them. He paused at Aaron and grinned.

"Glad you could come, Aaron," he said. In the weak glow of distant street lamps, his face appeared gaunt, chiseled. His eyes glinted out of bottomless pits of shadow.

His eyes darted to Clive, who was taking another hit from the joint. "Is that weed?" he said. "Hand it over."

Clive passed the joint to Dominic, who passed it to Casler.

Casler stood up, pressed the joint to his lips, and inhaled deeply. Then he breathed out a contented sigh and leaned through the window again. "Everyone out of the car," he said. "Time for introductions." He flicked the last burning ember off to the side.

Aaron opened his door and was overpowered by stench. There must have been a sewage treatment plant nearby. He tugged the cloak over his head and staggered to the other side of the car.

The other man was buzzard-like, and for a moment, his fierce yellow eyes targeted Aaron. He wore a gold cross around his neck and a woven sash similar to Clive's.

Casler wore dozens, all different colors and embroidered with ancient crests. They seemed to indicate his high status in the Juvengamy Brotherhood.

And Aaron became aware, more subconsciously than anything, that a spell-like power emanated from Casler's proud eyes. He beamed at all of them, and when he placed a hand on Aaron's shoulder, Aaron moved to stand beside him, feeling calm, blissful even—when a moment before he'd been certain the presence behind Casler's eyes was not human.

"Father Dravin, these are friends of my son," said Casler, herding them forward like children. "Dominic and Aaron."

The priest didn't smile. "Are they Brothers?" he said.

"Just guests," said Casler.

Dravin straightened his glasses and his eyes flicked to Aaron, but he said nothing.

They walked across the dead field, pitted with gopher holes, and through rows of expensive cars.

Moonlight brushed the back of Aaron's neck like a whisper. He shivered, with the sudden strange feeling he was being watched. He thought he saw motionless figures in all the cars, in the passenger seats, but it must have been an optical illusion. Aaron passed another car—and froze.

A blue Corvette, just like the one he had seen in front of Amber's house. Her father's car. Was this why her parents wouldn't be home tonight?

Aaron tore his eyes off the license plate, unable to recall the number.

Blinding light spilled from an open doorway in the warehouse, past the mangled, dented steel door.

Before they filed inside, Aaron saw the priest grab Casler's arm and stop him just outside the doorway. He stood on his toes and whispered in Casler's ear.

Aaron angled toward them and paused to listen, and because Father Dravin hadn't noticed him trailing slightly behind the others, Aaron heard every word of their whispered conversation.

"You expect them to believe you?" he said.

"Of course," said Casler, smiling.

"A child without a half?"

"Half death is a disease, Father, therefore it is curable."

"He would die of loneliness."

"*Loneliness* is not a clinical cause of death."

"There are other things," said Dravin. "Things from above. You could never make such a child persist."

"But Dravin, I *have* made such a child persist." Casler swung around, smiled at Aaron, and stepped into the bright warehouse.

Aaron's pulse quickened as he followed the men inside. *A child without a half* . . . so a cure for half death was possible, and Dr. Selavio was going to demonstrate it tonight. Aaron swallowed and tried not to think about the article he read earlier.

Hot air circulated inside the warehouse. A hundred folding chairs faced a podium, most of them filled, and Aaron noticed immediately what was wrong.

The chairs were filled by men—only men. Not one of them was with his half. They all wore the same red cloaks with sashes. The murmur of only male voices, like a constant growl, was a sound Aaron had never heard before.

The three of them, Clive, Dominic and Aaron, filed into a row near the front. Clive shook hands with the men around him.

Aaron scanned the audience for Amber's father, but there were too many faces, their identities lost under red hoods. Coincidence or not, the blue Corvette had gotten him to thinking about Amber and her disturbing, impenetrable life. There was so much she hadn't told him, and now, as Aaron sat in the cult's secret warehouse, her secrecy stung like betrayal.

A moment later, Father Dravin stepped behind the podium and took hold of the microphone. He peered around the room, hawk-like, until the conversations trailed off.

"Schrödinger's gift," he began. "The gift that keeps on giving. Your half is your slave; cherish her, and the depth of her loyalty shall touch your heart." Dravin smiled. "Please look to the brother next to you and recite the creed."

The din of low voices and sliding chairs filled the warehouse. Aaron crossed his arms and stared at the ceiling. Stupid cult formalities.

Dominic and Clive had already paired up. A hand gripped Aaron's arm, and he glanced over as a wrinkled old man settled into the seat next to him. The man started to speak.

"I am master and keeper of my half—" He paused. "Eh? You got to speak up son."

"Keeper of your *half?*" said Aaron in disbelief. "That's

how it starts?"

A deep chorus resonated around them as everyone else recited the creed.

"Eh?" The man cupped his hand behind his ear and leaned closer. "You don't *know* it? Listen closely," he said, and then his gruff voice articulated every syllable. "I am master and keeper of my half. So was my father, and so too shall be my son. Bind me to my birthright, brother, I shall bind you to yours . . ."

The old man was oblivious that everyone else in the warehouse had finished.

At last, there was quiet throughout the warehouse—an embarrassed, echoing silence. Aaron pulled his sleeve out of the man's iron grip. He caught Dominic's gaze and rolled his eyes, then slumped in his chair and tugged his hood until it covered his face.

Father Dravin nodded, pushed his glasses up his nose, and continued his talk. "Eighty years later, the clairvoyant channel is stronger than Schrödinger could have dreamed, and each new generation knits it tighter . . ."

So this was the Juvengamy Brotherhood—men who thought their halves were slaves. It made sense that Clive was here, but why Dominic? Aaron shifted, and his cloak peeled away from the chair, stuck with sweat.

"Unlike our bodies, clairvoyance lasts forever, which makes our commitment to forging strong channels at birth all the more pressing . . ."

Dravin finished an incomprehensible philosophical lecture an hour later, and there were sighs of relief as the men rose for intermission. They congregated along the back wall at tables laid with whisky and crackers. Badly in need of fresh air, Aaron slipped out a back door.

Outside, dark clouds swallowed the full moon. Before he could sift through his thoughts, though, Aaron heard a muffled roar of applause inside the warehouse. The door unlatched, and Clive poked his head out. "Harper, get inside," he said. "It's time for my father's demonstration."

Back inside the warehouse, chairs tipped back as the audience stood to cheer for Casler. The doctor leaned against the podium, let his hood fall to his shoulders, and flashed his dazzling grin. A dozen men lined up to shake his hand and congratulate him, but there were too many and he waved them all back to their seats. While his standing ovation roared on, he pointed to different people in the audience and winked.

Aaron squeezed into their row and sat in the empty seat next to Clive. The applause trailed off.

"A quick demonstration—" Casler boomed, and he produced two vials from the pocket of his cloak, a bottle of red dye, and an eyedropper. Each vial was half-full of a clear liquid. Then he hoisted a blowtorch onto the podium, crumpling Dravin's notes.

"May I have a volunteer?"

A palpable excitement rippled through the crowd as Casler picked his volunteer from a dozen hands—a man in the seat in front of Aaron—and handed him one of the vials.

"Hold that up so everyone can see," said Casler.

Aaron leaned forward, as the man held up a four-inch

long glass vial exactly like the one Clive had brought to the beach. A chill fluttered down his spine.

Casler stepped back to the podium and held up his own vial. It was open at the top like a test tube. "Mr. Lilian, is that vial sealed?"

"Yep."

"So there's no way for anything to get out?"

"I'm wondering how stuff got *in*," he muttered.

Laughter trickled nearby, but Aaron's body had gone rail stiff. He was sitting directly behind Amber's father—whose cloak, he noticed, was just as decorated as Casler's.

Casler grinned. "Excellent. Now watch closely."

He filled the eyedropper with red dye and held it over his own open vial. Before he released it, he peered stoically at his audience. "You are about to witness something spectacular—"

Then he squeezed the dye into his vial, and Aaron heard gasps, mutters.

"Mr. Lilian, hold that up so everyone can see."

Red dye swirled inside the vial in Mr. Lilian's hand, the same dye in Casler's vial.

Casler didn't wait for the chatter to stop. He lit the blowtorch and propped the open vial in the blue flame. The crowd waited anxiously. Half a minute later, the liquid boiled. The liquid in Mr. Lilian's hand bubbled also.

In two minutes, the liquid in Casler's vial had boiled away completely.

And the vial in Mr. Lilian's hand was also empty.

Casler smiled and collected the vial back from him.

"When I put dye in one, it colored both. When one boiled

away, they both disappeared—why?" He chuckled. "Because the molecules of both vials exist in a state of quantum entanglement."

The audience sat in dumb silence. Casler paced the stage. "But the demonstration was merely an analogy. I'm sure you've guessed what for—"

He peered around at them all. "The clairvoyant channel. Only instead of test tubes, you have living, breathing human beings. Instead of clear water, you have clairvoyance. Drop ink into a man, and his half will feel it."

"Dr. Selavio—" A hostile voice drawled from the corner. Dravin. "What do you suppose the halves feel if their clairvoyance boils away, as you demonstrated here?"

Casler held out his hand to silence the hisses. "A human being is not an open test tube," he said.

"Right. I suppose you'd have to cut a hole in one first," said Dravin.

"Nor are they made out of glass, Father."

"But you do have to cut a hole," said Dravin. "Am I mistaken?"

"Just poorly read," said Casler. "As I announced at Monday's press conference, I aim to *seal* the hole created by half death, not the other way around." Casler beamed at them, despite their somber expressions. And then he stared straight at Aaron. "In fact, I've sealed a boy who should have died—a boy who had no half."

The mutters trailed off.

"For eighteen years, his condition has been kept a secret, but now he sits in this very room. Now he will come before us."

Aaron wasn't sure he'd heard him right.

Casler scanned the wide-eyed and quiet audience. "I invited him tonight, although—" Casler looked in Aaron's direction again and chuckled. "I wasn't entirely sure he would come."

Sweat prickled on Aaron's face.

"On March thirtieth, eighteen years ago," said Casler, louder now. "I severed this boy's channel, sealed the leak—and saved him from half death."

Aaron watched in horror as his life unraveled before his eyes. The article. He should have known tonight was a trap, that he would be exhibited before the Brotherhood as Casler's twisted science experiment, as the boy without a half. An anomaly of the living world. There were a dozen seats between him and freedom—too many. They'd stop him.

Once again, Casler scanned his audience and stopped at Aaron, still beaming, full of pride. Others were turning in their seats, trying to get a look at him. "And now," he said, "let's have him come forward—"

Next to Aaron, Clive tensed. He was going to hold him if he ran. It was an ambush.

Casler raised his arm and pointed, and Aaron gaped, petrified, down the length of the man's finger as it bored into him like a spotlight.

Clive shifted again. He edged closer, his arms flexed.

But Aaron wasn't about to be taken by a cult in a dark warehouse and paraded as a freak.

A dozen seats. A dozen grown men. Aaron stood, and his chair toppled backwards. He balled his fists, ready to fight, as Casler spoke.

SEVEN
2 Days, 11 hours, 11 minutes

"I WOULD LIKE to present my son, Clive Selavio . . ." He saw that Aaron had stood and trailed off.

Aaron froze. Slowly, he stared around the warehouse at a hundred puzzled faces, and the thumping of his heart echoed, as if amplified over a loudspeaker. He faced the podium again, Casler—and they stared at each other in shock across three rows of blood red hoods.

Clive grabbed his cloak and tried to yank him back down. "Aaron," he spat. "Sit down! You're ruining it!"

Aaron no longer had a choice. He plowed toward the aisle, shoved aside knees, and stumbled. Clive grabbed his cloak and it ripped off his shoulders. Without it he felt naked, exposed, with only jeans and a T-shirt protecting him from a hundred pairs of gleaming eyes. He kept going, vaguely aware of someone rising behind him—and acutely aware of Casler's gaze drilling into the back of his skull.

Finally, he lunged through the door and stumbled into

the night. A moment later, Dominic ran onto the field after him.

"Number eleven, you can't just leave!" he yelled.

"Yeah—" Aaron spun, and his face burned with sweat. "Then stab me."

"This is a big moment for Clive. You walk out on him, you walk out on Dr. Selavio, you walk out on us," said Dominic.

"Can I throw a 'fuck you' in there too?"

Dominic just raised his eyebrows, then shook his head. "That's a big mistake, number eleven."

Aaron marched toward the street.

"A *very* big mistake," Dominic muttered, before slipping back into the warehouse.

Aaron walked under the blotted out moon, between dark, hungry-looking Cadillacs.

He had gotten it so wrong.

No shit the date in the article matched his birthday; March 30 was *Clive's* birthday too. Dr. Selavio had tested the device on his own son, not on Aaron . . . and, according to his speech, cured him of half death. A chill crept up Aaron's spine.

He was now outside the warehouse, missing the crucial truth—and in fifty-nine hours, he was due at the Chamber of Halves. Aaron reached the road and began to jog, then to sprint. Anything to burn off his adrenaline. The orange streetlights swam overhead, and a humid wind whipped his hair. He passed parked cars for several hundred feet, then his thighs gave out and he keeled over, gasping for breath.

A boy who had no half, Dr. Selavio had said—no doubt just rhetoric to play up his cure for half death. Because it didn't make any sense. Or did it? Technically, children were born halfless all the time. Those babies were always stillborn, though—

Aaron jolted upright, distracted by the car parked next to him. There was someone in the passenger seat.

He approached the window, heart pounding. But it was too dark to see. He leaned closer, pressed his forehead to the glass, and waited while his eyes adjusted. When they did, he jerked his head back.

For several agonizing seconds, a woman peered at him blankly through the glass, emotionless, her gaze eerily vacant. Aaron returned her stare, fighting the urge to look away—until he realized there was nothing staring at him. There was nothing behind the woman's eyes, no spirit, no life, only a lonely cavity where a person should have been. A hole.

And Aaron understood the hideousness of juvengamy.

The woman's half was in the meeting, whom she had joined with as an infant. After juvengamy, most of the clairvoyance linking their bodies he had come to possess. Hardly anything was left inside her. She was a shell, his slave, and he her master.

After school the next day, Aaron staggered out of Health into a humid Thursday afternoon, still haunted by the woman's ghostly eyes.

People said the discovery of halves had cured humanity of all that . . . The atrocities of war, slavery, crimes against humanity. Now there was a whole new kind of genocide.

Juvengamy.

It was the sacrifice demanded of all the Brotherhood's members. Now he understood why it was so illegal.

But worst of all, Amber's father was an honored member like Casler, of pure juvengamy blood and close to the potentate.

Which meant *what* for Amber?

While he drove home, the last sliver of sunlight smoldered behind a storm cloud, withering away to nothing—like his dwindling hope that she would be okay.

Once again, Aaron counted down the hours until he could see her. From his room, he watched the trees darken across the street, denied a sunset as rain clouds blackened the sky prematurely.

By midnight, though, the storm had blown south. After an evening of overcast sky, the stars were teasingly bright. Aaron parked on Loma Sierra drive and leapt from his Mazda, and Amber appeared in his arms. Her silken hair swirled around them.

Holding her was euphoria. The cool feel of her skin and the hot, summery smell floating off her body was enough to make his head spin. But best of all, she was safe. For now.

"If you kept me waiting thirty more seconds," she whispered, "I would have left."

"With who?" said Aaron. "Your other boyfriend?"

She gave him a slow, teasing smile. "Who said you were my boyfriend?"

Aaron winked and deposited her in the passenger seat. "I have a surprise for you," he said. "Buckle up."

"Where are we going?" she said.

"You'll love it, buttercup."

She glared at him. "If you call me buttercup one more time, you lose all boyfriend privileges."

"Oh, so I *am* your boyfriend?" he said.

"No."

"Right . . ." Aaron felt a smile tugging at his lips. "I just have the privileges."

Instead of driving back down the ridge, he took them farther up Loma Sierra drive. The street narrowed, and they flew around corners, blew through stop signs. He yanked the wheel and they spun onto Gibraltar road—the same road they would take to the Chamber of Halves on their birthdays.

For a moment, they glimpsed the Chamber between two peaks, white adobe towers drenched in floodlights, before they streaked out of view. Almost imperceptibly, they both tensed.

Aaron downshifted and carved his Mazda around switchbacks. As he shifted gears, Amber played with her hair and stared out the window. He floored it after the corners, burnt rubber, and sank the RPM needle deep into the redline. The engine screamed.

"You drive like Dominic," she said, taking her eyes off the window.

Aaron smirked, overly aware of her gaze, and jammed the stick into third on a straightaway. "The road's familiar."

He veered off the pavement and skidded to a stop, his headlights illuminating a patch of grass at the edge of a cliff. His door swung open.

"That was close," she said

"Nah, we had a few feet." He got out and circled to her

side to help her out. "Now close your eyes."

She was completely trusting as Aaron led her forward. He held her waist and stood her at the edge of the cliff.

"There," he said, and when she opened her eyes, she gasped and squeezed his hands.

From the cliff, they could see the entire valley, the harbor, the islands—a hundred and eighty degrees of moonlit Tularosa. The sea glittered in the moon's violet wake. Silver rain clouds billowed on the horizon. The city lights shimmered below them.

While Amber took in the view, Aaron unloaded a blanket from his trunk and spread it out on the grass. He lay on his back and waited for her to join him.

A breeze rustled the grass, infusing the air with the smell of sage, and a moment later, she lay back on the blanket next to him, shivering. He hugged her until she was warm. They watched the vast, calming reach of the constellations.

But tonight, solace evaded him.

"Have you ever wondered why halves exist at all?" said Amber. "I mean, why we're even entangled in the first place?"

"That's all I used to think about," he said. "Stuff like that gets to you when doctors tell you something's wrong with your half. You drive yourself crazy asking why this and why that . . . and why *me*." The stars winked out as a line of dark birds passed overhead.

She squeezed closer to him. "What do you think it is?"

"Maybe something out there." He nodded to the sky. ". . . or maybe we caused it."

"Do you think there's a loophole?"

"I think we're missing something obvious. Like why don't

animals have halves?" he said. "There's a simple answer . . . I *know* there's a simple answer."

"You just reminded me of this quote I really like," she said. "'The task is not to see what no one has yet seen; but to think what nobody has yet thought about that which everybody sees.'"

"Who said that?"

"I think it was Schrödinger."

"Nice. I thought you hated the guy."

"I'm not against halves; it's what we chose to do with it that scares me."

"Like juvengamy?"

Amber propped herself up on her elbow, then leaned in and kissed him. Her hair shimmered against the stars, translucent. "Can we not talk about that?" she said.

Aaron spotted a light moving against the stars—an orbiting satellite—and waited until it winked out before he responded. "Tell me about your dad."

"He thinks I'm with Clive," she said.

"Wow, I bet Clive's got it easy," said Aaron.

"I already told you, he's a family friend," she said.

"Since when?" he said. "Since he joined the Juvengamy Brotherhood?"

She sighed and rolled onto her back. "Are we *really* getting into this?"

"When did your dad join?" said Aaron, taking his attention off the sky to look at her. "Or was he born into it? Were you *ever* going to tell me?"

His accusation didn't surprise her, but it still stung. He didn't trust her. Amber closed her eyes, wishing they could just rewind. "Would you have told me?" she said. "If it was your parents?"

"But it's not my parents," he said.

"So why do you care?" she said.

He propped himself up, and moonlight revealed the concern in his eyes. "Is your mom like the rest of them?" he said. "Is she hollow like—?"

"It's not like that for my parents," Amber said quickly, not wanting to hear the rest of his description. "It hurt their channel, but at least they both got the same amount of clairvoyance. They're normal, they just can't stand each other."

"Why would anyone think juvengamy is a good idea?" said Aaron.

"I don't know," she said, "why would anyone think meeting at eighteen is a good idea?"

"Because it doesn't permanently damage you."

Amber felt her body tense up. "They don't think of it as damage," she said.

"Then what is it?"

"The natural form of halves," she said, and after a pause, added, "and a sacrifice for the potentate."

"That's sick," said Aaron.

Amber glared at him. "Can we drop this?"

"How do they get away with it?" he said. "It's illegal."

"There's more of us than you think," she said. "The United States Ambassador to the Chamber of Halves was a juvengamy baby, so are some of the Ambassadors from other countries."

"Jesus, how long has this been going on?"

"As long as everything else," she said. "The Brotherhood was founded the same year Schrödinger discovered halves."

"By who?"

"I don't know, Aaron. He was the Chancellor of Germany at the time . . . someone named Adolph Hitler."

"Never heard of him."

"Because he disappeared."

"And what about you?" said Aaron. "How do you fit into all this?"

Amber sighed. "Do I have to tell you everything about my life?" she said.

"Do you tell me *anything?*"

"Why should I?" she said, holding his gaze. "You hardly know me."

For a long time, he stared back at her, his eyes dark and cryptic. "Well it might have occurred to you," he said, "sometime after you kissed me and before you started wishing I was your half."

His words hurt more than she expected. She swiveled away from him and let her hair fall between them, hiding her face. "Actually, Aaron, you kissed me."

"Want to know what else?" he said, "I wish you were my half, too."

Her heart fluttered, suddenly in free-fall, and she forgot she was even irritated with him. If he wanted her to be his half—and she *definitely* wanted him to be hers—then nothing else mattered. "That's kind of nice to know," she said, catching his eye again.

He shook his head. "I'm sorry I said that."

"I'm not," she said.

After a silence, he lifted his gaze to hers. "I meant to ask you, what's the deal with Clive? I heard last night there's something screwed up with his half. Like he doesn't have one."

"I don't know," she said. "I wasn't there . . . *obviously*."

"You still think he's your half?"

"I only thought that because my parents and their friends said he was," she said. "They've been saying it for years. They're wrong, though."

"What changed your mind?" he said.

"They have to be wrong," she said, "because I think . . ." she lowered her eyes, and her heartbeat climbed to a blur when she realized what she was about to say. "because I think I'm falling for you."

There, she had said it. She peeked at his face, her pulse refusing to slow as she waited for him to drag her down and kiss her passionately. For a moment, the night retreated from his eyes and left them unguarded, he was *hers*—before darkness rushed back in and made him more inaccessible than ever. He sat up, and she saw guilt burning behind his pupils.

"Take that back," he whispered.

Amber felt her heart go still. "But it's true," she said, "we're only supposed to be able to love one person, right?"

"Yeah, so take it back. It's not me."

Now she glared at him. "Then who the fuck do you think it is, Aaron?"

Aaron tried to stroke her hair, but she wriggled away from him and he gave up. "Look," he said, his voice hollow, "my clairvoyant channel is supposed to collapse when I meet my half. It didn't collapse when I met you. In fact, it doesn't even hurt right now. Amber, I'm fighting not to fall in love with you because you can't possibly be my half. I'd probably be screaming in agony right now if you were."

The following morning, Aaron woke to the gong from the Chamber of Halves. The air was damp and yeasty, and beads of sweat clung to his forehead like leeches.

As he watched, a bluish hue crept along the dark horizon. It was six in the morning; he was due at the Chamber in twenty-nine hours.

Aaron rolled onto his side, and Amber's warm scent floated up from his bed. It had rubbed into his pores and rubbed off on his sheets—and then he remembered the previous night, how much he'd hurt her. He groaned and buried is face in his comforter.

Supposing Amber was right, though. Supposing they *were* halves. Everything would make sense that way. Doctors were pessimists; it shouldn't come as a surprise if they had falsely predicted the collapse of his channel when, in fact, nothing had happened.

Aaron closed his eyes, and for the dozenth time, he performed the calculation in his head. With a hundred thousand people in Tularosa, there couldn't be more than a few thousand seventeen year olds—merely a dozen of whom turned eighteen this Saturday. A few boys and a few girls. In reality, if Aaron and Amber were halves, their odds of finding each other were even higher. Clairvoyance brought halves together like magnets.

But the blue haze of dawn pried his eyelids apart. He already knew how it ended. He had known since his first nauseating sniff of the sterile, bleached insides of an MRI machine. He didn't get to have Amber. His channel wouldn't allow it.

Yet hope still leaked into his blood stream, itching in places he couldn't scratch. And he knew he had to see her again tonight, in case it wasn't their last night together.

And, in case it was.

At 6:25 that evening, Amber waited for Aaron with Tina and Buff outside the gate into Pueblo's rugby stadium. Sunlight slanted through the trees and tinted their faces orange. Amber had meant to keep her previous night with Aaron to herself, but she was on the verge of tears and Tina had no trouble prying it out of her. She was getting worse and worse at hiding her feelings.

"He's an asshole," said Tina. "We *all* knew that."

"No bullshit, Tina. Buddy was only trying to protect her." Buff stood tall in a crisp warm-up jersey, his hair neatly combed. He looked . . . cute.

"Well, she doesn't *need* his protection," said Tina.

"Somebody had to bring up the fact that tomorrow's their—"

Tina shot him a warning glare. "We're not talking about *tomorrow*."

Amber sighed. "You guys can just say it," she said. "Our birthday's in six hours. We shouldn't be anywhere near each other right now."

Tina and Buff flinched and averted their eyes. In other words, they couldn't have said it better themselves.

Amber stopped paying attention to them and scanned the faces of unfamiliar boys entering the stadium. She wished for once that she could be invisible. She hated being stared at when she felt like she was about to cry.

Why didn't Aaron think they were halves? The previous night, he had ruined her pride. Okay *fine*, so he was right. Amber knew she didn't get to have him. She was naïve to think she could just run away from her birthday, from what her parents had always told her. From Clive. But at least they could have pretended they were halves for one night. Tonight, after the game, she would have to confess the truth.

Tomorrow, when Aaron saw what she was supposed to become, he would wish she had never existed.

Finally, Aaron arrived at the gate, hair unkempt and skin bronze in the afternoon sun, looking more like he was modeling that leather jacket of his for a magazine than meeting friends at a rugby game.

Amber watched him, bubbly with excitement. Aaron nodded to Buff—who nodded stiffly back—then gathered her in his arms. She was breathless immediately, drinking in his smell.

Tina and Buff averted their eyes and headed down to the field.

"I'm sorry," Aaron whispered when they were gone, and she heard the pain in his voice. He was just as distraught over the previous night as she was.

And right then, as she looked up into his dark, sunset streaked eyes, feeling euphoric and implausibly safe now that he was here, Amber realized she was in love with him.

The wrong boy.

Aaron and Amber sat in the bleachers facing Pueblo's rugby field. Deep purples and maroons smoldered out on the horizon, the remains of their last sunset as seventeen-year-olds. Gone. A gentle mist settled in its wake.

The crowd groaned as Dominic Brees flattened the fullback and scored. Without Buff Normandy, Pueblo was getting ground to pulp. But Aaron's nerves were too occupied with Amber to care. His body felt rigid, his tendons strained like rubber bands about to snap. He couldn't relax, not around her. Not when he had fifteen hours left before his appointment.

He caught Amber peering at him.

"You're doing it too," she said, brushing her hair behind her ear. "You're risking everything for me. We *both* turn eighteen tomorrow."

"Amber, it's not a game of chicken," he said. "You have your whole life—"

"My whole *life?*" Her lips formed a cruel, haunted smile. "Wait and see."

A moment later the stadium roared with cheers. Fans screamed and leapt from their seats, but the two of them hardly budged. Their bodies stayed rigid, as if linked by a taut cord.

"You make me nervous," he said.

"I know." Amber's eyes reflected the misty halos blazing from the stadium lights.

Down by the field, though, he saw the flash of a green windbreaker, Corona's color. His gaze snapped to the bottom of the stands, and the skin burned behind his ears.

Clive Selavio was scanning the bleachers for open seats, and in that instant, his eyes locked on Aaron and Amber. His pale eyes narrowed in their sockets, and he barged through the first bench of fans and scurried up the stairs toward them.

❧

As Clive approached, the glare of the quartz lights eroded his scarred face. He reached the end of the aisle and cut toward them, gripping an unopened can of beer.

Amber finally noticed him, and the color drained from her face. He would reach her first.

Aaron stood, crossed her lap, and blocked Clive's path just as he reached her. "What the hell do you think you're doing?" he said.

"You don't mind if I slide in next to Amber, do you?" said Clive, drenching him with beer breath.

"The seat's taken," said Aaron.

"No, I believe it's free.

"I'd be careful in that green jacket," said Aaron.

Clive peered around at the red and white stadium and then held up his index finger, studying it. "Harper, all I have to do is touch the back of your skull, and a little more leaks out."

"What are you talking about?" said Aaron.

"And how long would you guess before you're empty?" He smirked. "My father can help you, you know." With that, he shoved past Aaron and squeezed into the chair next to Amber. She gave Clive a quick, hateful stare and flattened herself against the far armrest.

Clive's milky, lizard-like eyes surveyed the contours of her face as if she were prey. "Don't I get a kiss?" he said.

Though her cheeks flushed, Amber continued to stare vaguely into the distance. Aaron rolled up his sleeves and prepared to extricate Clive from the seat. He motioned for Amber to scoot over and dropped into the seat between them, facing Clive. Their eyes burned into each other.

"Harper, how many times must I warn you—"

"What was that your dad said about you on Wednesday?" said Aaron, interrupting him. "The boy without a half?"

"If you'd actually stayed," said Clive, "then you would have learned I got a new one."

Aaron felt white-hot adrenaline prickle into his blood. He didn't blink. Finally, Clive leaned around him and spoke to Amber again.

"Your father asked me to drive you home tonight. Apparently you've been sneaking off?"

Amber ignored him.

"Amber, I'm talking to you—"

Aaron yanked him back by his hood. "She doesn't want to hear it," he said.

Clive clamped his fingers around Aaron's wrists and pried them off his jacket. "You need to learn when to keep your ugly nose out of other people's business."

"You can't get a new half."

"*Can't* you?" said Clive, and he popped open his beer, spraying the seats in front of them with foam. He leaned around Aaron again.

"Amber, you still haven't done what I told you to do, and since you're going to be my half tomorrow . . ."

She was looking down now.

"Amber—"

Suddenly, she grabbed her bag, stood up, and squeezed past them. "I have to go," she muttered.

For a second, Aaron watched her hurrying down the stairs. Then he slapped Clive's beer. The can flew from his hand, spiraling foam, and landed several rows down. He rose and stumbled after her.

Aaron caught her at the gate and grabbed her hand. "Forget him," he said. "Come back to my house."

"Didn't you hear him?" she said.

"He's lying."

"*I* lied."

"I don't care," he said.

"I lied," she repeated, "because I wanted you instead. I wanted them to be wrong." Silver wisps of her hair sparkled against the stadium lights. "But it's just like Clive says."

It was the opposite of what she'd told him last night. Something had changed. Aaron felt the damp, chilly night clawing into him.

"He's *not* your half—" But the half time bell rang behind them, interrupting him and flooding him with shivers. Their time was up.

Amber kissed him, letting her fingers linger on his neck before letting go of him. "Clive and I have known since childhood," she said, her eyes cinders, extinguished of hope. "We weren't proper juvengamy babies because he was too sick when he was born. The operation would have killed him—it would have killed *us* . . . But I'm still his half."

The words pierced Aaron's heart.

"I'm sorry," Amber whispered. Then she walked away.

He was still standing in the same spot when Clive squeezed his shoulder.

"I do hope that meant something to you," he said, his pale eyes gleaming with triumph. "Because that's the last time you see her."

Aaron said nothing.

"You know, Harper, she's the one who's going to get hurt tomorrow, after what you've done to her."

Aaron swiveled away from him and leaned against the bleachers, just as Dominic Brees jogged over, dripping sweat and grinning from behind his plastic nose guard.

"Twenty-five to three!" he said. "Please tell me you guys saw that spin move." A loud clang made him look back, and his grin vanished.

"Enjoying yourself out there, Breezie?" came a voice from under the stands. Aaron followed Dominic's gaze to a large figure emerging from the shadows. Buff Normandy.

From his vantage point, Aaron saw Clive reach into his pocket and hand something to Dominic, which he concealed in his hand.

"It was better when you weren't too pussy to play," said Dominic.

"Bet you won't say that after the second half," said Buff. "Coach wants a fair game. He's putting me in."

"He can't do that," said Dominic. You're below the minimum GPA."

"Ever heard of extra credit?" Buff grinned and turned back to the field.

Aaron heard the click.

"Buff, behind you!" he shouted, but it was too late.

Before Buff could turn, Dominic lunged, the switchblade glinting in his fist.

No time to think. Aaron spun, off balance, and tackled Dominic, sank his shoulder into the rugby player's chest. They collided into the bleachers, into the sharp edges of the steel struts. Rusted metal bit into Aaron's ear and rattled his brain, but it was nothing like the clean slash of the switchblade down his forearm.

At first, he hardly felt it, just an eerie itch deep in his blood veins, but then came the hideous sensation of his flesh peeling open to the cold air. He grabbed his arm and staggered backwards. His hand came back warm and wet. In the dark, he saw nothing. Then every thunderous beat of his heart was like a douse of gasoline on the inferno in his arm.

Buff descended on Dominic and plowed his face into the cement. They rolled, grunting and kicking up dust. Dominic grasped for a crossbeam, caught one, and hauled himself to freedom. Corona's superstar was fast, but Buff was faster. In three steps, he overtook him and downed him again. Buff's fists were a blur.

"Buff! You're going to kill him!" said Aaron, now doing everything he could to restrain his best friend's arm. A few other rugby players sprinted over from the field.

"Normandy—" His teammates dragged him off.

"Security's just outside."

"Right—" Buff stood and straightened his jersey. "No more bullshit, *Breezie.*" He glanced at Aaron, his face cloaked in shadow.

Aaron tried to decipher his friend's expression, but his teammates were already ushering him back to the field, telling him they needed to bolt before the guards came. Reluctantly, Buff peeled his gaze away from Aaron. Feeling dizzy, Aaron fell to his knees in a patch of silver light.

Next to him, Dominic groaned and rolled onto his back. Aaron's eyes felt heavy as he watched his own blood drain into the dirt from the gaping slash above his wrist.

"*Number eleven*—" Dominic climbed to his feet and staggered over to him. "What the hell was that?"

Aaron ignored him, but a second later Dominic's wheezing face leered in front of him.

"You're about to go down a very painful road." He grabbed Aaron's sleeve and wiped the blood off his switchblade.

The outlines of Dominic's face blurred and started spinning, and Aaron had to shut his eyes.

"And you—" Dominic advanced on Clive next. "Couldn't even lift your pinky finger, could you?"

"I was unarmed," said Clive. "You had a knife."

"Oh yeah? Did Normandy have a knife? Did number eleven have a knife?" Dominic gurgled phlegm in his throat and spat. "I'm beginning to doubt your loyalty, Selavio."

"It's my *wedding* tomorrow," said Clive.

"Don't kid yourself," said Dominic. "A black eye would be

an improvement."

"It's going to be televised."

"So? You're not the one we'll be watching."

Clive's eyes shrank to slits. "You better get a real good look then," he said. "Because it's the last time you'll see her."

Dominic shook his head and slid the nose guard off his face. His curly hair bounced back into place. "Clive, I'm talking about your father. I don't give a damn about your half."

Aaron was still on the ground. Through the fog in his brain, he could barely hear Clive's tense voice.

"And what exactly about my father?"

"It's that machine he has in my basement that bothers me. I can't sleep with that God-awful racket."

"Then wear earplugs," said Clive. "Your parents agreed to let him test it."

"Don't even start," said Dominic, spitting again. "With all the rap they've taken for you guys, lying to the police and everything—"

"I'd stay out of it," Clive warned.

Dominic flipped the switchblade closed and leaned forward. "Selavio, I *know* that thing doesn't cure half death. If it did, Justin Gorski would still be alive." With that, he spun and hobbled back to the field. Before he was gone though, he yelled over his shoulder. "And if I was you, number eleven, I wouldn't fall asleep tonight."

Aaron was only half-aware of him. Later, once Clive left too, he ripped off a section of his T-shirt. With one hand, he wrapped the material around his arm, pulled it tight, and tied it off in a knot. Then he hunched forward and cradled his forehead in his palms. As the pain ebbed from his sliced forearm, he became aware of the slow smolder in his lips, leftover from Amber's last kiss. And he knew then.

He was in love with her.

EIGHT

0 Days, 12 hours, 18 minutes

DOMINIC DIDN'T PLAY in the second half, and with Buff now on the field, Pueblo won the first league game of the season twenty-six to twenty-five.

Back at home, Aaron scrubbed his arm over the bathroom sink. The wound had scabbed over, but the tension in his flesh threatened to rip it back open. He wrapped his wrist tight with gauze.

In twelve hours, he was due at the Chamber of Halves. In twelve hours, Amber and Clive would join as halves, and their souls would intertwine forever. Aaron forced himself to breathe, to exhale—and a nerve-racking moment followed when he wasn't sure he could fill himself back up again.

They had known since childhood.

His mom appeared in the doorway. "Phone call," she said, tossing him the cordless.

Nobody called him on their home phone.

"Hello?" said Aaron.

"Walter Wu speaking."

"*Who?*"

"Dreadfully sorry for the late call," he said. "I'm your authorized correspondent from the Chamber of Halves."

Aaron's stomach gave an odd shudder. "What's this for?"

The man cleared his throat. "Mr. Harper, how are you feeling?"

"Just dandy."

"Sick?"

"Yes."

"Stomachache?"

"Absolutely."

"Any pain at the back of your head?"

Aaron's mouth was already open to give an answer when he froze, and felt the hairs on his forearms slowly stand on end. "Mr. Wu, what's this for?" he asked again.

The man cleared his throat one more time then spoke in an high, oddly strained voice. "I think that just about does it. Tomorrow at eleven then, Aaron." And he hung up.

For several seconds, Aaron held the phone to his ear, listening to his heart's echo over the dial tone, before he set it down.

"You should get to bed soon," said his mom from the doorway, his dad behind her. "You want to feel rested in the morning."

"Get sleep while you can," said his dad, winking. "You'll be up all night tomorrow."

They both smiled at him, doing their best to act like he was normal, exactly like any other seventeen-year-old on the eve of his birthday—about to experience the best day of his life. It wasn't that easy, though.

Other parents spent months and thousands of dollars on their kids' eighteenth birthdays. But with all the MRIs and visits to the doctor, no one had time to prepare for Aaron's birthday. Here he was twelve hours from his appointment without a suit to his name, and all they could do was smile at him.

Though his intestines felt like they were being threaded through a needle, he managed to focus on Amber, on a final glimmer of hope. And as soon as his parents went to bed, he hurried out to his car.

The muddy sky had begun drizzling, and warm, oily droplets sprayed his cheeks.

His Mazda sputtered, caught, then lugged him up the street. Houses slunk by, dark as specters, and the liquid on his windshield glowed neon from their porch lights. The hulk of Mission Ridge loomed ahead of him, crowned with a strip of golden lights—Loma Sierra drive.

Amber's house.

She was Clive's half. Aaron counted raindrops, straining to numb the sting in his heart, but it was hopeless. He clutched the steering wheel and squeezed the color from his knuckles. At the game, Amber said they had known since childhood.

Pain exploded in his right arm, making him wince, and he watched as fresh blood soaked the gauze. The salty stench of an open wound coiled up his nostrils. But the pain was nothing compared to the rage and envy gnawing in his gut.

But Amber had lied before. In fact, she *always* lied. Aaron downshifted and sank his foot to the floor. No one knew their half before their birthday.

The sleek blue body of Mr. Lilian's corvette glistened in the rain. Aaron braked too late and plowed into its bumper. He cringed, jumped out of his car, and assessed the damage. Flakes of paint floated in the puddle between their cars. He leaned closer. *Blue* paint—thank God.

Amber didn't pick up her phone, so Aaron scooped up a handful of gravel, snuck around back, and trudged up a muddy hill until he was directly under her balcony—he hoped. Then he chucked pebbles against the sliding glass doors. It was absurd.

He heard a gasp, followed by a splash. But not from the balcony. The noise came from the hillside, from close by, from within arm's reach—

"*Aaron?*" It was Amber's voice. As his eyes adjusted to the darkness under the balcony, they focused on the wall right in front of him, where she stood inexplicably in polka dot pajama bottoms, rain boots, and an open hunting jacket. She was also holding a rake, sort of how you'd hold a baseball bat—

"Were you about to *hit me?*" he said.

"I should have," she muttered, reluctantly lowering the rake.

He looked her up and down. "And *this* is how you dress when I'm not around."

"You sound excited."

Then he noticed the plastic bin in a puddle at her feet, spilling cans and cardboard boxes into the mud.

"Taking out the trash?" he said, unable to prevent himself from smirking.

"Recycling," she said.

"No servants?"

Amber stepped in close, and he could see her eyelashes fluttering in the rain. "*You* just think I'm too pretty to be doing this kind of stuff."

"Makes no difference," he said.

"So you're admitting it?" she said.

"It didn't get you out of chores, did it?"

"Aaron, why are you here?" she said with a hint of impatience. Droplets sparkled in her hair, dripped off, and ran down her nose. The humidity brought out her smell, intensified it.

"Because you're lying about Clive," he said finally.

"And you're sneaking around in the middle of the night outside my bedroom," she said. "Want me to tell my dad?"

"Go. I'll wait right here," said Aaron. "It's about time he and I had a word."

"Fine. Don't move." She turned to leave, but Aaron grabbed her arm and tugged her to face him.

"Tell me you're not his half," he said.

Amber's eyes were luminous as they scanned his face. "Why do you care, Aaron? It's not like you wanted to be my half."

"So this is about last night then?" he said.

"When you broke my heart? Maybe," she said.

"I liked you better when you didn't listen to me."

"And I liked you better before you started trying to protect me," she said. "Because you can't."

"Amber, you don't want to be my half," he said. "My channel's about to break. I don't get to have what everyone else has." He reached up and wiped her dripping hair off her cheek. "You do."

"So all this meant nothing to you?" she said, watching him in disbelief. She sighed and pushed away his hand. "Can you go now? I have to get ready for tomorrow—" her gaze fell to the bloody gauze around his arm, and she stopped abruptly.

"I'm fine—"

"*Clearly* not, Aaron," She yanked him through a back door into her house, despite his protests. As soon as they were inside, Aaron heard shouts from another room. But not at him. It was Mrs. Lilian, hysterical, screaming herself hoarse at Mr. Lilian.

"Ignore them," said Amber, blushing as she pulled him up the stairs.

"Right." Aaron raised his eyebrows at the muddy footprints they left on the carpet. "And when they see me?"

"You run," she said, seating him on her bed. A piercing crash from downstairs made them both jump. The parents were hurtling china now.

Amber avoided his eyes and busied herself with the gauze around his arm, unwrapping it. Her hair tumbled loose and covered half her face.

Aaron caught pieces of her parents' argument before they lowered their voices, and they chilled him . . . *illness is getting worse, it's not my fault the potentate can't make the wedding . . . Oh yeah? Well unless we want to disgrace our bloodline, now our daughter has to spend her honeymoon at the potentate's palace . . .*

Amber's hands trembled as she peeled the last of the

gauze off his arm.

She went to her bathroom and brought back a warm washcloth. "Take off your shirt," she said.

"Amber, I really don't think that's necessary."

"Fine." She knelt in front of him and cleaned his arm. Her parents stopped fighting, and an unnerving silence followed. Amber rubbed the wound with Neosporin, and her fingers soothed the fire in his nerves.

And lit all different ones.

"You're making it worse," he said.

"This hurts?"

He stared at her. "Are you going to tell me what's going on?"

She smiled. "Do I ever?"

There was a knock on the door.

"Sweetheart, what are you doing in there?" It was her dad.

"Having sex," she said.

"I heard a man's voice."

"Could you come back later?" she said, her voice biting.

"Amber—"

"I'm naked!"

Aaron tensed, waiting for the door to open, but her dad's footsteps moved on down the hall.

"Now you really have to go," she whispered.

"I thought you wanted me to talk to your dad," said Aaron.

"I changed my mind," she said, a ghost of a smile crossing her face, and she raised her head to kiss him. "I like you better alive."

There was a creak outside her bedroom door. And then it

burst open. Aaron jumped up.

"God dammit, I knew it," said her father, stepping into the room. "Trespassing on my daughter and my property." He carried a semi-automatic rifle in his hands. It was all black, polished metal.

And Aaron was staring straight down the barrel's throat. "*Shit*," he said.

"Dad—NO!" Amber leapt in front of him.

"Baby, if you do not step aside, I *will* fire at him above your head." His eye narrowed behind the gun sight. "Son, I will escort you now to your vehicle. I did notice you were parked rather close to my Vette—I hope that's incidental."

It occurred to Aaron, as he scribbled out an uncashable twelve-hundred dollar check at gunpoint for the scratch on Mr. Lilian's bumper, that without Amber, life wasn't even remotely appealing. He wanted her to be his half.

As soon as Aaron made it home, he collapsed fully clothed onto his bed and stared at the four digits on his alarm clock. Two minutes until midnight. Then it would be Saturday, March 30.

And he would be eighteen years old.

He switched off his bedside lamp . . . darkness, except for the green glow of the clock's display. He pulled his arm back, and the gash itched painfully. His fingers scarcely resisted tearing into it.

One minute. Exhaustion weighed on his eyelids, but he strained to keep them open. All those nights he and Amber had stayed awake, all that time, and now the last of it had drained away. Gone. He couldn't fall asleep now.

Ten seconds. He counted the blinks of the colon between the eleven and the fifty-nine. Five seconds—*four—three—two—one—*

A violent crash from the front door jolted him upright. The sound of shattering glass. Instinctively, he clutched the back of his head.

Aaron stared at his bedroom door, toes tingling. He heard the distant toll from the Chamber of Halves, officially announcing his eighteenth birthday.

He listened carefully, his heart pulsing in his throat—and then he heard another sound from the hallway. Footsteps.

Aaron held his breath as the floor outside his door groaned under the weight of an intruder.

The door banged open.

Two figures rushed inside. They wore black beanies stretched over their faces.

"Surprise!" yelled one of them. He laughed, flipped on the lights, and yanked off his beanie—Dominic Brees.

The other one laughed too, and Aaron knew the voice—Clive Selavio.

Aaron stood up, adrenaline flooding his veins. "Get out of my house," he said. "I'm sleeping."

"Not anymore," said Dominic. "This is your payback for what happened at the game."

Clive rushed in from the side and clamped his hand over Aaron's mouth. "Shhh," he said, and Aaron could taste his sour breath. "Don't cry!"

Aaron slapped his arm away, grabbed his throat, and shoved him against the wall. "I said, *get out of my house.*"

Clive snorted with laughter and squeezed Aaron's wrist, dipping his fingernails into the open wound. Aaron winced and yanked his hand back. He threw in the weight of his other shoulder. They both fell.

Aaron seized the bedside lamp, snapped the cord free. Eight and a half pounds of hard porcelain. But Dominic caught him from behind. The rugby player's thick forearm coiled around Aaron's throat and dragged him backward.

Aaron slammed his foot into Clive's face and squashed Dominic against the other wall. They toppled over the bedside table, and his choke loosened. Aaron broke free, twisted, and buried his elbow into Dominic's jaw.

But Clive's clammy fingers closed around his ankle and yanked him off his feet. He crumpled onto the carpet and his attackers swarmed over him. A knee crunched into his back, and he felt the ice-cold prick of the switchblade poised at his throat.

"Don't move," Dominic hissed, his saliva splattering against his ear. Aaron twisted, but the blade pried into his skin, dangerously close to his jugular. He froze.

Dominic panted. "You made a mistake, number eleven, and now you're paying for it."

Aaron felt rope uncoil on his back. While Dominic held the knife to his throat, Clive bound his wrists and ankles and yanked the knots tight.

Dominic waved for Clive to switch the light back off. They were still for a moment, and they heard the creaking mattress from his parents' bedroom.

Of course. They weren't alone in the house.

"Dad!" Aaron yelled. "Call the police—" But Dominic smashed his head into the floor.

"Shut your trap!" he hissed.

Then they hustled him to his feet and out of his room. Aaron stumbled in front of them, his feet tied, praying he didn't trip—because Dominic didn't know just how close the blade was to slicing open his throat.

Outside, moonlight flooded the front yard through a gap in the rainclouds. They had driven the Beamer onto the grass and smashed the flowerpots. Dominic forced Aaron into the back, handed the switchblade off to Clive, and climbed into the driver's seat.

It felt like a bad dream.

Dominic floored it and popped the clutch, and the Beamer lurched forward. They missed the driveway completely, bounced off the curb. He shoved the stick into second, and for a heartbreaking moment, the screech of stripping gears rattled the car. The smell of burning clutch hissed from the vents.

"Want me to drive?" said Clive.

Dominic snickered. "You can't drive stick, Selavio." He checked the rearview mirror, and the car swerved. "His *head*, you idiot!"

Aaron felt Clive's slippery fingers drag a pillowcase over his face.

They drove for twenty minutes, and Aaron worked at the knots around his wrists. They were already looser; apparently, Clive was never a boy scout. Even blindfolded, Aaron knew where they were taking him. He could feel the static electricity when they entered Dominic's gate. He was aware of something else too. A sore spot, an itch. At the back of his skull.

Halfway up the driveway the Beamer pitched to the left, and they bounced along the lawn. Bushes whacked the bumper and scraped the sides. Through the pillowcase, Aaron saw tall, spindly shadows.

They were taking him into a forest.

A second later, he freed his wrists. And he didn't wait a second longer. In one fluid motion, he tugged the pillowcase off his head, yanked the door handle, and threw himself from the car.

Bad idea.

The car was moving faster than he'd thought. Much faster. His shoulder crashed through tree roots and splinters tore his skin. He tumbled, ate dirt, and collided face first with the trunk of an oak tree.

Numb with pain, Aaron leaned over and clawed at the knots binding his ankles, but the fingers on his left hand felt weak, feeble. The gash in his arm had reopened. The wound pulsed, and he couldn't get the rope around his heels.

Two pairs of hands seized his arms, and once again, the pillowcase smothered him. They hauled him into the woods, in and out of the toothed hollows beneath tree roots. Clots of fungus yielded under his face, squishing and splattering him with pus. The sugary odor nauseated him.

Then they jerked him to his feet, and the ground beneath him was solid—a slab of concrete. His toes hung off a ledge. Dominic pressed the knife to his throat, and Aaron realized they had taken him to an old water well.

Clive's hands fished through his pockets and removed his cell phone. He breathed into Aaron's ear.

"This is so you're not a nuisance on my birthday," he said. "While I fulfill my duty as Amber's half, you can cry your heart out in a dark hole—"

Aaron elbowed him in the solar plexus, and Clive keeled over, wheezing. He felt Dominic's foot crunch into his spine, and he lost his balance.

Aaron tumbled down the well's black throat.

His stomach squeezed up into his windpipe as dank, rotten air whistled past him. He crunched into the opposite wall, twisted, and kept falling. When he finally hit the bottom, his legs crumpled. His ear gouged into the stone.

Then, except for the violent agony in his limbs and the slosh of moldy water, everything was silent. But at least his bones weren't sticking out of his kneecaps. The well walls must have broken his fall.

Aaron pulled the pillowcase off his head, but it didn't help. Perpetual blackness caved in on all sides. He reached forward and his fingers collided with cold, grimy rock, inches from his face. The well was hardly wider than his shoulders. His eyes adjusted, and he became aware of the dark circle of sky, twenty feet above him.

Aaron untied his feet and tried to climb. He wedged his fingers into the slimy cavities between stones and then kicked off the ground. He hung for a split-second, his body trembling with exertion, before he collapsed.

As he panted to catch his breath, decay soaked into his

lungs, chilled his heart. The walls were too slippery. He'd never climb them.

In eight hours, he was due at the Chamber of Halves. Eight hours. And here he was at the bottom of a well. Clive and Dominic were *not* coming back to get him.

He was going to miss his appointment.

It was that simple.

Aaron pictured his nameless half waiting all alone in a dungeon at the Chamber of Halves, and he pitied her. Did she already know, as he did, that their channel was going to break?

Then the girl in his mind changed to Amber, and his stomach did cartwheels. He needed to be there in the morning for *her*. Suddenly, Aaron balled his fist and swung at the walls, tearing skin from his knuckles.

No way in hell did Clive deserve her, not in a billion years. In eight hours, Aaron would be there to teach him that lesson.

Just as soon as he got out.

Aaron squatted and raked the mud with his fingers. The air down at the bottom was heavier, weighed down and humid with infection, morgue-like. He half expected to find bones. But there was nothing so useful. He took inventory. Shoes, six feet of rope, shirt, pants, belt, and a pillowcase. Somehow, they added up to his escape.

But seconds passed. Minutes. His body cooled, and it became hard to think. The cold numbed his fingers, crept into the marrow of his bones. Then the shivering began. And it occurred to him, between convulsions, that he could die in this well.

Ten minutes passed. It was a terrifying kind of time, impaling him silently. Nothing came to him. He raked the bottom again. Still nothing. He searched the walls, probed for indentations, anything he could grip. Always nothing. Slowly, inexorably, the walls of his tomb were closing in.

After he traced the contours in the slimy walls enough times to memorize them, reaching higher and higher, Aaron finally discovered an irregularity.

Almost out of reach, he could just feel the lip of an opening in the side of the well. Maybe he could haul himself up. But then what? He'd still be fifteen feet underground. Still, it was worth a try.

Aaron stood on his toes and curled his fingers over the lip. He strained his forearms, and gradually, feeling like his tendons were going to peel from his wrists, he lifted the weight off his feet. But then his fingers slipped and he crashed backwards. When he held up his hands, they were frozen in the shape of claws.

Aaron tried everything. He backed into the wall, jammed his feet against the stone for leverage. He spread his arms and wedged his fingers into crevices. He untied his shoes and stood on top of them. But the inside of the well was caked with squishy moss. He always slipped.

And the blood had withdrawn from his cold fingers, the nerves throbbed. Aaron gasped for breath, and his chest stung with each lungful of frostbitten air. There was only one more thing to try.

Aaron squatted, tensed his thighs, and jumped as high as he could. He slapped his palm over the ledge. For a moment, he gripped the ooze, then everything slipped and he collapsed painfully to the bottom.

It was like volleyball. To get maximum elevation, you needed an approach, you needed to build momentum. But even if you were directly under the ball, you didn't just jump straight up. You executed footwork. You shifted your weight, and that got you a little higher.

Aaron closed his eyes and visualized a volleyball sailing over the net. An overpass. The other team's middle was already up, his arm cocked. Aaron had to get it first, he had to set his outside hitter. He'd done this a thousand times.

Aaron swung his arms and exploded upward. He got both hands over the top, kicked off the back wall, and pulled himself up until his eyes were level with the ledge.

It was a tunnel leading out of the well, scarcely large enough for a human. He was clinging to the bottom edge. Before his strength gave out, he wiggled inside the opening and collapsed onto his stomach, hands near his waist. His body shook from the exertion, but he had done it.

Except the tunnel went *deeper* underground.

Hopefully it surfaced eventually . . . as opposed to plunging three-hundred feet to tap an aquifer. He would just have to find out.

There wasn't enough room to swing his arms around in front of him, so he shifted his weight and scrunched forward. Darkness swallowed him, and the stale, extinct smell of moist concrete eroded his nostrils. With what little space he had, he made steady progress downward, half sliding, half crawling—deeper into the Earth.

Too deep. Aaron was about to turn back, thinking it was a dead end, when the tunnel leveled out. He breathed a sigh of relief and squeezed himself into the level portion of the tunnel. It was a tighter fit, and he felt his shoulders wedge against cold, damp concrete—and he had a terrifying realization.

It was only with the help of gravity that he had been able to slide down the tunnel. He would never be able to backtrack the distance he'd come. Either the tunnel led to the surface or—

There was a splash in front of him, and then liquid slipped under his torso and trickled between his fingers. Aaron lay still, panting. Had there been water in the tunnel all along?

He wiggled, moving only inches, and more water splashed against his chin. It was flowing from somewhere in front of him, submerging his hands and pooling underneath him. Sweet, icy droplets dribbled onto his lips—he knew the taste. Fresh rain.

It must have been raining again—no, *pouring*. The runoff from the hillside twenty feet above him was somehow draining into the well system, filling it up. Water gushed around him, drenching his shoulders now. Aaron strained against the cement, anxiety oozing in his stomach. He needed to lash out, tear the walls apart. But his arms were straitjacketed at his side.

And what if Clive and Dominic had already returned to find the well empty? They would assume he escaped and never check again. He was going to drown in this tunnel, alone.

Hours before meeting his half.

Aaron squirmed into the blackness, thrusting himself slug-like into the icy flood. Water rose in the tunnel, trickled down his back and sloshed up his nose. He stretched to keep his nostrils above the surface, but his head scraped the ceiling. His windpipe tightened in his throat. He coughed, but he couldn't fill his lungs. It was terror that kept him moving, terror that kept him arching his back and jamming himself deeper.

Then white foam crashed around him, and before he even had the chance to hold his breath, his face was plunged underwater.

Amber stuffed her hair straightener, skin lotion, and shampoo—the last of her essentials—into the duffel bag, and was all ready to run away. Except the zipper wouldn't close. She took out her socks. She'd be better off without the useless things anyway.

She took one last look around her bedroom, and the hollow feeling in her stomach deepened. Tomorrow, Aaron would meet his half and forget all about her while she would be trapped forever with Clive.

Unless, of course, she was nowhere to be found.

Amber hauled her bag down the stairs. Her mother was waiting at the door.

"Amber, darling, where do you think you're going?"

Her mother's voice made her flinch. "Isn't it like a hundred years past your bedtime?" said Amber, stopping right in front of her.

"André will be here at six."

"In the *morning?*" said Amber.

"You do want to get ready *before* your wedding, don't you?"

"Who says I'm going?"

Her mother ignored the comment, but her lower lip twitched. "Clive says he hasn't been able to reach you."

"That's because I blocked his calls," said Amber.

"You did *what?*"

"You heard me, mother."

In one sudden movement, her mom slapped her across the cheek. Amber glared at her, though the sting made her eyes tear up.

"The potentate arranged this for you. It's your duty. Now go to bed."

As her mother walked away, Amber could see the tattoo under the deep v-back of her nightgown—the tattoo they carved into her nine days after she was born that said she belonged to Amber's father.

Amber would get one too.

Defeated, Amber walked back upstairs and collapsed onto her bed. Her mother was right. The idea of running away from her half, from Clive, was almost laughable, like trying to escape from her own body. There was a part of him inside her—in a place she couldn't reach, otherwise she would have torn it out already. Their bodies were linked. No matter where on the globe she fled, he could always track her.

And now that their channel was mature, prolonged separation would be agony. After a few months of evading him, her body would start to wither. After a few years, they would both die. Being with her half wasn't a choice—it was a biological need.

Amber buried her head in her comforter and screamed. Why couldn't she choose her own half? She wanted Aaron.

And she wanted to hear his voice. Right now.

Hands trembling, she dialed his number. Maybe she could sneak over to his house and feel his arms around her too. Maybe they could run away together, abandon their halves and live like outlaws for a few bittersweet months—

"Hello, Amber," said a cruel, cold voice. *Clive's* voice.

Her stomach shriveled into a knot.

"Where's Aaron?" she said, her heart sputtering.

"Don't you want to talk to me?" he said.

"Clive, *where is he?*" she repeated.

"He's fine."

"Then put him on."

There was silence. "Why do you hate me?" he said.

"Why do you *think?*"

"But you love me too."

"Can we talk about this later?" she said.

"Amber, we were chosen to be halves," he said. "The potentate wanted *us*—"

Amber hung up the phone. Just like her mom said. *The potentate arranged this for you.*

What did it matter what the potentate arranged? She was Clive's half because of her own bad luck, not because the potentate arranged it. Halves were born, not chosen—

Or could they be chosen?

Suddenly, what both Clive and her mother said made perfect sense—not chosen . . . *faked.* She scrambled off the bed and brushed her hair from her eyes. She had to get to Aaron before tomorrow, before it was all too late.

Then her skin prickled. She felt breathless, like cold water was closing around her lungs.

Aaron.

Aaron was twenty-five feet underground, trapped in a tunnel full of water. His lungs writhed for oxygen. He thrust his head back, struck concrete, and raked his scalp to shreds. He scratched the walls, terrified, but there were no air pockets.

The closest air was back in the well, *minutes* away.

Aaron opened his eyes underwater, felt the sting, and glared up the submerged tunnel—wondering only which thought would be most fitting for the last few seconds of his life.

He chose Amber, fixed his mind on her, and just for a second pretended they spent their lives together. He imagined finding out tomorrow, on their birthday, that they were halves, that they always had been, always would be, *forever*—a spasm in his chest jarred him back to the tunnel. He couldn't hold his breath any longer, he had to breathe.

But he felt warm despite the death congealing in his skin. There was light up ahead, conveyed through the water like clairvoyance. But how far? Too far. And how long before his chest was rent wide open? Aaron fought the current and crawled forward, buoyed by the liquid, his brain slurry. Then his breathing reflex took over, his mouth sprang open.

He thrust his head back one more time. But this time, there was no ceiling. His mouth cleared the water and he filled his lungs with air. He felt a breeze on his face, raindrops. A circle of sky glowed twenty feet above him, pearl gray at the top of a vertical maintenance shaft. Fastened inside the shaft, a rusty ladder led to the surface. He grasped the first rung and climbed.

Aaron burst through a layer of roots and sprawled out on the grass under an oak tree, just beyond the meadow behind Dominic's house. He had never loved the taste of air so much. As rain kissed his cheeks, he gazed at the mansion through the trees. Golden strips of light sprinkled the meadow from tall, radiant windows.

Somewhere in there was Dr. Selavio, the man who could supposedly cure half death and treat a ruptured channel. Now that Aaron was here, he might as well investigate. Today *was* his birthday, after all. It was now or never. Plus he needed his cell phone back.

Still panting, he untangled himself from the roots and climbed to his feet, but before he took a step, something odd caught his eye off to his right, in a clearing between two oak trees. An oddly shaped mound glistened in the rain.

Aaron breathed in slowly, and he noticed the smell. Odor didn't carry in the rain. He shouldn't have smelled anything from that distance, just wet soil. Yet he did—a wretched smell slinking through the rain, impervious. And Aaron was certain the mound in that clearing was its origin.

Aaron edged closer, and details materialized under the raincloud's feeble silver glow. A glossy plastic sheet had been stretched over a lumpy mass. Droplets splattered on the material and drizzled off in the folds. A shovel stood propped against a tree beside a pile of mud, and an unfinished hole—a grave.

Suddenly, Aaron choked on the stench of rotting flesh. He clutched his stomach as the black fumes pried into his nostrils, scorched his sinuses. His knees jerked and he lost his balance, tripped forward and caught himself inches from the plastic. By then he knew what was underneath, and he realized it would be a mistake to visit Dr. Selavio.

The mound was a corpse wrapped in cellophane and turned on its side, a boy; he couldn't have been more than seventeen. Blisters festered on his waxy skin.

It was like someone turned up the volume inside Aaron's head. His heart drummed. The oak leaves crackled beneath him as he stumbled backward.

The boy had to be Justin Gorski.

But there was one thing about the body that disturbed Aaron more than anything else. Under the faint light from a nearly full moon that beamed above the clouds, it was clear.

It couldn't have been any clearer. Justin's head had been shaved, and a dark "X" had been drawn across the back of his scalp. And in the very center, scabbed over and crawling with maggots, a hole had been drilled into the back of his skull.

NINE

0 Days, 9 hours, 51 minutes

JUSTIN'S CORPSE PROVED Casler had committed murder—no, worse than that. He had punctured the boy's channel and drained his sacred connection to Emma Mist into a vial, killing them both.

And he claimed he *cured* half death.

Aaron turned away from the corpse and faced the house. A surge of prickly blood blurred his vision. Rain boiled off his skin, and he stumbled forward and crossed the meadow. He snapped off fistfuls of gnarled stalks, splinters and all, and wiped his face. He reached the door in the east wall of the house and yanked the handle.

The door creaked open, and he stepped inside a laundry room. Murderer or not, Aaron just wanted his fucking cell phone back.

As soon as he was inside, static scampered across his skin. The floor vibrated from the drone of Casler's machine. Once again, he noticed the sore spot at the back of his head, like a finger pressing out from the inside.

Aaron climbed the nearest staircase. He found Clive's room empty, but what he saw from the doorway knotted his stomach. There wasn't a square inch of wall exposed—Clive had plastered images of Amber's face into every last corner.

His collage of her was complete.

Aaron heard voices from the living room down the hall. Just as he spun and marched toward them, though, the voices faded. Aaron hesitated, hearing only his jerky pulse. He crossed the hall, backed into the shadow of an armoire, and peered around the corner.

Seated in a black leather couch opposite a fireplace, Clive and Dominic were speaking in low voices. In the glow of dying embers, their mouths hardly moved. Aaron crept closer.

". . . Father wants to test it again." Clive tapped something metallic against the coffee table then covered it with his fingers, which were trembling. "He's found a way to reseal the channel once he's made the cut, so that not that much leaks out."

Dominic swirled a glass of whisky, and the ice clinked and crackled. He shook his head. "Not after what happened to Justin."

"But he's fixed it—"

"Then he can test it on himself," said Dominic. "No one else gets involved."

"He needs someone who hasn't met their half."

Dominic's eyes narrowed. "And who might that be?" he said. "Me? Amber?"

Again, Clive tapped the metal thing against the glass. "He wants Harper."

"*Harper?* You're kidding."

"When my father examined him, he noticed something really weird about his channel. Said it looked like . . . like . . ." Clive whispered the rest, and Aaron missed it. *Damn.*

"I seriously doubt that, Selavio." Dominic drained his whisky and slammed it down on the coffee table. "It's been long enough. Let's go fetch him. You can tell him what you told me . . . maybe he'll even volunteer."

"*No*. He stays there until after my birthday."

"It's his birthday too, fuckface. We leave him down there, his family's going to sue us."

"I don't care. He thinks Amber's his half."

"So what? Maybe she is," said Dominic.

"She's *not*, okay? I just don't want him messing anything up—" Suddenly, the metal object slid from his hands and buzzed across the glass.

Aaron's instinctive reaction was to clutch his pocket, but his pocket was empty—of course. His cell phone was vibrating across the coffee table.

"Unbelievable," Clive muttered, lifting the phone. "That's the third time she's called him."

He cleared his throat and answered the call. "Amber, you should be in bed. If you call this number one more time—"

Even from across the room, Aaron heard the click on the other end.

Clive swallowed and laid the phone back on the coffee table, his knuckles white. "Unbelievable," he repeated. But then his head jerked toward the hallway, and his eyes widened. Dominic glanced back too—as Aaron, hands casually in his pockets, strolled into the light.

Aaron wiped his nose and picked at the dirt caked on his knuckles before he spoke. "You guys haven't seen my phone anywhere, have you?" He glanced up. "Ah—"

Aaron plucked his phone off the coffee table. "Must have slipped from my pocket," he said, "lucky you picked it up."

He winked at Clive and walked back to the hallway. Clive and Dominic didn't budge until he reached the top of stairs, probably too stunned. Finally footsteps sounded behind him, and Aaron spun, ready for a fight. Clive bounded toward him with Dominic at his heels.

As they closed the distance, the back of Aaron's head throbbed. All at once, the ache sharpened into a burn, scorching deeper with each step Clive took. "Jesus!" Aaron flinched away from him, clutching his scalp. "Get away from me!"

Clive halted, and a smirk crossed his lips. "Does that hurt your head, Harper?" His pale eyes gleamed. "I didn't even touch you."

"Alright, who's the fuckface bleeding on my rug?" said Dominic, kneeling over a red spot on the floor. "If this leaves a stain . . ." his dark eyes targeted Aaron, "you're *dead*, number eleven."

Aaron stared at the red spot, and a chill sank through his skin. He touched the back of his head, and slowly, hands trembling, lowered his fingers before his eyes. But there was no blood. His gaze snapped to Clive.

"Selavio, it's you," said Dominic.

"*What?*" Clive twisted, and another drop of blood struck

the carpet. "Where's it coming from?" Eyes frantic, he scanned his hoodie.

"No idea, but you're dripping all over the place."

Then, just like Aaron, Clive felt behind his head. He pulled his hand back and leveled his index finger in front of him. They all fell silent. A single drop of blood teetered on his fingertip and dripped to the floor.

"We need to get your dad," said Dominic.

"No!" said Clive. "We're not telling him a goddamn thing. I'm fine." He glanced at Aaron, and for a split-second, terror flared in his eyes—before he fled down the hall.

"Number eleven, get out of my house," said Dominic, and he raced after him, leaving Aaron alone.

Except for the melted ice rocking gently in Dominic's glass, there was no sign of life. Aaron felt his heartbeat pulsing in the back of his head. Clive hadn't even touched him; he was eight feet away, yet Aaron had actually *felt* his presence.

And was it just a coincidence that Clive had started bleeding at the same exact moment? Or was it some kind of backlash? Aaron didn't finish the thought, though. Around him, the living room lamps faded. The orange bulbs winked out, and blackness immersed him. They must have been on a timer.

He could feel Clive pacing in the back rooms, his movements pivoting in his skull like a compass needle. Aaron jumped at a scratch, a patter of footsteps. But only his own erratic breathing pierced the silence. He backed against the wall and tiptoed downstairs.

Aaron had only just reached the front door when a car's

high beams glared into the marble entrance hall. The headlights flooded the room with blue light.

Doors slammed, tires kicked up gravel, and lanky shadows arced across the ceiling as the car drove back down the driveway. Male voices approached the front door and the handle twisted. Aaron flattened himself against the wall just in time, as Casler Selavio and Father Dravin stepped inside, both of them in red cloaks.

It was four in the morning. What the hell were they doing here?

Casler flipped on the lights, and Aaron realized his hiding place wasn't a hiding place at all. He held his breath, but they didn't turn around. Casler led Dravin straight across the room, and they ducked into the wine cellar. For a moment, the aitherscope's silver orb beamed beyond the door before it clacked shut and silence flooded back.

Aaron let out his breath and headed for the front door, but he paused, hand poised at the handle. He glanced behind him. The wine cellar led to the dungeon.

It was four in the morning. Why were they even awake? So instead of leaving, Aaron followed them.

Aaron emerged at the bottom of the slimy stairs and tiptoed into the cavernous dungeon. While Dravin perused the laboratory, Casler booted up his laptop at a battered desk. The machine droned behind them. Its metal edges appeared blurry, almost transparent. Like a projection.

Aaron edged closer and slid behind a rack of medicine bottles.

"Just one more thing," said Dravin. "I was under the impression that only the water molecules in the two vials were entangled. But when you introduced the red dye into that first vial, it clearly colored both. Dr. Selavio, correct me if I'm wrong, but it seems the molecules of red dye jumped as well."

Casler smiled, pulled off his red cloak, and tossed it onto the chair. He wore his lab coat underneath. "You're very perceptive," he said, "but I'm afraid the demonstration was simply a magic trick designed to prove a point. The real fluid was pinched from me some weeks ago."

Dravin raised his eyebrows. "And it wouldn't be the first time Mr. Lilian did you a favor. May I ask how the trick was accomplished?"

"A pinhole in the top of the vial," said Casler.

"But a magician never reveals his secrets," said Dravin.

"I'm a doctor, not a magician," said Casler.

"It seems to me you're neither," said Dravin, setting his own cloak on the desk and stepping over to the machine. He wore a black, clerical robe underneath. "You're a politician. Is this it, then?"

"All two-hundred million volts of it."

"And what is the machine's secret?" said Dravin. "A pinhole in space?"

Casler's smile widened as he typed in his password. "Very perceptive indeed." He flicked the touchpad, and files flashed across the screen. "Although the entrance to the channel is slightly larger than a pinhole."

"And *where*, may I ask, did you find the entrance?" said Dravin.

"I'm afraid it requires drilling," said Casler. "It's on the inside of the skull, just behind the visual cortex. I give my son credit for the discovery—" He laughed quietly. "His *awful* headaches."

Dravin placed his palm on the machine and circled it slowly. "Dr. Selavio, how is this machine different than the machine you tested eighteen years ago?"

"This one reseals the hole."

"So the subject lives?"

"The *patient* lives," said Casler. "Forgive my sensitivity, Father."

"But he lived the first time," said Dravin.

"Not entirely," said Casler.

Dravin paused at the open panel behind the machine and peered inside. "I pray to God I never understand what you mean by that."

"You always were squeamish," said Casler. "Here, I've got it loaded. This is from that kid you met on Wednesday. It's a video of the inside of his channel, recorded directly from the aitherscope."

Dravin patted the machine and headed back to the desk. "You mean the rugby player?"

"The other one. The one who left early."

Aaron shifted to get a better view, and his wrist cracked.

Dravin whipped around. "Did you hear that?"

"Trust me, we're quite alone," said Casler.

Aaron stayed perched on his fingertips until Dravin's eyes finally returned to the laptop. Then he eased himself into a crouch, praying his slamming heart wasn't audible over the drone of the machine.

"Okay, watch this—" Casler played the video, and in slow motion, the screen displayed exactly what Aaron had seen through the aitherscope—three and a half seconds of flashing static—before it went blank.

"No regular clairvoyant signature," said Dravin.

"I noticed that too," said Casler. "Fairly typical for a patient who's sustained trauma to his channel, and that was my initial diagnosis. But I filtered out the static and . . ." he tapped a few keys, "I want you to watch it again, from my angle." Casler slid over, blocking the screen from Aaron's view.

The priest leaned in, and a moment later, his eyebrows furrowed. "Is that a branch?"

"You tell me."

"But . . . to where?"

"Father, I'm beginning to wonder . . . It's too much of a coincidence that this boy shares Clive's birthday."

"We checked the Registry, though," said Dravin. "No one was born opposite Amber—except, of course, your son."

"I know, I know . . ." Casler rubbed his temples, "but we knew the operation would affect both ends of the channel, both halves. We just weren't sure exactly how. Supposing the machine skewed the synchronization. The Registry might have clocked the boy's birth a few seconds late . . . or maybe even registered him as a stillborn. Stillbirths aren't always recorded accurately. Maybe that's why we didn't know about him."

Dravin nodded. "Then deal with him before he becomes a problem. And for your son's sake, don't speak of this again . . . not even to the potentate."

In the frail light, the shadows elongated under Casler's

high cheekbones. "Of course." He reached out and closed his laptop, his hands trembling.

"Clive seems very much in control of himself lately," said Dravin. "He's come a long way."

"Yes, he has," said Casler. "But there are still times when he lashes out—"

"As with all of us." Dravin straightened his glasses and focused on Casler. "You may wish to know your son has been chosen as the heir."

Casler rose from his seat suddenly. He shut his eyes and breathed deeply. When he opened them again, a tear slid down his cheek. "Thank you," he whispered. "I am pleased to hear that."

Dravin appraised him with cold eyes. "I only wonder if he's mature enough," he said. "If he can't control that half of his—"

"She *will* submit to my son," said Casler.

"Mr. Lilian is in full agreement that you should do everything in your power to make his daughter complacent for our heir." His lips curled into a smirk. "Quite a prize, she is. You won't tarnish her face, will you?"

"You won't even see the scar," said Casler. "It'll be at the back of her head, underneath her hair."

Aaron's shoulder bumped the medicine rack, and the bottles rattled.

Casler glanced at the rack, and his eyes narrowed through the gaps.

Dravin laughed. "Another one of your tricks, Casler?" He pulled his cloak around his shoulders. "Until tomorrow then."

"Do try to dress nice," said Casler, his eyes still on the medicine rack. "It's my son's birthday."

"It's the birthday of our heir," said Dravin. "Oh and Casler, about the bruises he had Wednesday—that will need to stop."

"That will stop when he obeys me and quits sneaking into my studio," Casler said loudly, peering intently in Aaron's direction.

As soon as Dravin left, Casler marched to the wall. Aaron watched him between two beakers, as he flipped a switch—and a hundred halogen lights ignited and blazed all around him. Their blinding blue glare grilled his skin.

"Now—" Casler's voice boomed. He faced the medicine rack, which was now hardly more than a stained glass window. "Let's find out who's sneaking around my studio."

As Casler swept toward him, Aaron coiled his fingers around the throat of a medicine bottle and yanked it from the rack. He cracked it against the floor, stood, and raised its jagged edge.

"Hold it there—" he said, as clear, chilled liquid dribbled down his arm and soaked into the gauze.

"*Aaron?*" Casler halted.

"Who'd you think?" said Aaron.

"I thought you were Clive—" Casler's face softened and he grinned despite the broken bottle in Aaron's hands. "Aaron, what brings you down here?" he said conversationally.

Aaron kicked over the medicine rack, and the roar of shattering glass echoed off the walls. Chemicals sizzled on the floor. "Why do you keep pretending?" he said.

Casler eyed the steaming liquid rushing toward his feet. "Pretending?" he said. "Did something I say upset you?"

Aaron's wet arm felt warm and itchy. "If you even touch her," he said. "I'll gouge out your son's eyes, I swear."

Casler smiled and stepped carefully around the steaming puddle. "Aaron, we're all very taken by Amber's charm," he said, "but you do understand how much of a nuisance her constant disobedience can be sometimes." His face blotted out the halogen lamps. "Just one tiny prick, though, and we can drain out the feisty parts. She won't even know anything's missing."

"You're out of your mind," said Aaron.

"I'm afraid this isn't my choice," said Casler. "A man's half must be obedient."

"So you're going to suck her dry?" said Aaron, and he pictured the woman in the car outside the Juvengamy meeting. That was what Casler meant by obedient.

"She'll be quite tame when it's done, and much improved, you'll see. Now was there anything else?" Casler grinned, and he stepped closer, teeth sparkling.

Aaron thrust the bottle forward, halting him. The cut on his wrist felt hot. "How about the kid you murdered?"

"Sorry?" said Casler.

"I saw the body," said Aaron.

"The body?" For a moment, Casler peered at him as if he was the crazy one, before his eyes flashed with awareness. "Ah—*that* body."

"There's more than one?" said Aaron.

"Just the one," said Casler, beaming at him. "I was

supposed to return it to the coroner—"

An invisible fire seared Aaron's wrist, and he dropped the broken bottle. His fingers tensed, clawlike, and he tore at the gauze around the knife wound. Singed hairs curled on his forearm, and the chemical smell of dissolving flesh parched his nose.

It was the liquid on his arm.

Casler rushed to his side and lifted his hand. His thick fingers probed Aaron's skin.

"Hydrochloric acid," he said, kneeling and rummaging through the bottles on the floor. He caught one as it rolled away, unscrewed the cap, and doused Aaron's arm.

White foam hissed out of Aaron's wound and off his skin, and the pain vanished immediately. Casler poured until the bottle was empty.

Then he sighed and squeezed Aaron's shoulder. "You had me frightened," he said. "Let's wrap this up so it doesn't scar."

Aaron stared at him in disbelief.

At that moment, Clive appeared at the foot of the stairs. "Father, are you busy?" he said.

"Always," said Casler, still examining Aaron's swollen forearm. "Grab a bandage for us, would you?"

Clive noticed Aaron in his father's shadow, and his eyes contracted into white slits. "Father, can I speak with you in private?"

"Get the bandage first," said Casler.

Clive's shifty eyes darted between them. "It's urgent," he said.

At first, Casler didn't say anything, but his fingers closed on Aaron's wrist, stiff as iron, and the low sound of his breathing rose over the machine. "Get us a bandage, Clive. Aaron's hurt himself."

"Father, you *must* listen to me."

Casler scrunched his eyebrows together, released Aaron's wrist, and stood to his full height. Slowly, he faced Clive. "I asked you for a bandage."

"Father, can you do it tonight?" Clive stuttered, pointing a trembling finger at Aaron. "Can you to put him in the machine tonight . . . *please?*"

Before Casler could turn around, Aaron raced past him and rushed the exit. Clive stood his ground, but at the last moment, shrank away from him. Aaron shoved him out of the way and lunged up the stairs. Up in the cellar, he flew past the aitherscope. The intercom clicked above him.

"Dominic—" Casler's voice thundered in every room, a hundred times louder than it should have been. "Make sure Aaron doesn't leave. He's hurt himself and I need to treat him."

Aaron was already at the entrance, the door right in front of him. Freedom. But as it turned out, Dominic Brees was drinking another glass of whisky in the kitchen when Casler made his announcement.

And Dominic Brees was the second fastest rugby player in the league.

Aaron heard two sets of footsteps streak across the dark marble. He reached the door first and yanked it open, but Dominic slammed into him and they both tumbled out onto the granite steps.

Aaron kneed the rugby player in the face and leapt up, and then there was nothing but cold wind whipping through his hair. He tried to hurtle a dead rosebush, jammed his foot ankle deep in thorns, and toppled face first onto the brick driveway. Dominic went the long way, but the dark blur of his torso closed in fast.

Aaron veered toward the wilderness on the far side of the property. His thighs burned, and his chest threatened to cave in, but he could hear Dominic right behind him, panting, his hot breath on his heels.

They plunged into the pitch-black forest. Branches materialized two feet in front of Aaron's face, like disfigured human limbs. Too late to duck. He lowered his shoulder and charged through them. Splinters showered behind him.

Then he shoved his foot against a root, swerved, and collapsed into the shadow of an oak tree. Dominic flew by, oblivious, and his muddy splashes faded into the distance.

Aaron waited until there was silence, until only the restless clicking and creaking of the forest could be heard through the trees, then he retraced his steps back to the driveway. Beneath luminous rainclouds, a breeze rippled in the meadow. He knelt at the gate and caught his breath, and inside his rib cage, his heart ricocheted like a bouncy ball.

But he shouldn't have rested so soon.

Aaron heard a click behind him. He spun, but too late. The fleshy hollow of Dominic's elbow clamped down on his throat. He felt the switchblade wedge into the side of his windpipe, and then he heard wheezing in his ear.

"How'd you get out of the well, number eleven?"

"I climbed out," Aaron spat. "It was easy."

"No way. Those walls are like a slip 'n slide."

"Yeah?" said Aaron. "My grandmother could have done it."

The knife's pressure increased and Aaron struggled to breathe.

"Sounds like you need a doctor," said Dominic.

"Fine," said Aaron, "take me back to him . . . play his little lapdog."

"Don't insult me," said Dominic. "I don't answer to any Selavio, and I never will."

"Then why'd you let him get away with it?" said Aaron. "He drilled a goddamn hole through Justin's head. I saw the body."

"I know what he did, fuckface . . . it's the same thing he's going to do to you." Dominic uncoiled his arm and shoved Aaron away from him. "Lucky for you, it's Clive's birthday today, which gives you a one day head start to leave the country. Now get off my property before I change my mind."

"It's my birthday too," said Aaron.

"No shit," said Dominic, "and you're going to wish it wasn't."

At four-thirty in the morning, Aaron scaled Dominic's gate then stood terrified on the dark road. In all directions, the street's gloomy houses were concealed behind knotted, cancerous growths of vegetation.

Instead of being sound asleep like the street's inhabitants, he was fifteen miles from home, alone, with six and a half hours to make his appointment—and all he could think about was Dr. Selavio's hideous plans for Amber.

First, he had to tell her.

Aaron dialed her number and pressed his cell phone to his ear, but he got her voicemail.

"You've reached Amber," she said, giggling. "If you want me to call you back, try leaving a message."

"Amber, pick up your phone. *Please.*" Aaron snapped the phone shut, and a little more of his hope evaporated. She was asleep like everyone else at this ungodly hour, oblivious to the danger she was in.

Or *was* she oblivious? How often had Amber told him nothing and pretended everything was fine? How often had she hidden her life from him so he wouldn't try to protect her? How often had she disregarded the future—because she didn't really have one?

The truth was, Amber had known from the beginning—and that was the hardest part to take.

She knew she was being molded into a prize for the Brotherhood's heir, domesticated. That the undesirable parts of her would eventually have to be removed. She never told him because she never wanted him to know.

Because after the operation, the scar at the back of her head would heal, but the hole inside her would not. Her eyes would be empty, extinguished forever of their dazzling flare—like all the other juvengamy women.

Aaron's stomach did queasy somersaults at the thought. He had to get her away from everyone. From Casler, from Clive—*from her father.*

With trembling fingers, he dialed her number again.

Again her voicemail.

Aaron slipped the phone back into his pocket. *Damn it, Amber*. He started walking.

He could go to the police. First they would interrogate Amber's parents, then her half, Clive. Both conversations would convince them that Aaron was just causing trouble, that he was just a boy who had fallen for the wrong girl. He had no proof.

And in six and a half hours, the entire Juvengamy Brotherhood would be watching her, the *heiress*. She would be untouchable. Aaron inhaled through his nose, and the stale morning air churned inside him. Its usefulness was rapidly ticking away.

Except there was proof. In the woods behind Dominic's house, the body. Proof that Dr. Selavio, the figurehead of Brotherhood, was a murderer. The police couldn't ignore a body—

Aaron's cell phone rang, interrupting his thoughts. Amber's ringtone.

He flipped open the phone. "Are you okay?"

"I have something to tell you," she said.

And she sounded deliriously, impossibly happy.

TEN

0 Days, 6 hours, 29 minutes

AARON'S PULSE FLICKERED. He shut his eyes and breathed in slowly. She sounded just like she was supposed to, like herself—*safe*.

"Tell me later," he said. "You have to get out of your house right now."

"Why did Clive have your phone?" she said.

"I got it back."

"*Obviously*," she said, her voice still bubbly. "Now aren't you going to invite me over so I can tell you?

"I'm not home."

"Where are you?"

Aaron stared at the moldy sky through a cage of dark, gnarled oak trees. Forty feet ahead, the pavement veered into the murky wilderness.

"I'm at Buff's house."

"You are *such* a bad liar—"

"Because I don't do it all the time like you do," he said.

"Just meet me at his house, *please*."

"Only if you tell me where you are," she said.

Aaron sighed and stepped up to a lonely mailbox. He lit the number with his cell phone screen. "Number twenty-two, Via Cordillera. It's out in the middle of nowhere—"

"Stay there," she said. "I'm picking you up."

Aaron peeled the phone from his ear and stared at it in disbelief. Was she serious? "Amber, stay where you are. Don't come anywhere near this place."

"I thought you wanted me out of my house?" she said.

"I'll come get you."

"So you're wandering around alone in the middle of the night, out in the rain, and you think *I'm* the one who isn't safe?"

"Good. You understand," he said.

"No, what I understand is that knowing *you*, Aaron, you'll probably get yourself thrown down a well or something. *Bye.*"

"Amber, don't—"

But she'd already hung up. He redialed her number and it went straight to voicemail. Great, she was being reckless. *Typical.*

Aaron kicked the mailbox, and droplets tumbled into the grass. The post wobbled sleepily. Aaron had only just leaned against the mailbox, too exhausted to speculate about Amber's good news, when he felt another twinge in the back of head.

Aaron's questions resurfaced. Had *he* caused Clive's bleeding? Or was it Clive's weak connection to his half, a symptom of the "loose forces," as his father called them? Was he sensing Clive again now, lurking nearby in the woods perhaps, *following* him—?

Aaron's thoughts blurred together as fatigue weighed down his eyelids.

A few minutes later, Aaron's eyelids sprang apart, and he found himself on the ground squinting into the silver glare of headlights. His jaw fell open as Amber's blue beetle pulled off the road and stopped just short of him.

He stood, yanked open the door, and stared in at her. "How fast did you drive?" he said.

She smiled. "Fast."

At four-forty-five on Saturday morning, Aaron peered around the dark street then slid in next to her, into soft, black suede. Warm vents glazed his skin. Her car smelled brand new, like toy plastic. The dashboard twinkled with purple LEDs, and in their glow, Amber's hair looked glossy, almost translucent. They both hesitated, as if they wanted to lean in and kiss each other. But the moment passed.

"What'd you want to tell me?" he said.

"Aren't you going to wish me happy birthday?" she said.

"It was my birthday first," he said, shoving his fingers through his knotted, grimy hair. "Just drive."

But her eyes froze on the fresh black blood trickling out from underneath the scraps of gauze still clinging to his arm, then darted to his tattered, bloodstained shirt.

"I'm fine," he said.

"Why do you always get hurt?" she said, leaning over him.

"Just drive—*please.*" Aaron glanced at the rear view mirror, and for a terrifying split-second, he thought he saw a figure cross the road. He swiveled and looked behind them, but the road was dark.

Amber followed his gaze. "Are you running away from someone?"

"See the pedal on the right?" he said. "*Push it!*"

"So you are running?"

"Amber, can I drive?" he said.

"*No*," she said, and the car glided forward. "I've seen you drive." Through the windshield, the high beams chased the shadows, which scampered back and crouched behind bushes.

Aaron sighed, and Amber's warm scent floated over him, confusing his nerves. Beneath him, the highway droned endlessly, and it would have put him to sleep but for the icy pricks of panic he felt across his skin. No, they *weren't* being followed.

Instead, he watched the speedometer. The needle climbed past eighty, then ninety. Then a hundred.

He raised his eyebrows.

"Do I scare you?" said Amber.

"Are you trying to?"

"Usually."

"Amber, I know what's going to happen to you," he said. "I overheard them. When you become the heiress, they're going to make you like the other juvengamy women."

"They're *not*." An orange street lamp streaked past them and illuminated her expression—a mixture of exasperation and helplessness.

"You know I'd give myself to Dr. Selavio before I let him do that to you," said Aaron.

"That's your *best* plan?" she said.

"What's yours?"

She took her eyes off the road to look at him. "Clive isn't my half," she said. "You are."

"Haven't we been over this?" said Aaron, scanning the deserted lanes in the rear-view mirror one more time.

"So? Isn't it your deepest, most erotic fantasy?" she said, turning back to the road.

"Be mature for five seconds—"

"And it's the truth," she said. "He isn't my real half. It's an arrangement."

Aaron glanced over at her. "Meaning what?"

"Don't you think it's too convenient?" she said.

"You and Clive?"

"We're two of the oldest families," she said. "Together we'd form a perfect bloodline."

The time had passed too quickly when she pulled in front of his house, leaving the engine running—and Aaron noticed the state of his front yard.

Runny sediment trickled from cracked flowerpots, mustard yellow, and drained in rivulets off the curb. On the lawn, murky rainwater rippled in the deep tire tracks left by the Beamer. And next to his front door, glass splinters dangled from a broken window. He watched as a breeze severed one loose and it shattered onto the porch.

"Keep driving," he said.

Amber gunned it down the street, and Aaron directed her to the botanical garden several blocks away. They parked in the vacant lot. In front of them, dark, muddy steps climbed into a grove. She killed the engine, and silence flooded in.

"A perfect bloodline," Aaron repeated, at last beginning to understand. "In other words, the bloodline of an heir."

"Clive and I weren't juvengamy babies because we aren't even halves," she said. "They're going to switch me with his half."

"But halves can't be switched," he said.

"What about faked?" she said.

"*Faked?* What do you mean?"

"Why do you think Casler wants to test the machine on you?" she said. "Because you're my real half. He wants you out of the picture, but still alive; he's going to drain your clairvoyance."

"But what about Clive's half?" he said.

"Wouldn't you have seen her by now?"

Aaron opened his mouth to protest, but stopped when he remembered Clive's tattoo. Suddenly, the mysterious absence of Clive's half made sense. She was hidden away somewhere, brain dead but still alive. Dr. Selavio had already operated on her, drained her, taken her out of the picture so Clive could pretend to be Amber's half. Now, in order to complete the switch, Dr. Selavio had to do the same thing to Aaron.

"So we're halves?" he said.

She bit her lip, waiting for his reaction, and as Aaron stared at her, he realized she had solved the riddle. They had chosen her for the heir, the perfect half—when really she belonged to Aaron.

"We have to run away," he said.

"I'm already packed," she said proudly, gesturing to the back seat where a huge, overstuffed suitcase was spilling onto the floor.

Aaron eyed the bag doubtfully. "Did you pack underwear?" he said.

"Check"

"Socks?"

"*Socks?*" she said. "That's the *second* thing on your list?"

Aaron stared at her. "You didn't pack socks."

"*You* didn't pack anything," she said.

The intensity of her green eyes stunned him. They were richer, he noticed, and all the colors were showing. The night was over.

Amber's cell phone rang, making her jump.

She stared at the caller ID, then silenced it. They both checked the clock—and caught each other. Five-forty-five in the morning. Suddenly, they staggered out of the car and into each other's arms, just starting to grasp that they were halves. A strip of pink stained the eastern horizon, their first day.

"What was that about your deepest, most erotic fantasy?" said Aaron, his skin igniting as he held her.

"You," she said, locking eyes with him, taking short, shallow breaths. "Where should we go?"

"Paris," he said, "then Spain, then Sicily—"

"I want to explore the coral reefs," she said. "Will you buy me a sailboat?"

"And what do I get?"

"Me," she said, batting her eyelashes.

"Don't push your luck," said Aaron, "or I might change my mind about letting you be my half."

"Actually, it's you who's on thin ice, buddy."

Through a hole in the clouds, silver rays pierced the canopy, glittered, and struck the soil. Sunrise.

"Come on." Aaron took her hand and led her up the muddy steps into the botanical garden. They collapsed on a bench between two dripping rose bushes, opposite a wall of mossy stones. As warm dew evaporated from the grass and perfumed the air around them, Amber curled up at his side. Their bodies melted together. Aaron filled his lungs, euphoric, unable and unwilling to calm the fire burning in every last nerve.

"Aaron, if I'm wrong," she whispered, "if we're not actually halves, will you promise me something?"

"What?"

"If I decide to do something you think is really stupid, promise me you won't try to protect me. Promise me you'll leave, that you'll go somewhere safe instead of trying to bargain with Dr. Selavio."

"Stop it," he said.

"Just promise me," she said.

"I promise we're halves."

Of course there was more to the story. But here, with Amber's silky hair flowing across his chest, everything was perfect.

And they fell asleep thinking they were halves.

While he slept, he had a nightmare that Clive came out of the shadows and took her. As he carried Amber into the morning light, they both looked like angels, perfect in every way. It seemed so vivid at the time, but he soon forgot.

On his birthday, Aaron woke up alone. It was daytime and his arms were empty. Like a single breath of air, she had gone. And from high, high above the hills, the sun's rays burned into his eyeballs and crushed his pupils to the size of pinheads.

But how high?

Aaron tore through his pockets and wrenched open his cell phone. His heart slammed against his chest. How high? A blank screen—the damn thing was out of batteries.

And it felt like being in a furnace. He squinted into the sun's glare. Sweat steamed off his neck. Was it nine o'clock in the morning?

Or high noon?

Aaron rolled off the bench and ran back down the trail. Her car was gone.

The morning with Amber was a distant memory, fading as if it had never happened. He clung to some details, but others vanished, dreamlike in their elusiveness. But worst of all was his memory of their conversation, the logic of why they were halves: dream logic.

Desperate, Aaron struggled to recall their plans. Were they running away first and working things out later? Or were they first going to the Chamber, confirming they were halves, and then running?

It must have been the latter. Amber had gone off somewhere to change out of her suitcase. Yeah, that was it. She would be waiting for him at the Chamber at eleven.

Aaron sprinted home, and he counted out exactly sixty seconds before he crashed through his front door. He stormed into the kitchen, into a blaze of golden sunlight.

But even when he shaded the numerals, he couldn't read the clock. They were stifled beneath a white-hot haze of glare.

Still wheezing, he dashed to his bedroom—his alarm clock. The display faced the wall. Clive must have bumped it the night before. Aaron stepped forward, his heart squirming in his throat, and flipped it around.

At first, Aaron just blinked at the digits. They looked backwards, like he was seeing them through a mirror. Nine-fifty-nine.

With effort, he determined he had one hour to get ready. He did it in half.

Thirty minutes until his appointment, Aaron twisted his Mazda's ignition wires together. The engine roared for a few seconds, then idled obediently.

He pressed down on the gas, and the car's acceleration made his insides squirm. But it wasn't nervousness, it was excitement.

As the streets flew by, he thought about his scar tissue, and the belief he'd held his whole life that when he finally met his half, something would be missing.

At dawn, gazing into Amber's eyes, he'd realized *nothing* was missing. He and Amber had entered the world at the same moment, destined for each other, halves. She was everything.

Twenty-one minutes until his appointment, he turned onto Gibraltar road and the engine lugged. He downshifted into second, and the surge made him dizzy.

Thirteen minutes until his appointment, his tires squealed

around the turnoff for the Chamber of Halves. Somewhere on the other side of the mountain there was another entrance, he would enter this one.

The driveway followed the top of a ridge between two lines of palm trees and then ducked through a stone arch into paradise. A miniature valley unfolded before him, blindingly green. A brook twinkled in the sunlight. Orchids blossomed in its sandy banks, and upstream, a waterfall sprayed off moss-covered rocks. The sparkling vapor rose like powdered crystals. Everywhere, clusters of cherry trees frosted the grass with pink petals.

A mile from the Chamber, Aaron started passing cars. Cadillacs and Mercedes. Their black bodies glinted in the sun.

Then, without warning, the Chamber of Halves was upon him. A towering castle of bleached adobe, nesting in the high cliffs above the valley—parting a great sea of silver mist.

Six minutes until his appointment, he pulled up to the entrance, double-parked a blue Corvette, and killed the engine. Silence closed around him.

As soon as he stepped out of his Mazda, a crosswind sliced through his tuxedo, making his knees wobble. The Chamber of Halves loomed in front of him, immense and impenetrable.

There were thirty-six steps up to the oak doors. But it felt like three hundred.

A man waited at the top. He wore the red vest and black slacks of a bellhop or valet.

"Welcome to the Tularosa Chamber of Halves, Mr. Harper." The man bowed and hauled open the giant oak doors. "We have you in a special office today. We'll let you know when it's time."

On March 30, three minutes until his appointment, Aaron stepped inside the Chamber of Halves, into the dry and decadent aroma of royalty—alone.

❧

The lobby was huge. Tapestries hung from a sixty-foot ceiling, from timbers carved of whole trees. Curving majestically up to the second floor, a staircase draped in purple carpet spanned the entire space. Velvet couches lined the walls, dwarfed under a mosaic of framed photos that reached the ceiling.

Photos of Chambers from around the world.

Their founding dates, most within five years of the discovery, were engraved alongside on plaques.

Aaron slung his jacket over his shoulder and strolled into the lobby. He leaned against the receptionist's mahogany desk, which looked to be proportioned for a giant.

He closed his eyes, and the thought of Amber sent shivers down his spine.

She was all his, forever. They were halves.

And in two minutes, they would be whole.

Then again, his sense of time could have been off by two minutes.

Aaron felt the eleven o'clock gong before he heard it, and his eyelids sprang open as the walls began to thunder. The roar of the Chamber's bell tower vibrated his bones, deafeningly close. In his ears, blood rippled and throbbed against his skull.

A searing pain shot through the back of his head, making

him wince, and at that moment, he knew everything was wrong. He couldn't catch his breath, the air was sluggish, burdened by the bell's lingering vibrations—the clairvoyance of things to come.

He glanced around, then started toward the stairs. It was all wrong, they had gotten everything wrong. Before he even made it halfway across the lobby, the elevator chimed, and its doors opened. Half a dozen photographers filed out, carrying flash units and tripods. They waddled to the foot of the stairs.

Aaron slowed and watched them. Then he heard footsteps, hundreds of them, marching down the stairs into the lobby. A camera flashed, followed by another. Soon the bursts came like fireworks, flooding the stairs with blinding light.

It was a formal wedding party, and Aaron caught a glimpse of the two people they were photographing at the front of the procession—and it felt like an eighty-pound dumbbell landing in his stomach.

The closer one was Clive Selavio. He wore a white tuxedo. And walking to his right, her arm linked with his—was Amber Lilian.

She had straightened her hair and put some of it up. Her lips sparkled, so did her long white gown, trailing on the steps behind her. She glittered with every flash from the cameras.

She stared straight ahead, her expression blank, detached.

Her father walked behind her, next to her mother, whom Aaron had never met. The woman's golden hair had silver streaks from age. She looked stoic, like a mannequin. Yet her eyes gleamed with pride.

Towering over the others, Casler Selavio walked in step behind Clive and next to Mr. Lilian, his huge arm firmly linked with his half, also whom Aaron had never seen. But judging by her blank stare, she was just like the woman he'd seen in the car. Empty. Another camera flashed and Casler's white teeth twinkled.

Dominic Brees came next, followed by hundreds more in crisp suits and gowns, including Father Dravin in full priest attire a few rows back. Most of the women had the vacant looks of juvengamy women.

Clive grinned for the cameramen as they circled him and Amber, flashing away. He put his arm around her shoulder and squeezed her closer. Her limp body obeyed like a rag doll. She smiled once, briefly, and the onslaught of flashes that bleached her face forced her to lower her eyes.

Aaron stared at them as they crossed the lobby, unable to draw breath, unable to pivot his frozen knees. Unable to save her. Between his eyes, there was only frigid, black confusion as every last drop of his conviction evaporated. There was so much they hadn't considered the night before, so much delusion. Of course halves couldn't be faked. He saw the truth now—in Amber and Clive's synchronized steps, in the identical sparkle of their bright eyes, in their equally perfect features—what he'd been blinded to for a month.

Amber and Clive simply *looked* right together.

After today, they would belong only to each other; the rules were different. When Casler's machine was through with Amber, she would become Clive's puppet, to do with as he pleased. There was nothing Aaron could do about it. Nothing.

That was the law of halves.

The paparazzi followed Clive and Amber through the doors. For a full five minutes, the procession filed through the lobby, until finally, the footsteps of the last couple echoed through the hall.

Gradually, the stabbing pain in his skull faded. But the pain in his heart did not.

"Mr. Harper—" The receptionist leaned forward. "It's time."

Amber felt Clive gripping her waist, holding her steady as they descended the thirty-six steps outside the Chamber of Halves, most likely unaware that his arm was the only thing keeping her vertical. Every step was a leap of faith, a petrifying free-fall, threatening to drain her already empty stomach onto the flashing cameras in front of her.

At the bottom she let unfamiliar hands guide her into a limousine, and she fell into a cold leather seat strewn with rose petals. Clive slid in next to her, and without warning they were alone, *unnervingly* alone—as the guests' chatter was muted outside the tinted glass.

The limo pulled away, leaving her stomach far behind. Clive was whispering something, sliding closer to her, touching her in places he shouldn't, but all she could do was fix her stare helplessly on the horizon and wait for it to stop spinning.

Clive had discovered her that morning, sleeping with

Aaron. Amber shut her eyes, but the memory had already stung her. The urge to cry out his name was unbearable. Even in the Chamber, she expected Aaron. Even after Clive entered, grabbed her hand, and led her wordlessly before their parents—and the roaring applause of the Juvengamy Brotherhood—she *still* believed it was an arrangement.

What finally convinced her otherwise was the image of Clive's pale blue eyes through the aitherscope during the confirmation.

The limo descended into the valley below and dropped them off at the Chamber Ballroom, where a hundred silk covered tables were set with crystal glasses and silver.

When the first course was served, shrimp salad over half an avocado, smothered in a thick reddish sauce, Amber took one look and barely managed to excuse herself to the bathroom before she threw up.

Clive followed her and banged on the door.

Amber coughed and stared at the watery contents of her stomach as they seeped down the drain, and another knot formed in her stomach.

She wondered vaguely about Aaron's half, but she couldn't hold the thought. Her stomach convulsed again. Good, the sooner it was all out, the better.

Just like the sooner they emptied her out with that machine, the better.

Clive banged harder, threw his weight against the door, and broke the lock. He swooped in and grabbed her shoulders.

"What's wrong?" he said.

"You're *really* asking?" she said.

"Is this how it's going to be, Amber?" he said. "Is this how it's going to be on our wedding night?"

"No," she said, "this is how it's going to be forever."

"Does it matter that I love you?"

"Clive, none of this has ever been about love," she said.

He stared at her. "It's Harper, isn't it?"

"Why does it matter?" she said. "We're halves, just like you always wanted."

"You used to love me," he said.

"Funny. I don't remember that," she said.

His blue eyes held her captive. "Well I do."

Aaron stepped into the special office and found Walter Wu cradling his forehead in his hands, gazing at a photo of his half through thick glasses. Aaron shut the door behind him and the man flinched, knocking the frame into his lap.

"Mr. *Harper*—?" he said, his eyes widening as Aaron lowered himself into the chair opposite his desk.

"Who'd you expect?" said Aaron.

Walter chewed on his lip for a moment, considering him carefully. Then he pulled off his glasses and massaged his bald forehead. "Aaron, you seem like an ordinary kid to me so I'll just get right to it."

In the special office, there was only a desk and a chair. No tapestries, no chandeliers, no paintings. It was an office for delivering bad news, for explaining complications.

And it was wrong to be here. It was wrong to meet his half. He was in love with Amber.

"Yes, perfectly ordinary," Walter added, and he didn't

look Aaron in the eye. He slid his glasses back into place and turned to the file that was open on his desk, "which is why your situation is so curious."

He flipped over one of the pages. "Of course, halves aren't born *exactly* the same time. Sometimes they're off by a fraction of a second, but *eighteen years?*"

Walter Wu shook his head and set the page down. "No, your situation is quite different." He looked up. "I'm afraid you don't have a half."

ELEVEN

Plus 1 minute

WALTER WU HELD his breath, his knuckles white on the framed photo in his lap as he waited for Aaron's reaction.

But Aaron only blinked.

You don't have a half. It was like saying he didn't have a mother, or that the sun hadn't risen that morning. It had to be a play on words.

"Sorry—" Aaron leaned forward. "I didn't catch that last bit."

"I assure you," said Walter, his breath leaking from the corners of his mouth. "To this day our very best psychologists continue to analyze the circumstances of your birth. They agree that you're extremely fortunate—"

Aaron raised his eyebrows, and Walter's face gave an odd twitch.

"In fact," said Walter, still unable to meet Aaron's gaze. "It's a miracle you're alive at all. Anybody else with your condition would be dead."

The man's words travelled slowly, striking Aaron's ear a full second after they were spoken. In the special office, across from Walter Wu, Aaron watched the answer to his life's riddle crystalize before his eyes.

He didn't have a half. And the opposite of what Walter said was true. To be dead—*that* would be fortunate.

Amber had been wrong. It wasn't a setup.

"So the two who just left," said Aaron, asking the only question that still mattered, "they're halves?"

"You mean the Selavios?"

At the mention of the name, Aaron's lungs tightened. He nodded.

"Actually, I confirmed them myself," said Walter. "I still have the aitherscope's printout if you'd like to see."

Aaron stared at him, swishing drool around in his mouth. Then he hunched forward, planted his elbows on his knees, and spit on the floor. While his saliva bubbled on the tiles, he listened to the clock's endless ticking.

Walter Wu stiffened, and his hand crept toward the telephone on his desk.

Finally, Aaron rose to his feet and left the office. The deep, purple hallways were lined with paintings of valleys and sunsets—scenes of life's beauty.

On Aaron's eighteenth birthday, he left the Chamber of Halves through a steel service door, peeled a parking ticket off his windshield, and drove home alone.

And he thought of Amber.

She had known all along that Clive was her half. All last week, all those nights together, she'd been living with an expiration date.

Aaron passed his house but kept on driving. Street names repeated. The hours blurred together. He couldn't face his parents—not without a half. Not alone.

Not when his final glimpse of Amber was branded into his eyelids, flashing every time he blinked. Amber, all dressed up as a prize for the Brotherhood's heir, for Clive.

At sunset, Aaron found himself alone on the cliffs overlooking the pink streaks at the ocean's edge. Alone, when the word itself meant nothing. And he wondered what they were doing to her.

Amber caught a glimpse of the Chamber's distant towers, soaring like sunburned fists as the last sliver of sunlight cleared the peaks—before she was led into the church.

The dying light slanted in through stained glass windows, dusting the empty pews. Amber and Clive walked in front of their parents down the aisle toward the priest waiting at the pulpit. They were no longer in their wedding clothes.

Clive reached Father Dravin first and knelt briefly in front of him. "Father Dravin, I present my half, Amber," he said.

Dravin turned his large, golden eyes on Amber and waited. She did nothing.

He straightened his glasses. "Genuflect on the left knee, sweetheart."

Amber was mystified as to what this meant until she felt her mother's hand on her shoulder, forcing her to kneel.

"Dravin, are you sure this is the best place?" said Amber's father. "If anything happens to her—"

"Then it would be best you waited outside," said Dravin.

"The potentate specifically requested my services. That should put your worries to rest." With that, he spun and signaled for Amber and Clive to follow him behind the altar, where two tables stood side by side in a circle of light.

"Shirts off," he said, moving to an open leather bag on a third table. He slid on latex gloves, then extracted three glinting scalpels. As he arranged his tools on a folded towel, Amber felt her throat tighten. She heard Clive's shirt fall to the floor then felt the heat of his gaze, but she refused to look at him.

Amber swallowed and pulled her own shirt over her head. Her loose hair swished across her back, prickling her bare skin.

Dravin glanced up at her and straightened his glasses. "The brassiere too, sweetheart."

Amber glared at him and climbed onto the table, and only when she was lying on her stomach did she unclip her bra.

Clive lay down on the other table.

Father Dravin walked between them, and Amber felt his fingers brush her back, trace her shoulder blades, and run down her spine. She tensed, hardly breathing. He leaned over Clive next and touched the scars on his back.

"Curious," he said, finally. "I understand now why this was to be conducted in private."

"Can you duplicate it?" said Amber's mother.

"Hers will be cleaner," said Dravin.

Amber felt something cold dab her back, and she squeezed her eyes shut, helpless against the shivers that followed.

"It's just alcohol, sweetheart."

The priest grabbed something off the towel and leaned

over her, blocking the light, and she gripped the front of the table. He pressed a sharp object against her spine. She winced, but it was just the tip of a pencil.

Dravin's hand curved up the side of her torso, where the pencil jerked over her ribs. He lifted the pencil, referred to Clive's tattoo, and made another arc below the first. By nightfall, the outline was done.

He picked up the scalpel.

Once again, his shadow swallowed her. He pressed the scalpel to her skin, moved it slightly—and then the blade sank in. Prickles surged through Amber's body, and her throat squeezed shut. As he sliced her skin, everything inside her screamed. She felt spasms of pain, electric shocks. Her body twitched.

Dravin dabbed at her back, and his rag came away spotted with blood. He went over the line twice, then started a second cut. Droplets of blood cooled on her skin and dribbled down the side of her waist. As the pain blurred into a prickly fog, she whimpered, and her tears pooled under her cheeks.

Her parents watched proudly as the priest carved the mirror image of Clive's tattoo into her back. Clive's clairvoyance was in her blood. *He* would prevent the cuts from healing, and they would form white scars forever branding her as his half.

When the incisions were done, Dravin reached for another tool—and Amber felt him peel away the strips of skin, exposing what was underneath to the cold, cold air.

"In the woods, you say?" said the deputy.

"I can show you where," said Aaron.

"A body?"

"Justin Gorski's, there's a hole drilled through his head. They're going to hurt Amber next," said Aaron, fearing what they might have already done to her.

The deputy scrunched up his eyebrows. "How old are you again?"

"I'm eighteen."

"Are you jealous or something? Where's your half?"

"There's a *body*," Aaron repeated slowly. "Casler murdered Justin Gorski, and he's going to hurt Amber next."

The police officer regarded him for a moment then rubbed his sleep-deprived eyes. "You're going to have to give me more than that," he said. "Our community values the contributions of Dr. Selavio. I can't start a criminal investigation based off a crack-pot story from a jealous seventeen-year old."

"Eighteen," said Aaron.

"Maybe you should spend some time with your half," said the deputy, and his eyes flicked to the picture frame on his desk.

Aaron followed his gaze to a photo of the deputy's half and their kids. A normal family. Except something in the picture was off.

Aaron glanced at the other photos behind the deputy, also of the same woman, then back to the one on his desk—and he felt a chill.

In each photograph, the deputy's half had the same blank look, like there wasn't anything behind her eyes.

The officer saw where he was looking and twisted the

picture away from him. He stood. "Let me show you out, Mr. Harper."

❧

He needed more proof.

When he was sure his parents were asleep, Aaron snuck into his house and tiptoed to his bedroom. He took a deep breath and flipped on the lights. His room was just as he left it.

Aaron hesitated in the doorway, breathing slowly, as the smell of sunscreen and vanilla floated over him—*her* smell. It was all over his clothes, floating out of his laundry hamper, just as strong as the first time they met.

He remembered meeting her at the bonfire. Now, on his birthday, if not for the throbbing in his lungs, if not for that smell, everything in between could have been a dream—Dr. Selavio's machine, the body, the vial full of clairvoyance.

There was no proof.

But as Aaron watched his wrinkled, mud-smeared jeans sway on the back of his chair, a terrifying idea took hold of him.

The vial was proof.

It had tumbled off his fingers. He knew exactly where it sank . . . He could recover it.

Before he backed down, Aaron opened the bottom drawer and closed his fingers around the hem of his bathing suit. Instinct pressed against the back of his mind, screaming at him. The vial was buried in the sand under thirty feet of water. He'd *never* find it.

But what if he could?

Could a vial full of clairvoyance save Amber's life? Could it give her a new half?

That was what truly scared him.

Entanglement

Aaron googled the word after he parked outside the Arroyo Beach Café, using their Wi-Fi and his mom's laptop, which he balanced against the steering wheel. The word was thrown around every five seconds, but he still didn't understand it.

The sun was just rising.

He clicked on the second link, a wiki page titled "Quantum entanglement," and read from the top.

> **Quantum entanglement** *(commonly known as* **entanglement** *or* **clairvoyance***) occurs when particles such as photons, electrons, and even molecules as large as DNA interact physically and then become separated such that each resulting member of a pair is properly described by the same quantum mechanical state . . .*

Fat lot of sense that made.

Aaron scanned the rest of the page, but none of it meant jack. Frustrated, he clicked on random keywords, jumping through page after page about halves until he ended up on a page titled "Quantum teleportation."

Aaron waded through more dense physics, again comprehending none of it, and he was about to slam the laptop shut when a sub-heading caught his eye.

He stared at the strangest phrase he had ever seen.

Entanglement swapping

A film of dust coated the laptop's display, catching the morning rays and obscuring the text. He grabbed his shirt and wiped the screen, and read the first thing all morning he did understand.

If Alice has a particle which is entangled with a particle owned by Bob, and Bob teleports it to Carol, then Alice's particle becomes entangled with Carol's.

At nine in the morning on Easter Sunday, Aaron peeled off his shoes and stuck his feet into the sand at Arroyo Beach. Fog whisked past him. The month-old charred logs from the bonfire had long since been broken apart and buried.

Entanglement swapping.

There was no way.

Aaron felt thunder against his back and glanced up to see a wall of white foam smash against the sand. The surf looked especially rough today.

But he had come prepared.

He threw down his backpack and extracted a pair of goggles, an underwater flashlight, and a package of eight neon dive sticks.

Aaron tore open the package with his teeth and jammed all eight of them into the pocket of his bathing suit. Then he slid the flashlight into his other pocket, took off his shirt, and stumbled toward the water.

A wave rose and smashed in front of him, stinging his eyes

with mist and parting around his ankles. The water wasn't nearly as cold as the night he swam with Clive, but it still stung. He stepped up to his knees in foam, and goose bumps rushed across his skin.

After he nearly drowned in the well, the thought of diving for the vial made his lungs ache. For a month, he had tortured himself brooding over its hiding place, knowing it was just out of reach—and knowing that it *could* be reached.

Now, wading thigh-deep through the ocean's thrusts, he wished more than anything that he never had the thought.

What exactly was he planning to do once he found the vial? Take it to the police? A doctor? Or find a way to use it himself.

Aaron rotated his shoulders, crouched, and charged through a mountain of water. He popped up on the other side and climbed another wave, struggled over a third, a fourth, then broke free of the pounding surf.

A vial full of clairvoyance could be capable of anything, but he prayed it never came to that.

Aaron swam as hard as he could, and his uneasiness reminded him, once again, that he had no idea what Dr. Selavio was up to. Or why he even filled the vial in the first place.

Around him, the fog thickened, blocking his view of the buoy. He slowed and treaded water, and a crisp breeze whistled in his ears. He patted his pockets to make sure he still had the flashlight and dive sticks before he started up again.

Soon he couldn't see the beach, just swells and white caps, and the same arctic gray in all directions. His arms throbbed with fatigue. He should have reached the buoy by now.

Aaron pressed on, but his strokes felt heavier, burdened by anxiety. He stopped again, now gasping for breath, and scanned three-hundred-and-sixty degrees of bleak horizon. A swell drove him skyward then gave out beneath him.

No way he'd swum this far, not at midnight, not after a volleyball game, and not in freezing March waters. He must have passed the buoy in the fog.

Aaron angled his body back to shore—or what he thought was shore—and once again lugged his arms through the brine. He had wasted his energy, and now he had precious little left to recover the vial.

But the fog thinned. For a few seconds, he glimpsed the beach—and the buoy?

Still beyond him. He'd hardly made it a third of the way.

A long time ago, Aaron had heard the water was seventeen feet deep at the buoys. Or was it thirty-seven? Aaron reached the buoy choking for breath, not sure he could manage five.

After catching his breath, he tugged the dive sticks from his pocket and released them all into the water. He watched them sink.

They were bigger than the vial, but their behavior would be the same underwater—they would *sink* the same. And if everything went according to plan, the neon dive sticks would roughly mark the area at the bottom where he should search for the vial.

Aaron stretched the goggles over his eyes and dipped his head underwater. A murky green abyss swallowed his gaze. There was no hint of the bottom, and the buoy's chain sank deep into the haze, eerily still.

Aaron raised his head, took a deep breath, and made the

plunge. Scraps of kelp materialized inches from his nose and whisked past him. He swam as deep as he could, until his ears throbbed. But there was no sign of the bottom.

Back at the surface, Aaron clung to the buoy, panting. But as he waiting for the hollow feeling in his chest to subside, he had a chilling thought. Even now, Dr. Selavio could be strapping Amber into his machine. Who knew how much time she had left.

Feeling sick and failing to push the thought from his mind, Aaron submerged his head again and scanned the teal gloom for any indication of the sea floor. Nothing. The bleak haze sank into infinity. It was hopeless.

No it wasn't. Aaron's eyes settled on the crusty chain swaying gently in the ocean's current—the chain that anchored the buoy to the bottom.

Aaron grabbed the rusted links, and slime oozed between his fingers. He dived again, this time climbing down the chain. Seawater rushed around him, squashing him. Still no sign of the bottom.

His heart thumped in his ears, like impacts from a baseball bat. The goggles pinched his sinuses. Again and again he plunged his hands through freezing water and yanked the chain, dragged himself deeper. A cold, dark midnight closed around him.

Without warning, a vast black wall materialized from the gloom in front of him—the bottom of the ocean. Three of the dive sticks gleamed in the sand: yellow, green, and pink. He slapped the bottom and scrambled back up to the surface.

Afterwards, he had to catch his breath for a whole minute.

Waves lapped against the buoy. If he could touch the bottom, then he could definitely recover the vial.

Aaron dived again. Three more times. He scoured the seafloor with his flashlight, and the dive sticks lit up in its beam. All eight of them.

But he never found the vial.

It should have been easy, like finding a glow stick at night. The vial held bright red fluid—or was it buried in the sand? Aaron clung to the buoy and caught his breath for the sixth time, and a gust of wind made him shiver.

He simply *had* to find the vial.

On his next dive, he swept his flashlight around a larger radius. For a split-second, just inside the farthest dive stick, the sand glinted. He flicked the beam back to the spot but saw nothing.

Aaron swam through flakes of dead kelp and brushed his hand along the bottom. He had to check now or risk losing the spot.

His lungs heaved, pulling at nothing. He already should have surfaced. Aaron raked his fingers through the muck, which billowed up in his face. He watched it settle. Bits of silica, grains of iridescent shells. In the flashlight's beam, it all glinted—he hadn't seen a damn thing.

Furious, he shoved off the bottom, and his hand struck something invisible. Then he saw it, skittering across the seafloor. The outline of the vial.

But Aaron's stiff fingers hardly obeyed him. The vial vanished against the sand. He lunged for it, but only knocked it farther away.

He needed air. The sea swarmed with black spots. His

lungs convulsed, tore at his chest. Aaron squirmed after the vial, but his fingers lost their grip on the flashlight and it nosedived into the sand—and the vial tumbled into the shadows.

Aaron stared at the narrow cone of light, the particles as they swirled like snow in front of headlights. The vial was gone. He couldn't hold the air in any longer, and bubbles exploded from his nose.

~

But light behaves differently underwater. The index of refraction of fused quartz is lower than glass. If the vial *had* been made of glass, he would have seen it. But it wasn't glass.

In salt water, a vial made of fused quartz was nearly invisible. At the bottom of the ocean, through a foggy pair of goggles, it would be like finding a poppy seed on a beach.

Yet right there, an inch from the flashlight and twinkling in its yellow beam, the vial had come to rest.

Aaron grabbed the vial, kicked off the bottom, and swam for the surface. Without the air in his lungs he was denser. He thrashed at the water, but it resisted him like syrup and he sank back after each thrust. The surface shimmered, miles above him.

But he kept going, willing the blood through his limp muscles. More air escaped his nostrils, deflating him further. His body was on the verge of collapsing in on itself.

Then he felt warmth on his cheeks, fresh air in his lungs, but by then he realized what was wrong.

His swim to the buoy, the dive sticks, the underwater flashlight—none of that mattered.

Aaron pried his fingers off the vial and looked straight through it. Of course he hadn't seen it underwater.

It was empty.

❧

The vial was Aaron's last hope. There was nothing else to do, nowhere to go. In a world where everyone was paired with their half, he was alone.

Aaron drove home ten miles per hour under the speed limit, took a shower, and charged his cell phone.

Sunday passed. Absurdly, the digits on his clock continued to change. Around five in the afternoon, when yellow-orange light slanted in through the windows, Aaron laid the vial on his nightstand and sat with his back propped against his bedframe.

Amber's perfume floated over him still. He wanted to feel her hair on his neck. He wanted to hold her, whisper in her ear. He wanted to see her green eyes sparkle.

Before they sparkled for the last time.

Aaron stared at the empty vial. Waiting. Just as he'd been waiting for his entire life.

Only there was nothing to wait for. His birthday had come and gone. He wasn't seventeen anymore. Now, for as long as he lived, nobody would ever break the silence between his ears.

But he would always be waiting.

❧

Aaron opened his eyes suddenly. He lay curled in a pool of sweat, still unable to sleep at three in the morning. Yellow haze trickled through the blinds from a solitary streetlamp. His heartbeat deafened him.

Then he felt it, like hot breath down his neck, something else in his bedroom—something *alive*.

Aaron kicked off his comforter and jolted upright. He scanned his room, wheezing, and his eyes narrowed on the black hulk of his nightstand. A single shiver crept down his spine.

The vial.

For a moment, Aaron lay very still, breathing in quiet gasps. There was something in it that woke him up. He snatched the vial off the table, jammed his feet into his shoes, and snuck into the hallway.

Outside, frozen moonlight drenched his yard. Aaron darted through the shadows and climbed into his car, parked just up the street. When he held up the vial, his breath misted on the quartz.

It appeared empty, but he knew it wasn't.

At three o'clock in the morning, nothing moved outside his car. The black contours of hedges were fixed, frozen in place. Not a single leaf rustled. Aaron might have been the only living thing in the world.

Except there *was* something moving outside his car.

Aaron sat forward, hardly breathing. One of the shadows had changed positions, drifted closer—*crawled.* But now he wasn't sure.

The road was too dark. The moon hid behind the trees, and the porch lights that hadn't run out their timers barely flickered.

Then he saw it again.

Across the street, a figure darted forward and sank into the shadows between two trees. Closer now. Aaron's heart pounded. Who was out there?

What was out there?

Aaron stared into the shadows, straining his eyes, but saw nothing. Then a soundless blur crossed to his side of the street—and he lost it at the neighbor's hedge, five feet in front of his car.

It was pitch black, and Aaron couldn't see a damn thing. He fumbled along his steering column for the headlight switch. Through the corners of his eyes he glimpsed motion, followed by eerie stillness. Then something hammered against his hood. The sound froze his blood.

He was only aware of a pale blur after that. Then a body slammed against his door, and he nearly jumped out of his skin. The handle rattled.

Crouching below the window, the thing outside yanked the door in every direction, trying to get in. And the driver's side door was loose. In a split-second, it opened. Through the crack, Aaron heard gasps, a flurry of movement. He grabbed the door just in time, wrenched back on the handle, and for a moment thought the tendons would spring from his knuckles before the door slammed shut.

Whatever was outside scampered back to its hiding place. Aaron didn't wait a moment longer. His fingers closed on the lever, and he flipped on his high beams.

Brilliant white light flooded the darkness in front of his car. Tree limbs popped into focus, leaves burned in the glare.

The shadows dissolved.

And his headlights exposed a human figure crouched in the bushes. The figure raised a hand to block the light, but not before Aaron recognized who it was.

At first he felt relieved, bubbly almost, and he was about to let out a sigh when he realized what he was seeing. After that, it was pure terror. Something was wrong. Something was very, very wrong.

Crouching in the bushes in front of his car, shading her eyes against the high beams and shivering in a thin hospital gown—was Emma Mist.

TWELVE

Plus 1 Day, 16 hours, 30 minutes

AARON BROUGHT HER into his car, started the engine, and cranked up the heat.

He flipped on the cabin light. Emma's pale skin was smudged with dirt. Her frightened eyes darted around the inside of the car, barely registering him, and Aaron noticed the sunken look to her cheeks. She hadn't eaten in weeks.

"Emma—" Aaron didn't know what to say. The last time he saw her she had been in a vegetative state, scarcely alive. Her half was dead; he had seen Justin's corpse just two nights before.

She should have been dead too.

"Emma, tell me what happened," he said.

She shook her head and hugged her knees to her chest. "I can't remember," she whispered.

"Do you remember me?"

She glanced up at him, and then buried her face in the gap between her knees. "Aaron, I shouldn't remember anything," she said.

"But you do," said Aaron. "Buff Normandy and I came to see you a few weeks ago. Do you remember that?"

"I wasn't there," she said, sniffling.

"Where were you?" he said.

"Nowhere."

"Are you hurt?" said Aaron.

She nodded. "I think there's a hole—" She pointed to the back of her head and swiveled so he could see. "Will you check it for me?"

Her hair was crusted with flakes of blood, and Aaron was afraid to look. But the scab was small. It was her half who had the hole drilled through the back of his head.

"It looks fine," he said.

"I can't feel him anymore. I think our channel broke," she whimpered.

"What do you mean?"

"I'm not supposed to be here." Her teeth chattered.

"Emma—" Aaron pulled her into his arms to keep her warm. She was lighter than he remembered, and he lifted her right off the seat. Her skin was cold and sticky against him. She smelled like disinfectant. "Emma, tell me what happened?" he said.

"I woke up earlier . . . I didn't know where I was—" her eyes froze on the vial, which Aaron had dropped in the center tray, and she trailed off.

Aaron looked down too. Miraculously, the vial was full now, glowing. The dazzling red fluid lit their faces, blinded them.

"But . . . but it was just empty," he said.

The vial's crimson reflection swam in Emma's tear-filled eyes. "Can I hold it?" she said.

He held it out to her, and she lifted it off his palm. Her eyes tracked the red fluid as it scurried from one end to the other, trying to get to her.

Then she handed it back to him, and tears dripped into her lap. "Will you hold it, Aaron? *Please*."

"What . . . *why?*" he said.

"Because you're warm."

Aaron stared at her as the words sank in. Suddenly, he understood. The significance of what he was seeing, what she meant. The vial held clairvoyance drained from her own half. She was holding what was left of it, still pulsing, in the palm of her hand. The part of her that belonged inside her half—trapped forever inside a cold glass vial.

Dr. Selavio had done this to her.

He had cut the other end of her clairvoyant channel out of her half. Now all she could feel inside her was the hole. The vial had been underwater for a month, and as long as it remained sealed, she was trapped, unable to die. This was Dr. Selavio's "cure" for half death.

Emma watched him, transfixed by the clairvoyance in his hand. Aaron didn't wait a second longer. He stumbled from his car and flung the vial to the road. It popped and bounced to the curb, leaving a red streak. He followed it, crunched the glass under his foot, and ground it into powder. The glowing fluid pooled and evaporated.

In the silence afterwards, Aaron heard blood jolting

through his ears. He climbed back into his Mazda next to Emma, who looked like she was about to throw up.

"Why'd you break it?" she said.

"I set you free," he said. "Now go find your half."

Aaron drove her back to her parents' house, let himself in, and carried her up to her bed. She was already asleep. By sunrise, she would be gone.

On the drive home, Aaron pieced together the facts, his mind a storm. Clearly, the vial alone hadn't kept her alive. The headache, the bleeding from her head, the coma . . . Until yesterday, her symptoms exactly matched those of half death. Yesterday, though, she woke up.

Yesterday. The very same day Aaron recovered the vial. It wasn't a coincidence. He recalled when he first handled the vial out at the buoy, how it brightened and appeared to fill up in his hands.

Aaron jammed the stick into third, and his Mazda screamed onto the deserted freeway. Emma's half died that night, yet she didn't keel over in class until weeks later. He also remembered the words of her father when Buff and Aaron visited her. How when she first felt her half go missing, something kept her going.

That something was Aaron, when he touched the vial right before it sank. Yesterday, he touched the vial again—and once again prolonged her death. Both times, *he* kept her alive

And he thought he knew why.

In the case of normal half death, her clairvoyance should have leaked through her half's dead body into oblivion via their channel. But Emma's channel was severed. She no longer had a half. Neither did Aaron. He and Emma were two loose ends, pulling at each other like magnets. Thus her channel had been rerouted to Aaron's, temporarily plugging the leak and waking her from a coma. If not for the scar tissue blocking Aaron's channel, they would have snapped together and become each other's halves.

Even if it didn't make them true halves, it probably would have been enough to convince the world—

A chill pierced Aaron's spine, and his knuckles whitened on the steering wheel. Of course. It *had* convinced the world. Eighteen years ago, Dr. Selavio did exactly that to Amber and Clive. He used the machine on both of them, severed them both from their original halves and made them snap together. They were fakes, just like Amber said. Clive's first half must have died. In response, the Juvengamy Brotherhood chose a pureblood replacement that would make him heir: Amber Lilian.

But Amber's true half was Aaron.

So why didn't he die? Once severed from Amber, Aaron should have lost clairvoyance fast, like Emma—a vegetable just days after she was severed. Maybe his severed channel had scarred over, sealing the leak, while Emma's had not. At least that would explain the scar tissue at the back of his brain . . .

Aaron skidded to a stop in front of his house and ran inside. The Monday morning sun burned streaks along his wall. He yanked out drawers and tore through his clothes, searching. Searching for *what?*

What the hell could he even do?

His eyes darted to his cell phone, still plugged in. Now fully charged. And still off. His cell phone had been off since his birthday, and he hadn't even checked his messages.

Aaron pounced on it, flipped open the screen, and waited for the messages to flash.

Two new voicemails.

He held the phone to his ear and listened to the first message from Buff. Apparently, Buff saw how it was and he didn't want to be best friends anymore either. Aaron closed his eyes and waited for the second message.

His heart pulsed against the plastic. When he swallowed, his clammy cheek smeared against the phone's screen. Aaron's heart had almost scuttled up his throat and into his mouth by the time the message finally played.

It was Amber, breathless, on the verge of tears. Terrified. "Aaron, it wasn't supposed to happen like this, I'm so sorry . . . *you have to run away*—" She was cut off.

Aaron shoved the phone against his ear, and the plastic dug into his skin. He wanted to hear everything—the brush of her cheek against the speaker, her heartbeat, the flutter of her eyelashes.

But it was Clive's voice that stabbed his eardrum.

"Aaron Harper," his voice drawled. "I do hope you get this message, for Amber's sake. She agreed to do some things for me she isn't proud of, just so she could call you—and you didn't even pick up."

The line clicked. Then silence—*silence*, leaking into his ears like the frozen, endless vacuum of outer space.

End of new messages.

Aaron closed the phone slowly. Every fiber in his muscles had gone limp.

Aaron called her phone.

It rang once, beeped, and then a recorded voice said, "We're sorry, you have reached a number that has been disconnected or is no longer in service . . ."

Aaron's hand trembled as he ended the call.

He dialed Clive's number, but Clive didn't pick up. He called from his dad's phone, from his house phone. But he knew it was pointless. Aaron jammed his cell phone into his pocket and paced his room. Each time his volleyball got in the way, he kicked it as hard as he could.

Then he yanked his phone right back out and jabbed the buttons with his thumb. His heart clanged as he scrolled down his list of contacts.

He paused at Dominic Brees, not sure why he even had the guy's number. Maybe Dominic knew where they were.

Aaron took a deep breath and dialed the rugby player. He lifted the phone to his ear. *Two rings—three rings*—It felt heavy now, unwieldy—*four rings—five rings*—

"Who the hell is this?" said Dominic.

"Put Clive on the phone," said Aaron. "I want to talk to him."

A pause. "You're too late, number eleven. They're not here anymore."

His heart sank. "Where are they? Is . . . is Amber okay?"

"You know, there's a rumor going around, number eleven . . . people saying they can't find your half or something—Dr. Selavio won't shut up about it. He keeps saying he can help you."

"He can start by making me and Amber halves again."

Aaron heard a girl's whiny voice in the background, then Dominic snapping at her. "Hang on," he said to Aaron, "Tina wants to talk to you."

"*Who?*"

"Tina Marcello, fuckface."

There was a long pause. Aaron clamped his cell phone even tighter and pain shot down his ear. A moment later, Tina spoke.

"Aaron, they left for their honeymoon," she said.

His lips went numb. "Where?"

"We don't know. They're *gone*."

Gone. The word was indigestible. "*Where?*" he repeated.

"After her birthday, it was like she gave up. She stopped trying."

Aaron squeezed his eyelids shut. "Does Clive answer when you call?" he said.

"Only for Dominic," she said, "but he won't tell him anything."

"Then you can get a message to her," said Aaron.

"How?" she said. "Her phone's disconnected."

"Yell the message into Clive's phone so she can hear it," he said. "Yell it *loud*. Blow out Clive's eardrums."

She was silent for a moment. "Yell *what?*"

Aaron lowered his cell phone to his chest and scanned his bedroom. His lungs stung with each shallow breath. *Yell what?*

Amber had already given up.

No—that had to be a lie. Amber *never* gave up. He pressed the phone back to his ear.

"Tell her I love her," he said.

THIRTEEN

Plus 1 Day, 20 hours, 42 minutes

"ARE YOU NERVOUS?" said Amber.

Clive dropped the cord from his hoodie, which he had been fidgeting with, and fixed his gaze on her. "I'm proud," he said.

"Of who? Yourself?" The limo drove over a pothole, and she felt a spasm of pain in her back.

"Of you," he said. "The potentate will be delighted to see how much you've matured since the last time we visited the palace. You're a beautiful girl, Amber."

"Can you please stop talking like them?" she said. "Like who?" said Clive.

"Like our parents."

Clive smirked, ignoring her comment. "Then again, I still have to teach you some manners . . ." he leaned forward, "and that's what the ten hour flight's for, Mrs. Selavio."

Amber felt her lip curl. She pressed her forehead to the window, but she could still feel his gaze. She loosened her hair, and a blonde curtain fanned out between them.

Clive's cell phone rang.

Amber listened to the ring tone, and her pulse quickened. She glanced up at him. "Aren't you going to get that?" she said.

"It's *them*."

The ringing stopped. The limo bumped the curb as they pulled onto the runway, and she winced again. She sat forward carefully, trying not to put too much pressure on her tender back. She resisted the urge to scratch the scabs. The less she scratched, the milder the scarring.

She felt the whine of jet engines through the soundproof, tinted windows, but heard nothing. The limo glided past small propeller planes and commercial jets, and beyond the private airport's control tower she could just make out the mountains through the rippling haze—the mountains where she and Aaron had stargazed two nights before her birthday.

The memory stung her, and she felt a sudden, throbbing pressure behind her sinuses. She had tried to call him, but of course he was with his half. Now there was no way to reach him. Since she blocked Clive's calls, she wasn't allowed a phone anymore.

Amber closed her eyes and held her breath, but Aaron refused to leave her mind. Of course not, he had to ruin everything in there first and turn her into an emotional mess. The limo parked next to the potentate's private jet.

"That's a Gulfstream G650," said Clive, nodding to the sleek, black aircraft. "Here to Italy without refueling."

"Does it look like I care?" said Amber.

Clive's cell phone rang again, just as the driver opened the door for her, and the scream of jet engines blasted her ears. Amber hesitated. What if it was an emergency?

"Could you give us a second?" she said to the driver.

He nodded, tipped his hat, and shut the door. Silence again. Clive's cell phone was still ringing.

Amber faced him. "Didn't Dominic just let you stay with him for an entire month?"

"He's the one who owes *me*," said Clive.

"For *what?*"

"For Father's services."

The phone went silent, then rang again.

Amber glared at him. "So you're just going to ignore them?"

Clive sighed and jerked the phone open. "What do you want?" he said.

In the soundproofed interior, Amber could just make out Tina's voice on the other end. "Can I talk to Amber?"

"I told you to stop calling," said Clive.

"Is she okay?"

"Tina, I didn't kidnap her," he spat. "She's my *half.*"

"Is she there?" said Tina.

"She doesn't want to talk to you," said Clive.

Then Tina yelled something. "*Amber*, Aaron said—"

But Clive slammed his phone shut before she finished. "Bitch," he muttered, and then he turned his phone off. "Harper won't be saying anything once Father deals with him."

It took Amber a moment to process what she'd heard, and a moment more to realize Tina had been trying to send her a message—a message about Aaron.

Was he in danger? Had Casler gotten to him?

The driver opened the door again, and the screaming jets scrambled her thoughts. She stumbled out into the haze of heat. Her hair lifted and blew across her face, catching the sun like strands of glass, blinding her.

She had to make sure he was okay. No, she had no right, he was with his half now—

Clive grabbed her waist and hurried her toward the jet's airstairs, and her shirt scraped across the still wet cuts on her back. The sting made her flinch.

Clearly Aaron's half wasn't keeping him safe. She was probably dumb and spineless. And ugly. Besides, what did it matter anyway if Aaron and Amber weren't halves? She was in love with him.

Amber halted in the plane's doorway. "I want to go back," she said.

Clive grabbed her wrist. "Not now, Amber."

She yanked herself free. "Did you hear me?"

"We *can't*," said Clive.

"Why not? Aren't you the heir?" she said, and she knew she was going to have to pay for this later.

"You think I do whatever I want?" said Clive, his eyes narrowing.

She stepped up the last step, and their eyes were almost level. "Unless you're scared," she said, and though her thoughts were a dizzying blur, she didn't blink. The operation. Casler could use her clairvoyance instead of Aaron's. Clive would never let her, but if she went straight to Casler—

"The potentate is expecting us," said Clive.

"Oh, so this is the *potentate's* honeymoon?"

"It's *ours.*"

"Then prove it," she said, and with a final, smoldering look she kissed him in a way she never wanted Aaron to know about.

❧

It was out of Aaron's hands now.

Later, Tina called him back and said she might have gotten through; maybe Amber heard. *Maybe.*

Maybe he was asking for too much.

Aaron stormed out of his house and down the street. He hurried through morning shadows, crisp with icy air. He headed nowhere, just away.

She was the most meaningful part of his life, yet for a whole month he had denied it, pushed her away, hurt her—when all along she was supposed to be his half.

But just to be sure, Aaron went over the details one more time. Eighteen years ago, Clive was about to die from half death, but Dr. Selavio split him from his half. He did the same thing to Amber, and the two of them snapped together—stopping Clive's leak. Dr. Selavio must have used his machine on Amber's mother while she was giving birth to Amber.

And Clive . . . he could have been older. Once his son was connected to Amber, Casler only had to fake his birth certificate. He could have been twenty.

With each passing hour, Aaron felt more feverish. His heart thundered, rattling his skull with every beat. In the evening, he knelt in his driveway and watched the sun bleed through the trees. The violet sky gaped above him, ready to swallow him whole.

And he waited.

Around three in the morning, he got a response. His cell phone beeped, and he barely heard it through the clammy fog of his own thoughts. A text message from a number he didn't recognize.

Tina told me. Next time, you can just send me a rose.

Aaron felt his heart lighten. He thumbed his reply with shaky fingers.

So you're back? How'd you do it?

Don't ask. Where are you?

Twenty minutes later, Aaron glided his Mazda through the parking lot at Arroyo beach and untwisted his ignition wires. His house wasn't safe.

Around him, glistening black cliffs towered out of view. And what if the texts weren't hers? What if it was a trap? Clive, with someone else's phone, maybe?

The night seeped in, ice-cold and surreal.

A few minutes later, headlights swerved into the parking lot—and Amber's powder blue Bug pulled up next to him.

A figure stepped out, and then it became real.

The first thing he saw was a shock of silver hair, shimmering under the quarter moon. He jumped out of his car, and Amber fell into his arms. Soundlessly, they held each other.

When his hand brushed her back, she winced and took quick, shallow breaths.

Almost as soon as they touched, though, she jumped away. Her eyes darted to the Mazda's empty passenger seat. "I forgot—"

He yanked her back. "There's no one there."

Her green eyes locked on his. "You came alone?"

"So did you."

"What about your half?"

"You're my half," he said. "You were right all along. They switched us. Clive's not even eighteen."

Amber searched his gaze. "Then why was it him at the Chamber?" she said.

"Clive's half died before you were born," said Aaron. "They used you to save his life. Casler split us apart and sealed your channel to Clive's so it would stop leaking. He made you guys into artificial halves—*I'm* your real half, Amber."

Amber's eyes widened and her mouth fell open. Then she flung herself into his arms and kissed him, convinced, and Aaron's lungs inflated with helium. He felt her shivering, though, so they climbed into his car. Moonlight dusted their faces.

"Run away with me," said Aaron, and he reached for the ignition.

"No," she said, brushing her hair behind her ear, "because then we'd just be pretending. I want to be yours completely."

"Amber, we have to leave—"

"And if they see me?"

"We'll blend in," he said, searching for the wires.

"You want *me* to blend in?" she said. "Now that I'm officially Clive's half, a lot more people are going to know I'm missing. They'll come after us."

"So we lay low—"

"You *are* aware that I'm the heiress of the Juvengamy Brotherhood?" she said.

"So?" Aaron peered sideways at her, and for the first time that night, he noticed the light behind her eyes was dimmer, clouded over. Scarred. "Amber . . . what happened?"

Slowly, she swiveled away from him and pulled up her shirt—and Aaron finally lowered his hand from the ignition.

Because all across her back, adhering to the side of her waist and crisscrossing her spine, were strips of blood-spotted bandages. Where he'd rubbed her back, fresh blood stains soaked into the gauze, spreading as he watched. By connecting the dots, he could make out the design underneath—the mirror image of Clive's tattoo, marking her as his stolen property.

She dropped her shirt and faced him, and the surf sparkled behind her. Aaron could taste the ocean's salt. And he had nothing to say.

"I wish they'd just empty me out already," she whispered.

"Don't ever say that," he said. "Those marks will heal after we switch back, after we become halves again."

She nodded, and some of her hair came loose and fell across her eyes. "What about the part of me they gave to Clive?"

"What part?"

"The part of me you should have gotten when we were

born," she said. "The part that would have made us halves. I won't get it back, will I?"

Aaron stared at her, and he could feel the hollow seconds between his heartbeats. She meant the vial's worth of clairvoyance Casler's machine had cut out of her. It was inside Clive now, not Aaron, and it would forever be missing if they tried to switch back.

"How much do you think I'll lose?" she said.

"We need to find someone who can help us," said Aaron, reaching for the ignition wires again.

"Who?" she said. "Casler's the only doctor who would know what to do, and he's the one who did this to us."

"We'll find someone." Aaron fumbled with the wires, but they bounced off his fingers.

"Wait—" She held his hand. "Can't we just stay here for a minute, together?"

He squeezed her hand and faced her. Amber lifted herself off her seat, slid over the gear stick, and climbed into his lap. Carefully, he ran his hands behind her neck, where her skin was cool, slippery. Her hair slid between his fingers. She kissed him.

And the universe paused to watch as they broke the law of halves. He could taste how utterly forbidden she was, how kissing her was tearing her inside out. She belonged to Clive now.

He felt it too, a prick at the back of his head as a little more clairvoyance drained out.

They did it anyway.

She pulled her head away and gasped. "Aaron, you have to run away before Casler gets to you."

"I'm not running unless you're with me," he said.

"Aaron—" She pressed her cheek to his, and her tears filmed between them. "No matter what happens, *don't* let him talk you into anything—"

But a squeal of tires cut her off.

They both jerked their heads around as a pair of headlights veered into the parking lot.

The vehicle pulled up behind them, engine growling. Its high beams glared in like searchlights, and the glass flared with white haze, opaque as frost. They had fogged up every last window. And it left them blind.

"It's Clive!" Amber scrambled back into the passenger seat, her whole body trembling. "He must have followed me here. *Drive!*"

The sharp ends of the ignition wires stabbed Aaron's fingers, drew blood. Silence.

He tried the next pair.

A black figure loomed outside Amber's window, shadowing her from the glare. The wires shorted, and Aaron's Mazda roared to life. The smell of his own burnt skin reeked in his nostrils.

"Hurry!" Amber mouthed.

Aaron floored it and popped the clutch. His car lurched, recoiled, and heaved them forward. The engine stalled.

He had started too fast.

"Lock your door," he yelled, staring into Amber's fear-soaked eyes. She just stared back, frozen.

"*Lock it!*"

She finally obeyed—just as the latch clicked. Outside, Clive grunted and vaulted over the hood, gorilla-like. He stomped across the metal to the driver's side door—which didn't latch.

Clive jerked the handle and it flew open, taking him by surprise. He staggered backwards, still gripping the handle as the steel bent under his weight. The hinges groaned.

A frozen gust whipped Aaron's eyes, and he yanked back on the door. But Clive had already looped his arm inside the car, preventing it from closing. His tendons swelled like tree trunks.

The door's hinges reeled on threads.

Clive's face plastered against the window, and for a split second, their eyes burned into each other. Then Aaron dropped his shoulder and sank his full weight into the door, broke it free completely, and tackled Clive to the asphalt. He hardly felt the crunch in his spine.

Aaron rose, and a black fog closed around him. The back of his brain burned under his skull, and every stroke of his heart fueled the roar. He bent his fingers around the car door, raised it, and cocked it behind his head. Might as well have been cardboard.

He swung the door like a baseball bat, as hard as he could. Clive jumped to his feet, but not fast enough. The sharp edge gauged into his chest. The result was a fleshy sound, like cutting steak with a blunt knife. The impact flipped Clive's body, and he landed with a slap.

Clive tried to crawl away, but Aaron followed and swung the door again, made it whistle—buried the steel into Clive's shoulder and knocked him clear off the asphalt.

Fury pounded through him. It scorched his veins. He couldn't stand the idea of Clive possessing any part of Amber. He swung again—*thwack*—and again—*thwack*—he swung until saliva foamed on his lips. *Thwack.* Until Clive's blood ran in purple rivulets

Thwack—Clive's body convulsed and went limp.

Aaron lowered the car door. He coughed for breath, and mucous frothed in his throat. The sea's salt tore into his lungs. He glanced behind him, at Amber.

And the door slipped from his fingers, toppling with a clang. She was keeled over and wincing in pain, shivering—because every blow into Clive had been a blow into her.

She was still Clive's half.

Aaron stumbled forward and skidded to his knees. "No—"

"Aaron, you have to go," she moaned. "Before he finds you."

Aaron was only half-aware of the groans behind him, the wheezing, the sound of a body scraping across pavement.

"I can't leave you here," he said.

"Just *go!*" she said.

But it was too late. Clive wheezed into Aaron's ear, his breath damp with blood. His finger landed on the back of Aaron's scalp.

When he pulled it away, an entire ocean poured out the back of Aaron's skull. Aaron crumpled to the ground. Stars spiraled above him.

Clive leaned over him, blotting out the sky. "You can't win, Harper," he said, shredded skin flapping on his lip. He gurgled blood and spat to the side. "I deserve her. You don't."

He limped around to the Mazda's passenger seat and smashed in the window, and he lifted Amber out of her seat. She no longer had the strength to resist. Aaron had taken that from her.

Then the very last drop of his consciousness slipped away.

Daylight dribbled between Aaron's eyelids and lured them apart. He stared at a ceiling, at flakes of plaster. *His* ceiling. He was in his bedroom, tucked into his own bed. Outside, the morning sun glittered through lime-green sycamores, glossy with dew. He watched their shadows thrust across his floor, wash up his walls, then recede like surf.

Aaron fingered the back of his skull. He had been somewhere. Not asleep, somewhere else. An abyss.

He heard voices from the other room. His mom and dad—and a third voice.

Aaron closed his eyes again, and his heart gave a sickening lurch. *Amber.*

She was someone else's half; her back was already scarred, yet she had risked everything for him. Just to see him. And all he'd managed to do was drain what little strength she had left.

Now Clive had her.

Aaron traced the cracks on his ceiling, and his lungs caved in a little more with each breath. Clive would never let her go. He would never give her back what had been cut out of her, the piece that now made them halves.

In fact, he wanted to take more out of her.

Aaron sat up and threw off his comforter. Plumes of lint ignited in the sun's beams, flared white-hot, then extinguished. *No*. Amber was supposed to be Aaron's half, not Clive's.

He had to find a way to switch her back before they strapped her into the machine and drained out the rest of her clairvoyance.

It was Tuesday morning, April 2, three days after their birthday. He heard voices from the other room. His mom and dad.

But there had also been a third voice.

At that moment, a man stepped into Aaron's room. A man who had to duck to get through the doorway, a man whose white lab coat drifted, cape-like, behind him.

Dr. Casler Selavio.

"*No!*" Aaron jumped off his bed and backed to the wall as the blood recoiled from his skin.

Casler waved him back down. "Sit, sit."

"*You*—" Aaron groped behind him for his bedside lamp, but only grasped air. The lamp lay on the floor at Casler's feet.

"Clive told me what happened," said Casler, pulling up Aaron's desk chair and sitting. He slid a folder out of his briefcase—Aaron's medical record. "This is all my fault."

"Where is she?" Aaron whispered.

"May I see the arm?" said Casler, glancing up at him with watery eyes. His ashy cologne filled the room.

When Aaron didn't move, Casler wheeled the chair

forward and reached for his hand.

Aaron yanked it out of reach. "What did you do to her?" he said.

"We weren't sure you were going to make it last night," said Casler, craning his neck to examine the inflamed skin around Aaron's knife wound. He pulled out a pen. "The arm's healing nicely."

"Is she okay?" said Aaron.

"Since your channel is unconnected, your clairvoyance is especially vulnerable to disturbance," said Casler, scribbling something in Aaron's file. "That's why you lost consciousness when Clive touched your head. In fact, now that you're eighteen and your channel's grasping for your half, I wouldn't be surprised if just being in the same room as him would irritate the back of head."

"Just tell me if she's okay," said Aaron.

"She demanded the same about you," said Casler.

"Yeah. Because she's my half," said Aaron.

Casler stopped writing, and Aaron could see the muscles working inside his temples. "Yes . . . yes she is," he said, as if only now realizing this was true. He glanced up, "which is why I'm going to make you halves again."

Aaron blinked. "What?"

"This wasn't supposed to happen," he said.

"And what was?" said Aaron. "You severed our channel and gave her to Clive."

"We didn't fully understand the machine," said Casler. "We thought if we severed an infant's channel during her birth, her would-be half would just connect to someone else . . . not that he would be born halfless. After Clive lost his half, we had to act fast."

"And how did he lose his half?"

Dr. Selavio stiffened. "It happened when they were four," he said. "Their juvengamy backfired. They were playing by an old well, and Clive just lost it all of a sudden and pushed her in. By the time we fished her out, it was too late."

"You mean he murdered his half?"

"It was an accident," said Casler. "He was too young to realize the consequences."

"So you severed his channel and rerouted it to another girl," said Aaron, his jaw twitching, "and *that* didn't have consequences?"

"I'm sorry, but I wasn't about to watch my only son die . . . not when I believed I could safely give him a new half."

"But why Amber?"

"I didn't choose her, Aaron. The potentate did. Probably because the Lilians and the Selavios are the only pure bloodlines left, and together, Clive and Amber are the perfect heir and heiress to inherit the Brotherhood. I didn't care, though. I would have taken anybody. When I heard you didn't have a half, though, I realized I'd done something terrible." Casler reached forward and touched Aaron's forearm. "Let me switch you back."

Aaron's skin prickled. There were too many reasons not to trust him. "You murdered Emma's half," he said. "I saw the body."

"I meant to explain that earlier," said Casler smoothly. "The boy died mysteriously. The cause of death was clairvoyant in nature, so the coroner requested me for the autopsy."

"Bullshit."

"I'm the best there is, Aaron."

"Then why'd you bury the body?"

Casler smiled and squeezed his wrist. "You and Amber love each other. You deserve to be halves."

"Last time, when you and that priest were talking, you wanted to drain her," said Aaron.

"No, she offered that herself," said Casler.

"She didn't," said Aaron.

"Yes, I believe she wanted to donate her clairvoyance to less fortunate victims of juvengamy, but Clive wouldn't let her."

"She *didn't*."

"Maybe you don't know her as well as you thought," said Casler, his eyes twinkling.

"Well, that's because you didn't tell her the consequences," said Aaron.

"No, she knew," said Casler.

"And she still wanted to?" said Aaron.

"Apparently, until she discovered you."

Aaron stared at him, and then he shook his head. "You're not going to switch us back. You'd have to sever Clive's channel. He would die."

Casler smiled. "That's why I need something from you, Aaron. You survived eighteen years with a severed channel . . . and I think I know why. Since you and Amber were severed at birth, your channel retained its malleability, allowing it to heal despite incredible trauma. Amber's too, hence the scar tissue near the entrance of her channel—"

"Wait, she has the same scar tissue?"

"She didn't know until recently. It's where the wound

healed after you two were split apart, and yes, it matches yours. You see, the machine is useless on adult patients. It's like cutting through glass and trying to press the pieces back together; it won't seal. However, your clairvoyance acts like glue. With a tiny sample, I could reseal Clive's severed channel. He wouldn't have a half, but at least he would be alive, and that's all I ask for. Before we do it, I just need a tiny sample."

"Of my clairvoyance?"

"Just a thimbleful. You won't notice it's gone. If you prefer, I could take out a bit of Amber's—"

"You're not taking anyone's clairvoyance." Aaron narrowed his eyes, but it was Casler's hypnotic voice, the way the man's eyes bored gently into him. Aaron wasn't sure he wouldn't do anything the man asked. "But hypothetically, you *could* switch us back? Would you use the machine?"

"I have to bend space a bit to reach the opening," said Casler. "It's nothing to worry about."

"What about the part of her Clive has?" said Aaron.

"Which part?"

"The stuff you took out when she was born."

"Amber will get it all back," said Casler. "Actually, *you'll* get it."

Aaron's heart slowed, skipped beats, then slammed double-time inside his chest to make them up. "Will it hurt her?"

"Only a prick."

Casler was lying, obviously. Yet as Aaron peered into the depths of his calm eyes, he wondered again if he had gotten Casler wrong from day one. When he said it, it felt so real, so tantalizingly close; Aaron and Amber could be halves again.

All Aaron had to do was give in, believe. Trust—just for a moment.

Aaron took a deep breath. The man was a doctor, after all. Trust was easy.

"When I look through an aitherscope," said Aaron, "I want to see her eyes. I don't want any of Clive left inside her—not a trace. And no drilling through anybody's skull."

"It's a deal." Casler returned the folder to his briefcase and rose to his full height. "Come as soon as you're ready. She'll be waiting."

Casler's explanation was plausible. His reasoning made sense. His facts agreed with what Aaron already knew; there were no contradictions. Maybe he could put Aaron and Amber back together again.

Maybe every last stinking word was a lie.

But Aaron also realized how much danger she was in. Amber was Clive's second half. Clive had already killed his first.

In the middle of pacing, his phone rang. The same number Amber texted him from the night before.

"Hello?" he said, and even though it probably wasn't her, his heart quivered with anticipation. Just the thought of hearing her voice. Suddenly, his doubts vanished, replaced by a dizzying euphoria. He was about to blurt out that Casler was a hero, that he was going to make them halves again, when she spoke.

"I know about the deal you made with Casler," she said, her voice biting.

Aaron could tell something was off, and his heart chilled.

He answered carefully. “He said he could reconnect us.”

“I don’t care,” she said. “We’re not supposed to be halves.”

“What?”

She sighed. “You were just a fling, Aaron. It’s not like I wanted you to be my *half*. I wasn’t thinking last night; I’m sorry.”

“But we talked about this,” said Aaron. “Casler severed us—”

“Casler lied to you,” she said. “All he wants is your scar tissue, and even if he could make us halves, I wouldn’t want him to. I know I said things before, but I don’t actually want to be your half, Aaron . . . I’m happy with Clive.” She paused, waiting for him to answer.

But he couldn’t.

“Are you even going to acknowledge me?” she said.

“*Amber* . . . I . . .” His voice choked up.

“I know I hurt you, and I’m sorry. Obviously, what we did together hurt me too, but will you please let me get on with my life?”

“You’re lying,” he said finally. “You’re trying to protect me. I know what we had.”

She sighed again, more exasperated this time. “I knew you would say that. I liked you too, Aaron. I even thought I loved you at one point. You were fun, and I really needed that during that time of my life. You helped me through a lot. But I’m eighteen now and I have a half. What we had is over . . . and I want you to promise me you won’t try to contact me again.”

“So you love Clive?”

“Of course I do, he’s my half,” she said. “I told you that

like a thousand times. Aaron, will you please just promise me?"

Aaron shut his eyes and loathed the words that came out of his mouth. "If you love Clive, then yes. I promise."

"Trust me," she said, "you'll be happier without me screwing up your life. Bye, Aaron."

Then she hung up.

At ten forty-one on Tuesday morning, three days after his appointment at the Chamber of Halves, reddish sunlight slashed through the dust and scorched Aaron's retinas as he crossed the street to his doorless Mazda. He would drive away. No idea where. He would just drive. He pressed his phone to his ear, and one more time, he listened to Amber's terrified message, the one she left while his phone was off.

"Aaron, it wasn't supposed to happen like this—I'm so sorry—*you have to run away*—"

He slid the phone off his cheek, and it occurred to him in stabbing thrusts. That message was his last memory of her. They weren't halves, they weren't supposed to be. They had no connection to each other. She didn't love him.

And that was the end of it.

Casler had tried to lure him into a trap; it hadn't worked. Sure, he could toy with her clairvoyant channel, cut her open, reconnect her like the plastic pieces of a marble maze. But not to him—*never* to him. Amber didn't even want them to be halves.

In this world, he had no right to love her. Casler could drain her into a vial, and Aaron had no right to stop it. She was Clive's half, and in the eyes of the Juvengamy Brotherhood, his property—his *possession.*

Aaron's cell phone rang again.

He let it ring in his pocket, thinking instead about the half-baked plan he had been formulating when Amber called. First, he would have driven to Dominic's house and made sure she was okay. Then he and Amber would meet Dr. Selavio in the dungeon. Aaron would volunteer for the machine first. Amber would go next. When it was done, they would be halves again.

They would leave here and travel somewhere faraway, like Spain, or Sicily.

Thinking back, it was all a delusional fantasy. Every second he spent with Amber—*fake*. His body had been confused, fragile. It hadn't been love.

Aaron eased himself into his car, taking shallow, pinched off breaths, and his phone rang again. Only this time he felt goose bumps forming along his forearms.

Aaron dragged the phone out of his pocket. It was Tina.

"What is it?" he said.

"Aaron—" Her voice crackled over the speaker. "It's Amber, she's in trouble!"

"What do you mean?"

"She heard Clive's father visited you," she said. "She's scared he's going to hurt you—"

Aaron's heart jerked. "What did she do?"

"Amber made a deal with him," she said. "He promised to leave you alone, but now she has to go through with it."

"Go through with *what?*" said Aaron.

"They're doing it in fifteen minutes," she said. "The

machine . . . they're going to drill into her head and drain her clairvoyance. They're going to make her like the other juvengamy women!"

FOURTEEN

Plus 2 Days, 23 hours, 45 minutes

"NO—" HE GASPED, "talk her out of it, tell her she can't."

"We tried," said Tina, "but she's not thinking straight. She heard Casler say he could use your clairvoyance to make his machine work, and she freaked out. She volunteered herself instead."

"But she knows what it will do to her," he choked, barely forming the words. "She doesn't have any left to give."

He heard Dominic's voice in the background, and then the rugby player came on the line. "Number eleven?"

"I'll volunteer. Just tell her she *can't*."

"She's not listening to anybody, fuckface."

Aaron squeezed his eyelids shut. "She never does."

"Dr. Selavio's warming up the machine right now. They're doing the operation at eleven."

Aaron held the phone away from him, stared at it. It was a nightmare, surreal. His heart sounded far away, buried, and the whole world rippled when it beat. He pulled the phone back to his mouth.

"I'm coming right now," he said. "Why the hell didn't Dr. Selavio wait for me? We had a deal."

"Amber made him swear not to contact you," said Dominic, "and he decided she would be better anyway. She'll let him take more out."

"Jesus. Just tell him I'm coming," said Aaron. "And tell him we had a deal." He flung his phone onto the passenger seat and reached for the ignition.

What the hell was Amber thinking?

The operation would drain her body of something she could never replace. She would be docile afterwards, helpless, pathetic. She would follow Clive around like a pet, taking orders and feeling sad when she was reprimanded, happy when she was rewarded. Never defiant. On the outside, she would still be the same girl—Clive's trophy—with only a tiny scar at the back of her head to remind her that she was hollow.

They would do this to her, and in fourteen minutes, she was going to let them, all just to protect Aaron, a boy who wasn't even her half.

He had to stop her.

Aaron ignored the burn of the ignition wires, and his Mazda fired to life. Fourteen minutes. On a bad day, the drive to Dominic's house could take twenty. He wasn't going to make it in time—

Aaron hadn't even found first gear when a figure loomed to his left. He glanced up as two large hands closed on his collar and dragged him out of the car.

“Amber, turn around,” said Dominic. He stood in front of the cellar door, swirling a glass of whisky—blocking her.

Amber stopped just short of him. “What are *you* doing here?”

“Trust me, you don’t want this,” said Dominic.

“You mean *you* don’t want this?” she said.

“No one does.”

“It’s my choice,” she said.

Dominic scanned the entrance hall behind her and raised his eyebrows. “No Selavio?”

“I’m all alone,” she said. “Does that excite you?”

“Nah.” He tilted his glass, and the ice crinkled. “My birthday’s in five weeks.”

“Am I invited?” she said.

“Depends on how much of you is left.”

She sighed. “Can you *please* move?”

“Seriously though,” he said. “He’s going to stop you.”

“Clive?”

“Number eleven.” Dominic wrinkled his nose and sipped his whisky.

Amber felt a twinge in her heart. “He won’t. Not anymore.”

“Let him volunteer instead of you. He’s already halfless; no one’s going to miss him.”

Amber glared at him. Then her eyes flicked to his glass. She snatched it from his hand and poured the rest on his head.

He flinched, then shook the liquid off his letterman

jacket, kind of like a wet cat. "If that leaves a stain," he said, "you're paying for it, Amber."

She smiled sweetly. "Can I go now?"

He stepped to the side. "Don't let me stop you."

Before he changed his mind—or she changed hers—Amber pushed through the door. In the cellar, the silver haze of the aitherscope made her feel see-through. She held her breath until she was safely past it.

Her stomach still hadn't unknotted from her final, heartbreaking conversation with Aaron. On the phone, it had taken all her strength not to burst into tears, not to cave and confess she loved him. But somehow, she had to push him away. It was the only way to protect him. Whether or not they were supposed to be halves hardly mattered. Even if Casler agreed to reconnect them, the operation would be her second switch, and she wouldn't survive it—at least not all of her.

And she never wanted Aaron to see her like that. As long as Casler left him out of it and promised never to touch him, he could do whatever he wanted to her. In fact, the more he took out the better. When it was done, she wanted to feel nothing.

She couldn't stand another excruciating minute as Clive's half. Up until now, he had kept silent about his father draining her clairvoyance, though she knew it terrified him. In his own way, he did love her; he wanted to own her just the way she was, not hollowed out like other juvengamy girls. He wanted her to love him in return, to *really* love him, and he knew that would only come from the feeling, thinking, self-aware part of her, from the part she would be missing after the operation—but Amber would rather throw it away than let him have it.

Clive had never let her see his father's studio before, and before today, she had never wanted to. She took the stairs one at a time, not sure how deep they went. She reached the bottom and peered into the darkness, and when her eyes adjusted, she felt her brain go numb with panic.

It wasn't the white hospital room she'd expected.

Amber traversed the dingy cave and found herself under a huge machine, suddenly terrified—suddenly aware of everything she was about to lose. The thing hummed above her, dripping oil, and she could already feel it pulling at her, trying to get inside her.

Aaron was slammed against his car, which had stalled in first. He felt the edge of the doorframe cut into his back as he stared dumbstruck into the wild eyes of his best friend, Buff Normandy.

"Don't touch me," said Aaron.

"Buddy, you can't go," said Buff.

"You don't even know where I'm going."

"Tina called me and told me what happened," said Buff. "You made a deal with that doctor."

"In thirteen minutes," Aaron spat, "she'll be worse than dead. Let me *go*—" Aaron slapped Buff's hands aside and rushed the car, but Buff grabbed his shoulder and slammed him against the rear door again.

"No bullshit!" he said. "Not after all the things you told me about him."

Aaron was aware of every heartbeat, every second Amber didn't have. He glared into his best friend's eyes. "Do you know what she'll be like when they're through with her?" he said. "She'll be a pretty little shell—that's all!"

"It's a trap, Buddy. You know that."

"He wants clairvoyance," said Aaron. "It's either mine or Amber's."

"Says who? Make him use his own shit."

"Just get out of my way," said Aaron.

"Buddy, she's not even your half—"

Aaron shoved Buff backwards, and his friend stumbled to the ground. Then he climbed into his car.

"I'm not coming with you," said Buff, climbing to his feet.

"I don't want you to," said Aaron, "you'd only get someone killed." He restarted the engine and burnt rubber. Behind him, black fumes boiled off his tire tracks. Buff chased him down and kicked his bumper before he squealed down the street.

So much for friends.

Aaron drove a hundred and ten on the freeway. He passed cars as if they were parked. The wind tore inside the cabin, ripped at his clothes and blinded him. His Mazda leaned dangerously around curves, right at the edge of traction. At this speed, it was like cornering switchbacks.

So Casler lied about making them halves again. Why? All he wanted to do was drain their clairvoyance. But he clearly preferred Amber's.

The needle on his fuel gauge teetered on empty, then crossed it. There was enough fuel to get him there, to Amber—and that was all he needed.

Grassy hills swam around him, shimmering pollen-green under the bright sun—as green as her eyes had been when he sat next to her at the bonfire, more than a month ago, and gazed into them for the first time.

He didn't have the strength to face the rest of his life without her, alone. Halfless. He had to stop her, even if it meant giving up his own clairvoyance so she wouldn't have to.

Half a mile from Dominic's house, he felt it. A cold patch in the air. Static electricity. The hairs on his forearms rose and swayed, as if swept up in an underwater current, and there was no question as to the source.

At ten fifty-seven, Aaron mowed over the dry brush outside Dominic's gate, scaled the wall, and sprinted up the driveway. He felt the ground buzzing through the soles of his shoes. He circled the house.

At ten fifty-eight, the laundry room door creaked open, and Aaron slipped inside. It was like swimming through needles.

Only the house was empty.

He ran upstairs, Clive's room—empty. The bed had been made, the walls stripped bare. As if he never lived there. He ran downstairs and checked the kitchen. Through a broken window, a breeze fanned the stench of rotting fish. It wafted over him, warm and nauseating. Flies swarmed over piles of crusted-over china, oil-smudged paper plates, and dripping take-out boxes. Sunlight burned streaks through the humid haze.

Perhaps they were already down below.

At ten fifty-nine, Aaron plunged through the aitherscope's frozen glare. At the end of the corridor, the jagged stairs dropped into the Earth. His eyes watered from the gases rising out of the dark shaft.

Aaron took a deep breath, then stepped down.

And he found Amber at the bottom.

Suspended from the ceiling, dim bulbs flickered red-orange in wire cages. Moisture gleamed like blood on the rough cavern walls.

She was sitting on the operating table, dwarfed under the machine's pulsating mass. She held her legs against her chest, and her hair fell loosely in front of her eyes.

She was waiting.

Above her, the machine idled, purred—it did something to the air, made it ripple. The edges of the black steel blurred in and out of focus, as if the structure itself was oscillating between worlds. A single green indicator light blinked on the side.

It too was waiting, like Amber. Waiting for the surgeon.

"Amber!" Aaron yelled, but the machine's hum swallowed his voice. He ran to the operating table, and his footsteps faded behind him. Only when he touched her arm did she glance up.

Her mouth fell open. "Are you *dumb?*" she whispered. And suddenly her eyes glistened with tears. "You can't be here!"

"I can't let you do this," he said, his breath misting.

"You think everything's about you, don't you?" she said. "I meant what I said on the phone . . . and I don't need your permission." Her eyes darted to the stairs then back again, almost imperceptibly. "It's not like you're my half."

"Maybe I am," he said. "The only reason you called is so I wouldn't come."

Suddenly, her tone changed. "Aaron, *please*—" She glanced behind him again, her eyes panicky. "Do you think I want you to see this?"

"See what? The operation? Or *you?*" he said. "After they're finished with you."

She just glared at him.

"Get off the bench," he said.

"So now you're ordering me around?"

"I'll drag you off the bench if you prefer."

"I already made a deal with him," she said. "I made him promise, and *you* can't do anything about it."

"Promise what?"

"To leave you alone," she said.

"In exchange for *this?*"

"He said it's completely painless."

"I'm sure," he said. "And what about after?"

"Isn't that the best part?" she said, smiling weakly. "Clive can do anything he wants to me and I won't remember a thing."

"You'll remember what's missing—" Aaron felt an itch at the back of his head, and he glanced back at the stairs. They were empty. "We need to get out of here," he said. "It's eleven o'clock."

"Did you hear what I just said?

"I'm sorry," said Aaron. "I made a deal with Casler first."

"Too bad. He likes me better."

"I'm not worth you throwing half of yourself away," he said, and the itch in his scalp became a burn. "Now let's leave while we both still can."

She opened her mouth, but at that moment, Dr. Selavio, Clive, and Dominic emerged from the dark stairwell, and the halogen lights ignited like blue suns around the perimeter of the cave. They made the dimmer bulbs look like burned out cinders.

"Dominic said you'd come," said Casler, flashing his dazzling white teeth. He stepped up to the operating table, set down a worn leather bag, and rested his hand on Aaron's shoulder. He beamed at Amber. "You're free to go," he said. "Aaron's volunteered to take your place."

Figuring he'd play along until Amber was in the clear, Aaron nodded. As soon as she was out of the dungeon, he'd run for it, blockade the cellar door, and light the house on fire. Then he and Amber could split the country."

Amber glanced between the two of them, horrified. "You *promised*," she said to Casler.

"Clive, why don't you take her upstairs," said Casler, opening his medical bag. "She'll be safer up there."

"But *Aaron's* supposed to be safe!" she said, and as Clive limped forward, she scrambled backward off the operating table. Clive circled the bench, grabbed her arms, and lifted her off the table.

"Let *go!*" Amber tore at Clive's hoodie, and for a split-second, Aaron glimpsed the scabs on Clive's shoulder—the ones he'd made the previous night with the car door—before Clive swung her around and clamped his palm over her mouth, choking off her screams.

Aaron felt his muscles tense, but he held himself back. He just wanted her out of the dungeon.

Clive paused halfway to the stairs and glared at Aaron. His pale eyes burned between his slitted eyelids, challenging him—*daring* him. Then Amber jerked her head against his chin, knocked him backwards, and broke free.

She ran to Aaron and grabbed his hands.

"Are you crazy?" she gasped, as Clive struggled to his feet behind her. "Why are you doing this?"

"Because I'm in love with you," said Aaron, "and I can't stand the idea of him taking away everything that makes you who you are. Now go upstairs."

Amber blinked, and for an instant her eyes were completely unguarded, exposed. "No," she whispered, and moved closer.

Casler sighed. "Can *somebody* get her out of here?"

Dominic appeared at her side. "Come on, Amber. Upstairs where it's safe."

But Amber ignored him. Her green eyes never left Aaron's. "I want *you* to be safe," she said.

"There's no point if I don't have a half," said Aaron, and he winked.

She looked confused.

"Just go upstairs," said Aaron, and he tugged his hands out of her grip.

"But you're the only thing that matters," she said. "You can't let him do this to you!"

It took both Clive and Dominic to drag her toward the stairs. She squirmed and clawed at their arms, and her hair whipped behind her. "We had a deal!" she yelled.

"You're right," said Casler. "I just don't need your end anymore."

"Casler, you double-crossing liar," she gasped.

"Please—" He gave a weak smile. "Call me Dad."

While she kicked and struggled, they dragged her out of the dungeon. As soon as she was gone, Aaron breathed out a sigh of relief.

Casler leaned over his medical bag. "Now," he said, extracting a surgical mask, latex gloves, and a syringe. "Let's begin."

"You think I'm stupid?" said Aaron. "I'm not donating my clairvoyance either." He started toward the stairs, ready to sprint if Casler pursued him.

"If you're thinking of running away with her, it won't work . . ." said Casler.

"That wasn't the plan."

". . . because she and Clive are still connected. They need to be near each other constantly, especially in the beginning. If you kidnap her now, she'll get separation anxiety. She'll get sick. Eventually, she'll die. I don't think you want that, Aaron."

"No shit." Aaron slowed and glanced behind him. "That wasn't the plan. I just wanted her off your operating table."

"And I agree with you," said Casler. "As her half-father, I didn't want to let her donate anything, but since she's eighteen, it's her choice. Aaron, I didn't lie to you this morning. I *did* want to make you two halves again, but Amber wouldn't let me. She insisted I leave you alone. As I said before—and as you can clearly see—her decision to donate clairvoyance is separate from her decision not to be your half."

The words stung. Aaron spun around to face him. "She thought it was either her or me."

Casler smiled. "Trust me, I'm not taking anybody's clairvoyance without their permission. No, the real reason is that as Clive's half, she's facing a lot of pressure to conform. She wants the operation done so she can be like the other girls in the Juvengamy Brotherhood. Just a thimbleful . . . I'm not willing to take out any more than that."

"This is getting really sick," said Aaron.

Casler nodded, his face somber. "I know. I don't like the influence the Brotherhood has on her either . . ." He scrunched his eyebrows, brooding. "There *is* another solution."

Aaron stared at the doctor, hardly knowing what to believe anymore—and still clinging to the hope that somehow he and Amber could end up halves again. "Bullshit," he said.

"I can make it safe for you two to run away together. As much as it would hurt Clive, I want her to be with her original half . . . and I want her to be safe."

"If we're not halves, then how?"

"Right now, we just need to sever her channel," he said, and seeing the look on Aaron's face, he added, "we'll put Clive in the machine. Remember, her channel can heal like yours. You won't be connected like halves, but at least she'll be free."

"Forget it," said Aaron. "You're not cutting her channel again." He marched toward the stairs, but Casler called after him.

"Once you leave, Aaron, she's just going to come back down here. She gets what she wants, you know."

Aaron hesitated. He was right. She would come back down here, and *anything* was better than that. The next instant, Casler stood over him.

The man grinned, flashing a row of perfect white teeth as he slipped the white mask over his nose and mouth and snapped the gloves into place. "Keep her safe," he said, "and bring her back in a few months. I'll make you halves then." He winked.

Casler's cologne filled Aaron's sinuses, calmed him. Tempted him. He knew it was wrong, though. But even as he edged away from the doctor, his brain scrambled for a reason—*any* reason—to trust him.

"You'd really put Clive in the machine?" said Aaron.

"All I need is a tiny sample of that scar tissue so he'll survive without a half."

"No way. You're not drilling a hole through my head."

Casler chuckled. "That was for the *autopsy*, Aaron. It's a noninvasive procedure. I'm going to give you an injection that dissolves some of that scar tissue into your bloodstream. Then, all I need to do is draw a sample of your blood. Then you're free to go . . . and I'll take care of the rest."

"That's it? Just two shots?"

"Just two shots."

Aaron considered the risks. When it was explained like that, his doubts seemed absurd. All the guy wanted was a sample of the scar tissue; he had made that clear from the beginning. If Aaron complied just this once, it would at least get the guy off his back and buy him more time with Amber.

Also, he would force the doctor to show his hand. The worst Casler could do, short of injecting him with poison, would be to tranquilize him and strap him into the machine anyway. And Aaron wasn't that stupid.

He felt his mouth widen into a smirk. "I'll do it on one condition," he said. "You inject yourself first."

Casler peered into his eyes, then ruffled Aaron's hair with his palm. "Gladly. I think this is the right thing to do, Aaron."

And Aaron knew it wasn't.

"Any allergies I should know of?" said Casler, as he rummaged through his medical bag. His voice was deep and soothing behind the mask. He was a doctor, after all.

Aaron shook his head, gaping in disbelief as the doctor filled two syringes with a clear liquid. This was actually happening.

"Okay, I'm injecting myself." Casler rolled his sleeve up to his elbow, plunged one of the needles into his own forearm, and drained the plunger. Then he lifted the second needle.

Aaron swallowed hard, wishing he hadn't agreed to this, and averted his eyes as Casler rolled up his sleeve.

"There—" Aaron hardly felt the prick. Then Casler daubed his arm with a cotton ball and slapped on a bandage. "Give that a few minutes. Then we'll draw the blood."

Clive limped into the dungeon, his cheeks scratched up and swollen.

Dr. Selavio stared at his son. "Was she too much for you to handle?" he sneered.

"No, Father."

"If you ever embarrass me like that in front of company

again—"

"I'm sorry, Father," he said.

"Learn to discipline your half," said Dr. Selavio. "I didn't give her to you as a toy."

Clive's pale eyes flicked to the machine, still humming in the background.

The chemical was taking effect. Suddenly woozy, Aaron lowered himself to the floor. A thousand suns wobbled above him, the quartz-halogen lamps. Their blue glare pierced his pupils.

"I want more," Clive blurted out, his eyes still on the machine.

"More of what?"

"More of her clairvoyance."

"You have enough," said Casler. "Now help me start the machine."

Aaron stared at his hands. They had paled to the color of frost. He felt his own blood pooling at the back of his head, as if he was hanging upside down. Meanwhile, Casler barked orders to his son, completely unperturbed. The stuff was only affecting Aaron. *God damnit.*

"Alright Clive—" Casler wheeled a chair in front of his laptop and typed something fast. The screen spit out line after line of green code. "Let's spin."

At the machine, Clive coiled his fingers around a massive switch and shoved. At first it didn't budge. The tendons bulged in his forearms, and his shoulder trembled with exertion. Then the switch chunked into place.

The halogen lights dimmed, sputtered, then failed completely. They were plunged into midnight.

Aaron's blood continued to pool at the back of his skull. He wanted to scratch it, but where? The itch was inside him.

The lights flickered back on.

Then the oscillations began.

From the machine's belly, the first revolution struck Aaron's chest like a shockwave and knocked the breath out of him. It echoed off the granite walls. The second revolution hit his skull, the third his heart. Faster and faster. The machine revved up, growled.

The bulbs rattled in their aluminum funnels. Dust and bits of granite sprinkled from the ceiling. The revolutions blurred into a deafening drone. The pitch climbed.

"Clockwise—two degrees," Dr. Selavio shouted to Clive. Meanwhile, his fingers blurred across the keyboard. "Keep the field stable."

Clive spun a wheel on the side of the machine.

Aaron stared at its looming mass. Its edges flickered, blurry, sometimes not even there. Sweat dripped into his mouth. No way Casler was putting his son in that thing.

"Clive, watch the drift," said Casler, his voice closer. He appeared over Aaron, his gaze radiating warmth. "How you feeling, bud?"

"What the hell did you inject me with?"

"A chemical agent. Like I said, it's dissolving that scar tissue into your bloodstream. Give it three more minutes."

"How much is going to dissolve? A sample, or the whole goddamn lump?"

Casler just smiled, patted Aaron's shoulder, and returned to his station. And Aaron had his answer. Of course. The chemical agent was dissolving the scar tissue that had kept

Aaron alive for eighteen years—dissolving *all* of it. Casler was simply removing the plug from Aaron's severed channel. Without the scar tissue, Aaron would suffer half death. Of course the doctor was immune; he had a half.

Three minutes. Aaron had three minutes before his clairvoyance started to evaporate, before his soul leaked into the gaping hollow at the back of his head.

Well played, big man. If there was any flaw in Casler's execution, it wasn't that he had gone through all the trouble of starting the machine, then not used it. It wasn't that he'd lied unnecessarily. It wasn't even that every smile and every word that crossed his foul lips stank of treachery. It was only that he might have warned Aaron, given him half a minute, thirty seconds—just to contemplate his own death.

And to remember Amber.

Aaron collapsed on the floor, muscles limp. His cheek slapped cold stone. He could already feel something flowing out the back of his head, but the sensation was painless, surreal. Peaceful almost.

The machine whined ever faster, but Aaron had already done what was required of him. At least Amber was safe.

Fatigue weighed on his eyelids, closed them.

"Clive—" It was Casler's voice, somewhere high above him. "Bring Amber back down here, would you? The machine's ready for her."

FIFTEEN

Plus 3 Days, 0 hours, 12 minutes

AARON OPENED HIS eyes. The machine wobbled in and out of focus. It was his imagination, he hadn't heard right. Dominic was upstairs. This was his house. The rugby player wouldn't let Casler touch her.

Even so, the fight would be two on one without Aaron. He willed himself to move. First his pinky, then his whole hand. But with each passing second, his body weakened. He didn't know how much longer the scar tissue would hold out.

"Clive, go get her," said Dr. Selavio, "or is that too much for you to handle?"

"You said we wouldn't," said Clive.

Casler peeled off his mask and gloves. "I'll get her myself."

But Clive intercepted him on his way to the stairs. "Father, she won't be the same afterwards—"

"She'll be *obedient!*"

Clive didn't budge. "But you *promised,*" he said.

Meanwhile, Aaron twisted, scrunched every muscle and dragged himself an inch across cold, grimy stones. His heart missed beats. Even his eyeballs slumped in their sockets.

Above him, the machine screamed like a jet engine.

Dominic reappeared at the foot of the stairs. "You guys trying to wake the dead, or something? Turn that shit down."

"Would you bring Amber down here?" said Casler.

Dominic's eyes flicked to Aaron, crumpled on the floor, then to the machine ten feet away from him, still unused. "What's going on?"

"We're doing Amber instead. Aaron doesn't have enough scar tissue left."

"No, you're not, fuckface. It's number eleven or no one."

"Boys, she'll be fine," said Casler.

"*Fine?*" said Dominic. "She'll be just like your half—the goddamned walking dead."

"That's extremely rude," said Casler.

Dominic stepped around him and leaned over the laptop. "I'm turning this thing off."

"Amber *wants* the operation." Casler rested his hand on Dominic's arm. "You know that."

"Bullshit," said Dominic, scanning the green lines of code. "That was for number eleven."

Aaron inched closer to them, stronger now.

"Dominic—" Casler moved his hand up Dominic's arm and massaged his shoulder. "She's going to be fine, I promise."

Dominic shrugged off his hand. "That's a lot of promises, and I haven't yet seen you keep one." He lowered his eyes to the keyboard and started typing. "I'm turning this thing off and calling my parents."

It happened very quickly after that.

Casler's hand jumped two inches to the left, and he closed his giant fingers around Dominic's throat. "Dominic—" he whispered, his smile barely faltering. "*Please* don't touch my things."

Dominic gurgled and scratched at the bulging tendons in the man's wrist, but Casler only tightened his grip. In a split-second, though, Dominic clicked open his switchblade and sank the knife into the side of Casler's neck.

Finally, Casler dropped him. He stared at the rugby player, bewildered, then struck him in the temple. Dominic flew backwards and landed in a heap. Casler pulled the knife from his neck and dropped it on the floor, and blood dribbled into his collar. But it must have missed his jugular.

Dominic was crawling away, choking for air. Casler followed him and stepped on his back, flattened him. He held out his hand. "Rope, please."

Clive brought him the rope coiled on the floor next to the machine. Dr. Selavio knelt and unwound it, tied Dominic's hands behind his back, then tied his ankles—and Aaron could tell the father's knots were much stronger than the son's.

"Clive," said Casler softly. "Get Amber."

"But Father, you promised we wouldn't," said Clive, close to tears now.

"And *you* promised she'd obey you," said Dr. Selavio. "Look what happened on your honeymoon."

"I said I'd deal with her," said Clive.

"Yeah? Do you think the rest of us want to see bruises on

her face?" said Casler.

"I don't care what the rest of you think," he said. "She's *my half!*"

Casler yanked him forward by the sleeve. "Then keep the part I take out in a vial. Wear it around your neck if you want."

"Father, that's not the same—"

"This is because you and that brat stood up the potentate," Casler spat. "Now go get her."

"Soon, I'll be potentate," Clive muttered, lowering his head.

"Yes, you will. But until then—" Casler unclasped his fingers from Clive's sleeve and touched Clive's cheek, brushing his fingers along his jawline and lifting his chin so he could look him in the eye, "you're still my son. Now bring me your half."

Aaron saw Clive's neck muscles tense up as he swallowed. "As you wish, Father." Then he headed for the stairs.

Casler swung Dominic over his shoulder and followed his son up the stairs. Then the dungeon was empty.

Now it was just Aaron. He was the only one left standing between Amber and the machine—and he *wasn't* standing. In fact, his three minutes were almost up.

He had barely managed to prop himself up on his elbow when Casler returned and leaned over him.

"How you doing, kiddo?"

Aaron strained to speak. "You piece of shit."

Casler brushed Aaron's cheek with the back of his hand. "I'm sorry I lied to you," he said. "But you were supposed to die on the delivery table. I'm afraid Amber belongs to the heir of the Brotherhood now, my son. As long as you're alive, Aaron, you're a threat to their future. I'm sorry."

Aaron stared at him, dumbfounded. Casler had completely lost it. "Just . . . just let her be."

"I have to fix her first," said Casler.

"She's perfect."

"She disobeyed. They were supposed to spend their honeymoon at the potentate's palace, but then—you heard what happened."

"I heard . . . Clive . . . cold feet."

"Aaron, it was *her* fault," said Casler.

Aaron's lungs rose and fell, still hollow. "It was my fault. I made her come back."

Casler lowered his eyes. "Unfortunately, she makes her own choices." He laughed quietly. "And she doesn't realize that Clive will do anything for her."

"Except stop you," Aaron wheezed. Then his arm buckled and his shoulder crunched into the floor.

Casler leaned closer, his eyes full of concern. He glanced at his watch. "You're running out of time.

"Still all here," said Aaron, fighting the weight of his eyelids.

"You know, Amber's truly lucky her channel can heal itself, because that's what makes this operation possible. For anybody else, once we drilled that hole it would be a one way road."

"What about mine?" said Aaron. "Why isn't mine healing?"

"Oh, it is," he said, "but it's not instantaneous like it was during birth. Like all organs in the body, the channel needs time to heal—a few days or so. Unfortunately, you won't have anything left by then."

"What about Amber?"

Casler smiled. "We'll drill a nice small hole so just the right amount of clairvoyance leaks out by the time her channel heals—I'm aiming for about two-thirds. It's a slow leak, so naturally, she'll still be herself at first. I wish you could see what she's like after the operation, when she's flawless—ah, here she is now." He stood up, and his eyes beamed with pride. "Isn't she stunning?"

"Amber, don't come down here!" Aaron tried to shout, but she didn't hear.

She bounded down the stairs in front of Clive, streaked across the dungeon, and knelt in front of him. Her golden hair shimmered under the lights.

"Aaron, he *didn't*, did he?"

"He's doing . . . the operation on you," said Aaron, struggling to push himself off the floor. "Get out of here."

Amber tugged him into an embrace, squeezing herself against him. "As if I'd leave you," she whispered, and for a moment, the tension in her body thawed. "I lied. I *do* want to be your half."

Clive just watched her from the stairs, the corners of his mouth held firm. Only his eyes betrayed his torment.

"Amber, there's no deal," said Aaron, feeling stronger now that they were touching. "He betrayed us."

"He betrayed *everybody*," she said.

Then Casler rose up behind her, blotting out the lights.

His eyes gleamed as he snapped another pair of latex gloves into place and slid the mask over his mouth.

Aaron tried to push her off, but it was too late. Casler's shadow swooped forward. He grabbed Amber around the waist, swung her onto the operating table, and held her down with one hand as he strapped her in. She shrieked and kicked him in the nose, wriggled free. He dragged her back, yanked straps tight across her stomach, her chest, her legs. Then he adjusted her body until her head lay directly at the focal point of the machine's metal spike.

When it was done, Casler wheeled over his chair and sat beside her. He stroked her cheek and brushed the hair out of her eyes. "It'll all be over soon," he said. "I promise."

Amber glared at him. "Take whatever you want," she said, "but leave Aaron alone."

"It's too late for him," said Casler.

"No it *isn't!*" Amber strained against the straps, but nothing gave. Her body tensed, and then she collapsed, out of breath. "It isn't too late for him," she moaned.

Casler gave a sad smile, kissed her cheek, then pulled out another syringe. He rolled his chair behind the machine, where panels were missing, and extracted a loop of tubing coated with a sticky lubricant—*mucous.*

"Be gentle with this one," he said soothingly to the machine, "She's the potentate's favorite." Then he injected the syringe into the tubing. The tube pulsed vein-like between his gloved fingers before slithering back inside the machine.

Casler wheeled himself to the laptop, which flashed with an endless stream of green numbers. "Is everyone ready?" he said.

The machine wobbled, staticky, more like a projection than a solid object. Amber watched the quivering mass above her, too scared to look away.

And from out of the shadows, Clive was watching her. Aaron gathered one thing from the flicker in his pale eyes. He knew how much of his half would be missing when it was done. Clive averted his gaze, though, quickly wiped his eyes, and resumed his position beside the machine. "Go ahead, Father."

Casler typed a command, then hit enter. "There—"

The entire cavern lurched. The machine groaned, as if suddenly encountering resistance. And Aaron knew why.

It was drilling into Amber's clairvoyant channel.

He tried to climb onto the operating table, to Amber. But his fingers slipped. Again, the icy floor slapped his cheek.

Casler leaned back in his chair. "Keep it stable, Clive. Ninety seconds until we reach clairvoyance."

Aaron's three minutes were up. The resistance at the back of his head waned to a sliver, then nothing. Just the cold of empty space. By now, he should have been somewhere else. The golden fields of paradise, Elysium—the abyss.

Somewhere else.

Not here in this dungeon with his cheek glued to frostbitten bedrock. Yet, by sheer willpower, his clairvoyance held. Miraculously, though it felt like a vacuum cleaner had been plugged into the back of his brain and turned on high, it held.

And if he could just hold it for another ninety seconds,

he could fight. Aaron closed his eyes. First one arm, then the other. Then his leg. He dragged himself to his feet. His muscles wobbled, but they too held. He could hold anything for ninety seconds.

He could hold his breath for ninety seconds.

Fury constricted his pupils, and blood tingled in his fingertips. He wheezed, clenched his fists, and staggered forward, willing the strength back into his muscles.

"Counter-clockwise—three and a half degrees," said Casler. "Eighty seconds."

Aaron hooked his fingers over the backrest of a chair, grabbed the seat, and hoisted it over his head.

"Back it off, Clive. You're drifting—two degrees clockwise." The machine groaned behind him. "Keep it stable."

"Father, watch out!"

The steel leg struck Casler above the eye. The impact knocked him off his chair. He dropped like a felled sequoia, and Aaron was on him before he hit the ground.

Seventy-five seconds.

Aaron landed with all his weight, sank his knee into the man's back. He grabbed the first thing in reach. An old monitor. Fifty pounds of CRT, glass, and plastic. Cables snapped like roots as he dragged it off the desk and thrust it down on Casler's head.

The concussion gave a meaty thud, and Casler's face plowed into jagged stone. The monitor rolled off him, and a deep gouge oozed in its wake, right behind his ear.

Seventy seconds.

"Aaron—behind you!" Amber yelled from the operating table.

The fight was two to one—he'd forgotten.

Aaron glanced up as Clive swung. He jerked his head back, and the serrated end of a rusty pipe grazed his cheek. Clive's pale eyes gleamed. He swung again. Aaron backed his head into the desk. Nowhere else to go.

The blow deafened him, right on his ear. Slammed his head sideways. The pain made the cavern flicker. He scurried away, but the pipe clipped his shoulder. His left arm buckled, and he crunched into the floor, banged his lip. Salty blood gushed into his mouth.

Sixty-five seconds.

Behind him, Clive coiled his arm back.

"Clive, *don't!*" Amber yelled.

He swung again. Aaron heard the whistle and rolled just in time. Where his head had been, the stone floor exploded into shards.

The pipe buzzed from the impact. Clive winced and clutched his wrist to keep from dropping it. He raised the pipe again. Swung.

Sixty seconds.

Aaron curled into a ball, cradled his head. He felt a crack, the sound of a broken rib—just below his heart.

Then another. The pipe stabbed into his lower back, bruised his kidney. And another. Deep into his shoulder.

"*Stop it!*" Amber shrieked.

"Clive—that's enough!" yelled Casler from somewhere behind him.

One more. Payback for the night before.

"Clive—" The blows stopped.

Fifty-five seconds.

A shadow loomed above him. The halogen lamps winked out. Casler, his eyes glossy and bloodshot.

Aaron tried to crawl, but the man's dense fingers sank into his shoulder and yanked him backward, stood him on his feet.

"Aaron, get up." Casler's eyes darted across his face, concerned—*loving* almost, as a reddish-black stain spread on his mask.

"You're bleeding," said Aaron.

Casler spun him around, and his thick arm clamped down on Aaron's throat, choking him. "What you did to me was pointless," he said.

"Yeah? Cry me a river," said Aaron.

Fifty seconds.

Aaron jerked his head back, but Casler's jaw was too high. His skull hit the man's chest with zero effect.

"Shhh—" Casler squeezed Aaron tighter and stroked his forehead, smoothing back his sweaty hair. "It's okay," he said. Then he carried him to Amber's side.

"She's going to be fine," he whispered. "Look—here she is."

And there she was, in a lake of blonde hair—all strapped in. Her eyes glittered under the halogen lamps, the most dazzling green Aaron had ever seen.

They stared at each other. Too afraid to look away. Amber mouthed, "I love you." He mouthed it back.

Forty-five seconds.

"The potentate gets to keep the part we take out," said Casler. "We'll have Amber present the vial herself, as a gift. The potentate will be so proud of her."

Aaron tore at Casler's knuckles, but it was like scratching steel poles.

"Hold her hand," said Casler, and he yanked Aaron's wrist down and forced their hands together. Through her palm, Aaron could feel her shivering.

The machine's whine was quieter now, hypersonic.

"Clive, how much time?" said Casler.

"Forty seconds."

"Aaron—" Casler breathed into his ear. "Stay with me for forty seconds. Look into her eyes. Imagine how beautiful she'll be without flaws."

Amber squeezed his hand, and they never broke eye contact. They couldn't.

Thirty-five seconds.

He felt Casler's head turn. "Four degrees, Clive—counterclockwise."

"How can you tell? Let me check the laptop."

"Just do it," said Casler. "We want a nice clean hole so too much doesn't leak out. She should be fashionably obedient, not brain dead."

Thirty seconds.

Then her eyes would wink out. And that would be the last thing Aaron saw before he died.

But a lot can happen in thirty seconds.

Clive never made the adjustment he was supposed to—the four degrees bit. Amber glanced in his direction, and her eyes widened. Aaron heard the thump.

He and Casler turned at the same time, as Clive collapsed,

unconscious. A purple line of cuts bled above his ear, as if his scalp had been stamped.

Then a figure appeared behind Casler, and suddenly Aaron was free. He landed on solid ground and spun.

But it wasn't Dominic, and it wasn't his parents. It wasn't even Tina.

It was Buff Normandy.

All six-four, two hundred and forty pounds of him. The white Pueblo Rugby logo glowed on his sweatshirt as he pried Casler's arms off Aaron's throat, his eyes fierce.

"No more bullshit," he said, then he slammed his fist into Casler's jaw—brass knuckles and all.

Casler's head whipped sideways, and his surgical mask snapped free. Blood sprayed everywhere. And only then did Aaron see the damage he had caused him earlier with the monitor.

His lips were shredded, split open. Foaming.

But Casler moved fast, terrifyingly fast. He dropped his shoulder and plowed Buff into the desk, snapped it clear in half. But Buff wasn't the best rugby player in the league for no reason; his feet were quick. Casler went down first. Buff and Aaron descended on him together.

Buff landed his second blow—and winced. He must have punched wrong, because he rolled off to the side and massaged his fingers. Casler rose from the haze of splinters, his thick limbs swaying like battering rams. But Aaron was there. He thrust down his elbow, nearly broke it on Casler's skull. The man grunted.

Twenty five seconds.

"Buddy, hold his arms!" said Buff, sliding the knuckles onto his other hand.

"Not happening—"

Casler's fist struck Aaron's chest, and he felt his feet leave the ground. He landed on his back and gasped for air.

Casler leaned over him, his face twisted and bloody, and actually held out his hand.

"How about we talk this out?" he said. "Call off your friend."

"Stop the machine," Aaron spat.

"Aaron, you're *dying*," said Casler.

"You first," said Aaron.

Twenty seconds.

Casler tried to smile, but his shredded, foaming lip twisted his face. Blood collected in his laugh lines. "You and Amber would have been perfect together," he said proudly. "So *obstinate*—"

The machine roared. They looked up at the same time. Something was off.

Because Clive hadn't made the adjustment—the four degrees counter clockwise. The field drifted. It was a feedback loop. Once unstable, it slipped. Four degrees became five, then six. Then ten.

A grinding screech of metal split the air. The cavern lurched, then sank a whole foot. The ground tilted, and racks of beakers slid away, capsized. Bottles exploded in fumes.

Yet the machine stayed statue-still, its edges solid, anchored. It was everything else that shook.

Casler stumbled towards the machine. Aaron grabbed his

ankle and yanked him back, got a mouthful of boot heel. More blood.

Once again, he found himself on the floor, his cheek cemented to frozen stone. Clive's body—Aaron blinked. Clive's body was gone.

But there was something else right in front of him. An inch from his nose, still bloody. Dominic's switchblade.

The hilt felt good in his palm.

Casler stepped up to the machine and closed his fingers around the wheel. But Buff tackled him, crunched his face into the floor, and delivered two left-handed punches, his fists a blur. The brass knuckles ripped into Casler's scalp, muddied his skin into red pulp. One more would kill him.

Aaron rose to his feet. He could smell the high voltage, the raw odor of ozone. Arcs of electricity splayed tendril-like from the machine's core, sizzled, and vaporized. His hairs lifted and pointed toward the operating table, where Amber lay perfectly still, watching it all in horror.

Maybe the machine would break. Maybe she would be safe.

Maybe it would screw her up worse.

Fifteen seconds.

He had to free her. Or shut it down.

To his left, Buff raised his arm, torqued his body, and took aim for the brittle part of Casler's skull. This one would kill him.

Except Buff never landed his punch.

The halogen lights died, blackness swallowed them. *Clive*, in the shadows. Buff missed his target, and Aaron heard the scrape, then his friend's yelp as his fist struck bedrock.

But there was still light from the dimmer bulbs. Aaron's eyes adjusted, and he saw Casler rise again. His wounds steamed and tinted the air deep crimson. Casler gripped the wheel. He was going to right the machine.

Aaron jumped on him. He landed on his back, looped his arm around his neck, and pulled the switchblade as hard as he could. The knife sank an inch into Casler's throat, then stopped, as if he'd reached steel cable. Warm blood spilled down his wrist, but it wasn't enough. Aaron dropped the switchblade, and it clinked on the stone—he couldn't do it.

Casler fell to his knees, and saliva dribbled down his lip. "Tell my son to be patient and loving," he gurgled. "She'll be completely helpless at first—"

Aaron grabbed the switchblade and finished the job, and Casler collapsed dead at his feet.

Ten seconds.

Above the machine, the cave ceiling liquified and rippled. Over the operating table, a blue arc of electricity hissed from the tip of the metal spike, coiled through the air and slithered, snakelike, towards Amber's head. She watched it grow, trembling, her eyes wet and terrified. It brushed her cheek, and she squirmed against the straps, pressing herself flat.

But there was nowhere to go. The blue tendril slithered through her hair towards the back of her head, singing the blonde strands in its path.

Aaron flung himself to her side.

Her eyes lit up. "Aaron—" she moaned.

"Buff," he yelled, "turn it off!"

Five seconds.

The movement of Aaron's hands was flawless, precise.

The blade cut true. One strap, then another. He was the best setter in the league, after all.

Buff grabbed the giant switch on the machine, and he screamed. He yanked his hand back as putrid smoke poured from its socket.

Four seconds.

"It's all melted—" yelled Buff.

"Help me get her out!"

Three seconds.

Aaron stole a glance at her. She was staring into his eyes, calming herself by it. Biting her lip.

Then her head was free and she skirted away from the blue snake. It followed her.

Two seconds.

Buff appeared at his side, wheezing, and grabbed the straps around her waist. His knuckles whitened.

But he couldn't possibly tear them with his bare hands, not a chance—yet the fabric splayed. His arms flexed, blood dripped from his palms onto her stomach, and then the strap tore completely. He'd done it.

One second.

That left one more strap to cut, and then she could slip free. Aaron had the tip of the knife at its edge. She was going to make it out—

Then Aaron felt Clive's hot breath on the back of his neck, his cold finger on the back of his scalp. And Aaron's limbs turned to mush.

Just one more strap. But he didn't have it in him.

Clive reached around him, calmly took the knife from Aaron's hand, and plunged it into his stomach. Slippery blood gushed over his hands.

Clive's voice rasped in his ear. "She's *mine*, Harper!"

Zero.

Amber was still strapped in.

The machine ground to a sickening halt, and they were plunged into silence. Then there was only the ringing in Aaron's ears, like the gentle beat of an insect's wings.

The electric arc coiled, flickered neon blue, then sank into the back of Amber's head.

Aaron tried to block it, but there was nothing to block. The electricity slipped through his fingers and stung her.

He watched her eyes widen with panic, then confusion. She writhed, twisted against the strap as the arc of electricity groped inside her for the opening.

Then pierced it.

The tendril pulled out of her head slowly like a long, thin fang. A single drop of blood sizzled at the tip and then evaporated.

Her channel had a hole now.

Like Aaron's. She grabbed his hand, and their gazes locked. Her insides were being drawn toward the back of her head. But unlike Aaron, she wouldn't be allowed to die completely. They would reseal her . . . half empty.

She struggled to hold his gaze.

Buff grabbed his shoulder; he hadn't seen Clive. "You're bleeding!"

Aaron ignored him. Amber's grip slackened, and her eyeballs rolled to the side, unfocused.

"*Amber—*" he croaked.

"Buddy, you can't save her," said Buff. "I'm taking you out of here!"

Then Aaron collapsed, and his cheek struck frozen stone. And Amber's limp fingers slipped from his hand.

Before he lost consciousness, he saw Clive out of the corner of his eye, his arm inside the machine.

Clive pulled out a quartz vial, four inches long and rounded on both ends. The red fluid dimmed before their eyes—the clairvoyance from Amber, from his own half.

Clive's hands trembled, and the vial tumbled from his fingers. He fell to his knees, clutching his stomach.

The machine had cut out too much.

&

There was a moment Aaron would remember afterwards when he was taken over by a feeling that had no self-consciousness. Five days ago, in her bedroom, dust floated between orange shafts of sunlight, blazing like flecks of magnesium. Amber slid closer to him. Their faces were inches apart. Up close, her eyes were layered, freckled like jade crystals.

She was right.

In five days, something would be missing. In five days, his connection to his half would be uncertain, unlikely even. In five days, his channel to his half might not even exist.

But Amber was real now.

&

A white room.

Aaron yanked aside a bed sheet and sat up into a beam of sunlight, and he felt the knife wound twist in his stomach.

He was in a hospital bed closed in by white curtains. Buff was wedged in a tiny chair by the window, watching him carefully.

He raised his eyebrows. "Buddy?"

"What the hell is that look?" said Aaron.

He sighed relief. "I thought you were toast."

Aaron touched the back of his head. Not even a scab. How was he still alive? *Later.* "Where's Amber?"

"Buddy, uh—" Buff lowered his eyes, "listen—"

"She's okay, right?"

"We ran out of time," Buff said quietly.

"But—" Aaron paused, and his throat kinked up as those terrifying last few seconds replayed in his mind. "I . . . I couldn't cut the last strap."

"No one could have," said Buff.

"Where is she?"

He shook his head.

Aaron closed his eyes and counted to five, but nothing changed. *No*—he leapt off the bed, swatted the curtain aside, and hurled through the sterile corridors. He spun around a corner and collided with a nurse.

He grabbed her arm. "Where is she?"

"Pardon?"

"Amber Lilian—where? *Quickly!*"

"D-d-down the hall," she said.

He sprinted, and his heart thudded in the pit of his stomach. He pushed through another curtain, and there she was. Unconscious, pale, wrapped in sheets.

The steady beep of her heart monitor was the only sign of life. He moved into Amber's room and knelt by the bed. She appeared normal, untouched. Perfect. The ordeal could have been a dream.

A stiff hand landed on his shoulder. He whipped around, ready to fight.

It was Dominic, badly bruised. "He's dead," he said, coming in to stand next to Aaron. "They're collecting his body."

"Dr. Selavio. I know. I killed him," said Aaron.

"No, Clive."

Aaron stared at him. "Clive's dead?"

"The machine was off balance. Apparently, it severed his half completely."

"Why didn't he stop it? He knew what it was doing to her."

"I think he wanted more of her clairvoyance. We found him with the vial. He must have thought he could drink it or something—"

"I don't care what he thought." Aaron fell to his knees again beside Amber. "Just tell me she's okay."

"I'm not going to lie to you."

Even though the words sank in, there was nowhere for them to go, no place in his brain where they made any sense. They were in love with each other. Everything was perfect. It was all a bad dream.

He kissed her forehead, and the salty taste of her skin seared his lips. "We're going to make it out of this okay, I promise," he said. "Just open your eyes—" That was when he noticed the odor of singed hair rising off her pillow. A spasm shot through his lungs. "*Amber—*"

The beep of her heart monitor continued, unfluctuating, mechanical, without a jitter to indicate she knew he was there. He realized he was crying when a tear fell on her sheets.

"Amber, *please—*" A heaving in his chest sealed his lungs and choked off his words, silencing him. His hands trembled.

Dominic grabbed his shoulder. "Don't do this to yourself, number eleven. You know as well as I do what happened. Even if she wakes up, there's not going to be much left. She's *severed.*"

Aaron swatted his hand away. "Can't you just leave us alone for two fucking seconds!" Tears burned in his eyes. He turned his back on the rugby player and wiped them away. "Wait outside," he said, failing to keep his voice even. "I just want to be alone with her right now."

Dominic retreated a few feet behind him.

Shivering now, Aaron studied the curvature of Amber's cheeks, glistening and sweaty, statue-still; her eyelids, still closed. And he would have given anything to see them open, to see the spark in her green eyes one more time. "I couldn't cut the last strap," he whispered. "I couldn't get it in time." Another spasm shot through him. "Amber, all you have to do is open your eyes."

His closed his fists on the sheets to stop his hands from shaking. Another teardrop tumbled into the fabric. He folded the damp spot under, and he felt the material rip under his thumbs. Aaron cupped his hands over his face, loathing each breath that slipped through his fingers, giving him life that didn't belong to him. Life he should have given to Amber.

It was impossible to think that he would have to go on without her, that she could just be gone. She looked fine, untouched. Aaron turned to Dominic, his sinuses ringing. The ceiling reeled above him. Gone.

"Why didn't Clive stop it?" he said. "He was supposed to be her half, why didn't he try to save her?" Aaron sniffled. "And why isn't he here right now?"

"He's dead, fuckface, they took his body."

"Who took it?"

"It was that guy we met. The Brotherhood's not going to be happy about losing Dr. Selavio *and* their heir, trust me."

"What guy we met?" said Aaron. "Quit sidestepping and spit it out."

"Chill. It was that priest," said Dominic. "Dravin, I think."

The curtain rustled, and Buff squeezed into the room, followed by Tina.

"Friends and family only," Dominic muttered.

Buff walked past him and elbowed him in the head. "Whoops."

Dominic spun, grabbed Buff's collar, and had his fist cocked behind him when Amber stirred.

Her eyelashes fluttered. Everyone held their breath. A nurse entered to check her vitals. He paused and watched her too.

Amber's eyes opened. She sat up, blinked, and stared around at her visitors.

Aaron bit his lip so hard he drew blood. His heart

thundered against his eardrums, making him wince with every beat.

"Amber," he said, "are you—are you—"

Then she wrapped her hands around his neck, leaned forward, and gave him a long, passionate kiss on the mouth. Right in front of everybody. His lips caught fire.

The nurse did a double take, checked his clipboard, then stood awkwardly in the corner—because he was witnessing a girl kiss a boy who was not her half.

Amber pulled her head back, and Aaron had to catch his jaw. Her green eyes sparkled as if illuminated from behind. Aaron's body felt weak and jittery, his lungs like they were filled with helium. Relief.

"Did I answer your question?" she said.

"No, I think you need to kiss me again," he said.

"In your dreams." Amber glanced up at the four other people crammed into her room watching them, and she blushed furiously.

Almost as if she couldn't feel the hole. Aaron caught Buff's eye, and his friend understood.

"Well, I better get off to the fields," Buff said loudly. "Cal trains year-round."

"Go back to Junior League Rugby," said Dominic, following Tina and the nurse into the hall.

Once they were alone, Amber locked eyes with Aaron. "So . . . neither one of us has a half," she said. "Does that mean . . ."

"No idea," he said, his heart still in free-fall at the mere sight her—right now, a mess of tousled hair and big bright eyes.

She bit her lip, clearly deep in thought. "Hang on," she said. "Kiss me again."

Aaron kissed her, and he realized she no longer felt forbidden. Her skin felt divine, charged. Just touching her stole his breath, scalded his nerves, almost like—

Of course! He pulled back, just as Amber's eyes brightened with the same realization.

"How?" was all she said, her jaw suspended.

"Casler unblocked my channel!" he said. "It was supposed to kill me, but the machine severed your channel too. We were two loose ends; we must have snapped together."

Amber stared at him. "So we're—"

"Yes," he said. "We are."

"You mean, you and I, we're actually . . ." she trailed off, unable to form the words. "I want you to say it."

"Amber, we're halves . . . just like we're supposed to be."

It was obvious now. He could feel her weighing down his heart, how close she was. He wanted to leap into her body, memorize her. He saw it in her eyes too—her desperation to close the gap between them. To make up for eighteen years apart.

They were two halves of the same soul.

EPILOGUE

Plus 3 Months

"BUDDY, JUST LIFT it from the back," said Buff.

"No way—" Aaron's golden arms flexed against the solid brass. "You got to pull from the front."

Aaron collapsed, pulled off his goggles, and wiped his forehead. He gasped for breath. The sun kissed the tops of their heads.

He grinned and high fived his best friend.

Behind them, the Bermuda surf was already washing away the deep gouge they had left in the sand.

Buff peered at him over the top of the corroded brass eye-piece. "Let's go down and get the rest of the treasure."

"Give me a minute," said Aaron.

Aaron gazed at a cluster of palm trees. They had grown right up to the water's edge. Some fallen coconuts floated in the shady shallows beneath them. Beyond the palms, the white shoreline curved out of sight on its way around the tiny island.

Their 28-foot sailboat, *Endless Honeymoon*, was just visible around the bend—a wedding gift meant for Amber and Clive that she had managed to hold on to.

Buff's half, Daisy, scampered out of the jungle. The little redhead hardly made it up to Buff's biceps.

"That is *so* cool! What'd you guys find?" she said.

Buff picked her up with one arm. She giggled and tried to escape.

"Buddy, care to explain our find?" said Buff

"It's an aitherscope, probably eighty years old," said Aaron, beaming at them. "We found it in the wreck."

"Aitherscopes didn't exist eighty years ago," she said.

"Yeah, Buddy, don't you remember that lecture?" Buff dropped her in the sand, flicked some sludge off the eyepiece and pressed his eye to the lens. "I wonder . . ."

"Buff, there's no way—"

"Yep. Still works," said Buff.

Daisy looked through next, and her eyes widened. "Buffy, it's your *eye*!"

Buff turned the color of a ripe plum and tackled her onto the beach.

Buffy.

Aaron had to hold his nose to stop from cracking up. He tried the aitherscope after Daisy, while the two of them rolled around on the sand. It didn't hurt anymore, not like it used to.

Static.

"Still nothing," he muttered.

Then somebody jumped at him from behind. He spun and caught her, and she tossed wet blonde hair out of her eyes and kissed him with salty lips.

"Want to see what I got you?" Amber whispered in his ear, still panting from her dive. She leaned over, exposing her glistening back, and half of a faint white spiral caught the sunlight under her bikini top.

Even though Clive was dead, the scar hadn't fully healed. It was now a permanent reminder to both of them of how close she had come—and how they weren't like other halves. They had earned the right to love each other, and for that, every second they spent together was precious.

Amber held out a starfish for him. "Isn't she cute?"

Aaron glanced between Amber and the starfish. "I do see the resemblance."

"Oh, do you?" She brought out a sea cucumber next. "Well this one looks like you."

Aaron narrowed his eyes at the slimy, spotted slug. "Good to know you're not just with me for my looks," he said.

"Actually, it's mostly just your looks," she said with a sly smile. She peered sideways at the aitherscope. "You know, I haven't looked through one of these since my birthday."

She leaned toward the eyepiece.

And Aaron's heart clawed itself into his throat. He grabbed her arm. "Amber, forget it—"

But it was too late.

"Wow," she said, blinking into the eyepiece. "Aaron, that isn't your eye."

"Whose is it?" he croaked.

"It's just static."

Aaron exhaled his relief. "Come on," he said, grinning. "I saw an underwater cave we can explore."

Amber wrapped her arms around him again. "Is it private?" she asked.

"It's an underwater cave."

She bit her lip. "So *really* private?"

"That's why we're exploring."

The ocean glittered in her eyes. "Is that *all* we're going to do?"

❧

The first sign that something was off came late July, when they were back in Tularosa. Aaron sensed it first. They were walking out of the Arlington Theater, oblivious of the crowd—when he felt a gentle tugging at the back of his skull.

Then he saw him.

For an instant in a shop window's reflection. Across the street, standing in the shadows. A gray hoodie, pale blue eyes.

Aaron spun, but there was no one.

Just shadows.

Aaron took a deep breath and squeezed Amber closer to him. It was only his imagination.

People didn't live on after half death.

Only Aaron did that.

Dan Rix lives in Santa Barbara, California with his half, Laura. This is his first novel, which he started writing in college while procrastinating his architecture studio work.

A Message from Dan Rix

Whatever it is that brought you to *Entanglement*, I am honored to have you as a reader. In asking you to come on this journey, I've taken some of your time, and that's a debt I won't forget. My sincere hope is that I've given you something in return. Something to remember and think about. Maybe a little truth.

If I have, then you and I have something in common—and I want to offer you this challenge: let's not part ways.

Because the truth is, you and I co-authored *Entanglement.* My part was minor; it was you who brought the world to life, you who made the characters speak, you who stood by them to the end.

I'm asking you to take pride in that. So before anything else, I need you to do something. Hop on your laptop and give *Entanglement* a review on Amazon. You will make the difference. Do it now, while the story's fresh. After you leave a review, come join me at danrixauthor.blogspot.com. And let me be a part of your life.

I can't wait to hear from you.

Dan Rix

Acknowledgements

Following the advice of other writers, I kept this book a secret for four years. At least I thought I did. Right now as I write this Acknowledgements page and think back on all the names, I am humbled by the many people who gave me their unquestioning support and encouragement, and in so doing, gave me my strength.

Below is a list of people who had no cause to believe in me, yet did.

I owe my success and happiness to my beautiful girlfriend, Laura Carlson. She is my constant inspiration, and this book is a product of her unconditional faith in me. I also have the good fortune of being in love with the best damn independent editor in the world. Almost every big breakthrough I had in creating *Entanglement* is a result of her (if you're a writer, she's at www.americaneditingservices.com).

I am indebted to my parents, Ann and Paul, for never teaching me the word "impossible." Because of them, going after my dreams is a given, not a wish. They were also my two most loyal readers throughout.

I need to thank my brother, Steve, for coining my pen name and for encouraging me to ditch the nine to five and go after this thing with everything I had. It paid off like he said it would.

I must thank my friends Sukhee Basetti and Noah Lehman for reading the book and giving invaluable feedback. They went above and beyond the call of duty. I have to thank my friend and roommate of many years, Keith Salvado, for his infectious excitement for the book. He made me feel like I had an accomplice.

I want to thank Tamra Carlson, for knowing I would succeed and supporting Laura and me with Costco runs when money was short. I want to thank Brian and Teresa Carlson (who also supported us during hard times) for their generosity, and for being proud of me before I had anything to show.

I want to thank my former agent, Kim Perel, for her valuable world-building edits that gave the book the final edge it needed.

I also want to thank everyone who approached me at the 2012 San Francisco Writers Conference. Your words of encouragement and excitement for *Entanglement* (then titled *In Half*) fuel me to this day. I wish I could thank each of you personally. I also need to thank everyone on Agent Query who edited my query letter and told me they couldn't wait to read the book. I printed out those comments and taped them up on my wall.

And I want to thank you. For taking a chance on me, for investing a few days in this book. For making this all worth it. I hope you enjoyed the story.

14190505R00194

Made in the USA
San Bernardino, CA
18 August 2014